Tangled Up in Blue

J.D. Brick

ISBN: 098393911X
ISBN 13: 9780983939115
Library of Congress Control Number: 2015908224
Jackie Papandrew, Largo, FL

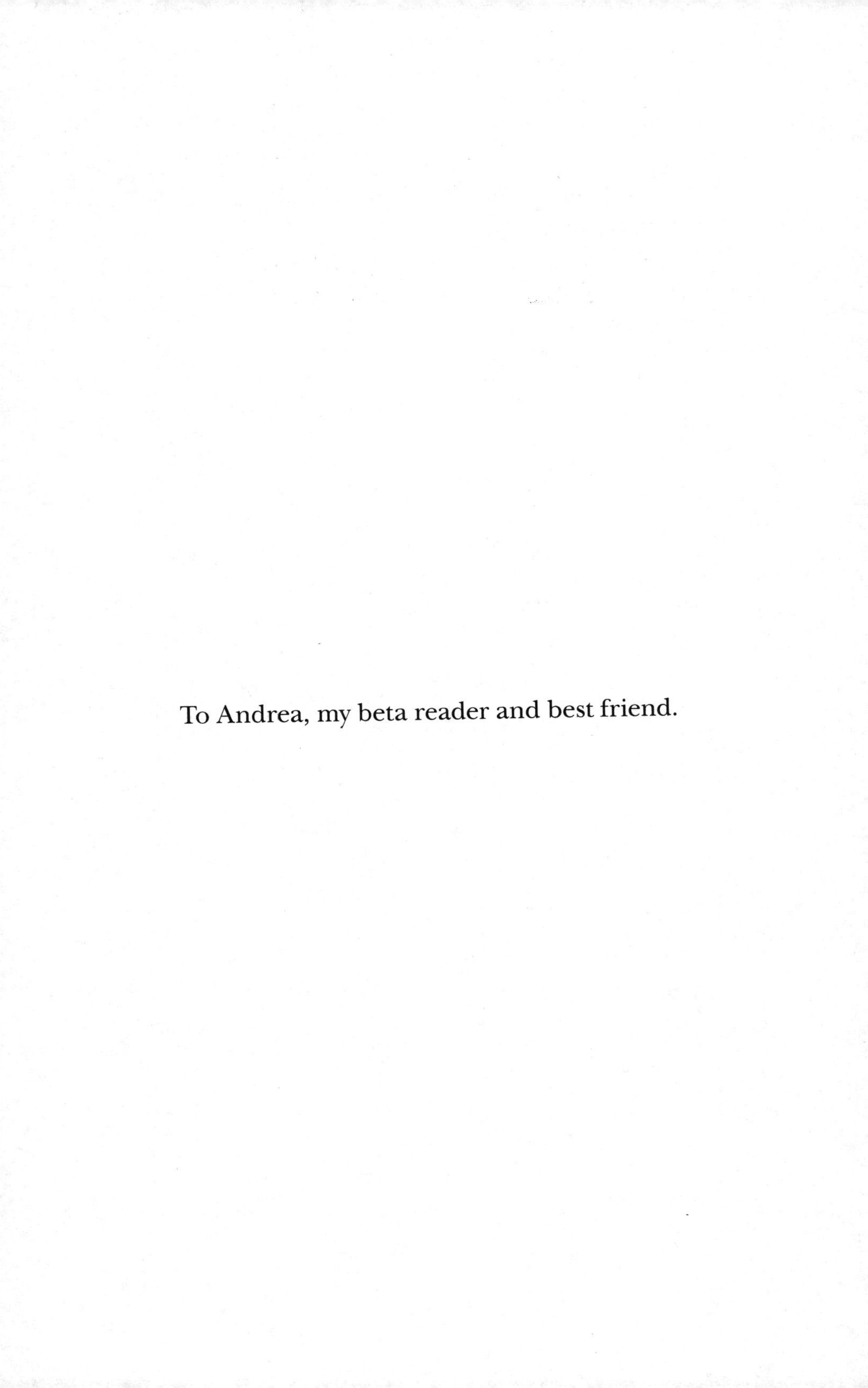

To Andrea, my beta reader and best friend.

TABLE OF CONTENTS

1

A BOY NAMED BLUE

Keegan

I just can't win for losing. The horrible voice that threatened to kill me a few hours ago is still scalding my eardrums when I pull up to my new home and see a tatted-up bunch of trouble sprawled on the front porch. He's lying on his stomach, wearing only jeans, his forehead pressed into sagging boards, his body blocking the front door. He's got a beer bottle hooked over one finger. He's got a great ass.

Even though I'm staring at him through the windshield, I can tell he's got a great ass. And sculpted arms, crawling with ink. And why the hell am I even paying any attention? I want nothing to do with guys like him.

I've already been driving around for hours. Kendra, the only one of my new roommates I've spoken to, told me not to show up too early. The clock in my car says it's exactly 10 AM. Surely that's late enough. All I want to do is move my stuff into my room and go to pieces without anybody seeing me.

I hear Mr. Hot Drunk Mess calling out as soon as I step out of the car.

"Max. C'mere Max. It's okay. You can come out now."

He doesn't really sound drunk. His voice is tender, deep, melodious. It's a nice voice. I close the car door, maybe a little harder than necessary, and stand there squinting as I look toward the house. Even with my sunglasses on, the bright sunlight seems to magnify my hellacious headache. Lack of sleep always makes me miserable.

It takes me a minute to focus, and when I do, I see that Great Ass is on his feet, his hands wrapped around two of the porch posts. The bottle sits on the railing. He gives me this warm, mischievous smile that moves from his lips through his five o'clock shadow to cobalt blue eyes, and my stomach flops around like a fish out of water. My stomach's never done that before around any guy, not even the preacher's son who took my virginity the night of my high school graduation. Especially not him.

"You our new roomie?" Great Ass asks me.

Oh God. He lives here. I hadn't even bothered to ask about the other roommates. I'd just assumed they were girls.

"Um, yeah, I guess I am." I can't stop staring. He's all washboard abs and jacked-up biceps. There's a tattoo right in the middle of his chest, but I can't see it clearly.

His grin deepens, and he steps off the porch and walks toward me, sticking out his hand. "I'm Blue. Blue Danube."

I stand there stupidly, freaking tongue-tied, not moving until I finally force myself to whirl around and yank open the rear car door. I pull out an overstuffed egg crate and turn back around. My new roommate is still standing there with his hand out, an amused expression on his face.

"Oh, sorry. I'm Kee… Did you say your name is *Blue Danube?"* My face is burning, and my brain seems to only be working at half-speed, so his earlier words are just now registering. "Isn't that a dance or something?"

"It's a song, actually, one that people used to dance the waltz to about a million years ago." His smile fades, and a muscle twitches in his jaw. "It was my old man's idea. You know, kind of a Boy-Named-Sue thing. I guess he figured if naming his son after an 18th-century ballroom dance didn't toughen him up, nothing would."

His name is Blue, and he's got these ridiculously *blue* eyes? He's got to be wearing colored contacts.

Blue Danube startles me by tucking a stray piece of hair behind my ear. My ponytail is barely hanging on, but I don't have a free hand to fix it.

"Kendra said you'd be moving in today, but she probably didn't expect you this early. I'm pretty sure I'm the only one up."

"Oh. Sorry. Should I come back later?" Why did I say that? No way I want to come back later.

"No, no. You're good." He smiles disarmingly, and I break into a sweat. Even though it's the end of October, it's hot outside, and I'm wearing shorts and a tank top. His eyes saunter over my body, obviously checking me out. "You're certainly an improvement over the last girl who was in your room. Not to be mean, but she was, um, not as easy on the eyes as you."

He's not even trying to be subtle. But it won't do him any good. I've got enough insanity in my life. No way I'm adding falling into bed with a horny roommate to the list. Even if he's a *hot* horny roommate.

"Geez, look at me just standing here like an asshole. Let me help you." He reaches for the crate, rubbing his arms against mine as he pulls it away, and I start tingling in places people don't talk about at parties. *Crap.*

Blue sets my crate on the porch. Some of the porch's boards are rotted through, and the siding on the house looks like it is about to fall off. It doesn't look anything like the online ad. No telling what shape my room is in.

I've heard of the house, of course. Everybody on campus knows about The Canadian Embassy, although no one seems to have a clue where the name came from. Embassy parties are legendary, which is why it's so ludicrous that *I* am moving in. Me, pretty much a party virgin. Pretty much a regular virgin too, if you don't count that one time. And I don't.

I'd been so desperate to move out of the dorm, I would have taken anything. Off-campus housing is notoriously hard to find at Ikana. I didn't have much choice in the middle of the semester.

"I assume you have more stuff in your car?" Blue ignores the steps and jumps the short distance from the porch to the bricked-over front yard. "Man, it's so damn hot. You'd think it was August instead of October."

He wipes an arm across his forehead, and my eyes, without any permission from my brain, register the way his fine abs move up and down. For a boy named after a waltz, my new roomie sure has a rockin' body. That tingly place inside me flares up like it's been splashed with propane.

"Uh, yeah."

My old Nissan Maxima has all my worldly possessions inside. I'd just thrown everything into it in the middle of the night, frantic to get away before another threat sent me right over the edge. I only had one egg crate and no time to get boxes and pack up my dorm. I figured I could organize everything once I got into my room at the Embassy. I hadn't counted on a swoon-worthy guy wanting to carry my stuff over the threshold.

Blue opens the passenger door and a whole embarrassing pile of stuff—including the 50-page police report I'd wasted time printing—spills out on the ground.

Blue draws back for a moment. "Whoa, you, uh, don't believe in boxes, I guess."

"I had to leave in a big hurry. It's a long story."

I rush over to where he's standing, then crouch down and begin picking things up, avoiding his eyes. Blue squats besides me and put his hand over mine. He's so close I can smell his aftershave or whatever it is that's giving off this musky, citrusy scent that makes me want to bury my face in his chest and breathe deeply.

"Hey, roomie," he says, quietly, "it's cool. Boxes are overrated." Then he scoops up an armful of my stuff and gives me a smile that sends a shiver through my soul.

Blue's face gets a little blurry. *Say something, you idiot.* I'm making a fool of myself before I even set foot in the house.

"You still with me, roomie?"

I shake my head, then start nodding rapidly. "Oh yeah, yeah, I was just, um…" And then he hits me with that smile again, and I can't even finish my sentence.

Blue turns toward the front porch. "Let me introduce you to your new home."

I grab as much as I can carry and follow him up the porch steps, shaking my hair out of its ragged ponytail. As he bends down to add my crate to the other stuff in his arms, I notice the scars all over his back. *Holy shit.* What happened to him? I also notice the tattoo on his right shoulder: dog tags, with something written on them. And then I hear what sounds like a dog whining.

Blue stops short and looks down at the hole in the porch where he'd been lying when I first pulled up.

"There you are," he says to the hole, and I twist my head to see who he's talking to. A long black snout sticks up through the boards and a pair of brown eyes look up at me.

"Oh. Is that who you were talking to when I first got out of the car?"

"Yeah, that's Max." His voice is tender again. "I forgot to lock him in my room last night, and all the noise scared the shit out of him." He whistles and raises his voice. "It's okay, Max, come out of there."

The dog disappears from sight. Blue chuckles. "He has to go back out the way he got in there. He'll show up in a minute." He shifts the load he's carrying to free up a hand, then opens the front door with a flourish. "Welcome to the Canadian Embassy!"

He waits for me to go in first. But then he holds up his hand to stop me. "Wait. I just realized I don't know your name. I need to announce you properly." Another adorable grin. This guy is not going to make it easy to stick to my brand-new, No Hookups with Roommates Policy.

"Keegan," I manage to answer. "Keegan Crenshaw."

"*Keegan.* I like that."

I smirk. "It's the name of the bar where my mom and dad met." I roll my eyes and shake my head. "My parents."

He laughs, then tries to bow as he ushers me in, dropping about half of what he's carrying. "The Canadian Embassy welcomes Keegan Named-After-A-Bar Crenshaw."

I step through the door, and my feet touch hardwood floors that are dusty and dull, but still have enough character to give me a pang of nostalgia. The huge main house at the Cooke Ranch, where I spent most of my childhood, has gleaming wood floors that my brother and I used to love to slide along in our socks. My grandmother would get so angry at us, like we were doing any harm. The woman can get mad over almost anything.

The living room floor squeaks with each step we take into the house, and my flip flops stick to the boards. "I guess there's no sneaking in or out of this house," I crack. I sound nervous.

We cross the room and set my stuff on the stairs that rise from the middle of the far wall. To the right of the stairs is a breakfast nook with a small table and a couple of chairs that look like they might collapse if sat on. Beyond that is the kitchen, with a lot of dishes piled in the sink. To the left of the stairs, I see what I assume is a bedroom. The door is closed, but I can hear someone singing, if you could call it that, with a voice that reminds me of the bullfrogs we used to hear at night when all the windows were open at the ranch.

"Hey, does whoever's in that room," I point toward the bedroom door, "make a habit of…" I don't even finish the sentence because I've stopped and am staring in amazement at one corner of the living room, where two beer kegs sit surrounded, as if in homage, by dozens of red plastic cups. The cups are in various stages of the typical red-cup life cycle; some are crumpled or smashed, others lying empty on their sides or still standing half-full.

With the unscreened windows that line two sides open and a hot wind blowing through, I can smell the stale beer left in the cups and, obviously, all over the floor. Nothing else in the living room. No furniture, not even the battered, mismatched thrift-store stuff you see in most college residences.

"So, you had a party last night, I guess?" I look at Blue as I pull off my sunglasses and tuck them into the front of my shirt. "You moved the furniture somewhere?"

Blue seems to choke on something, slapping his hand to his chest and looking down at the floor with a weird expression on his face. Then he slowly bends down to pick up a drum stick. "Sam will be looking for this." He sticks it into his jeans pocket and gives me a tight smile. "No furniture in this room, makes it easier for the bands to set up."

He laughs when my jaw drops. "You do know we have parties here on weekends with live bands, right? Even sometimes during the week. The Embassy's known all over campus for its parties. You have to have known that."

"Well, yeah, I knew it was a party house. But I didn't really know it was *every* weekend. Or that you had live bands. Wow." I sound less than thrilled.

"Last night's band was really a good one," he goes on. "The lead singer's kind of a douche, but he's got a great voice. We must have had 100 people just in this room."

Shit. I've made a huge mistake renting a room in this place. It is going to be very hard to keep up my straight As and do a kick-ass job as editor of *The Daily* if I am living in a 21st-century version of *Animal House.* I've fought too hard to get the top job at the campus newspaper to screw it up now. I always do bone-headed things when I'm in a panic. I must look dejected because Blue taps me lightly on the chin with his fist.

"C'mon Keegan. Surely a girl named after a bar knows how to have a good time."

Every time he turns that flirty grin on me, the one that lights up his eyes, I get that tingly feeling again. It's really starting to irritate me. And I don't like that he's already felt free to touch my face twice, within a few minutes of meeting me. The guy seems kind of pushy.

Blue yawns and stretches. "Only problem with Embassy parties is cleaning it all up the next day," he says, rubbing his stomach.

My tongue almost jumps out of my mouth, deciding on its own that it wants to trace the muscles on that stomach. I can feel myself blushing. Blue grins again as if he knows what I'm thinking.

"What did you mean earlier when you said 'a boy named Sue thing'?" I need something to say.

"You know ... Johnny Cash."

I give him a blank look. No idea what he's talking about.

"Come on now, girl. Wait. You're telling me you've *actually* never heard of *A Boy Named Sue*? The *song*? The song by Johnny Cash? It's about a father who tries to toughen up his son by giving him a girl's name? There's no way you haven't heard of it. No fucking way."

I shake my head. It's hard not to enjoy his playful horror. I'm pretty sure I've heard of Johnny Cash, if only in a vague, my-parents-might-have-mentioned-him kind of way. But I haven't heard of the Sue song Blue's talking about. I'm kind of having fun playing dumb, though.

"Johnny who?" I ask. All on its own, my face spreads out in this absurdly big smile.

Blue sighs and puts on a cowboy drawl. "Well, little lady, you are in need of some teachin' and you've come to the right place for it." He turns toward the stairs. "Come on. Let's get you unloaded, and then maybe I'll go back to cleaning up all this crap. That's what I was doing when you pulled up. Well, that and trying to find Max. It'll probably be hours before our other two lazy-ass roommates are awake."

We're about halfway up the stairs when I ask him who lives in the room with the blaring music. A couple of steps behind him, I am trying not to stare at his perfect butt. Naturally, I can't take my eyes off it.

"I hate to be rude," I say, "but whoever's in that room should maybe stick to singing in the shower, if at all. Ugh. Sounds like a dying cow."

Blue freezes, then very deliberately sets my belongings down again on the stairs before turning to glare at me.

"Okay, Keegan Crenshaw, let's get one thing straight right up front. No one criticizes the great Bryson, not in this house." He doesn't look like he's kidding. "In case you haven't figured it out, that's *my* room. And anytime I'm home, my room will be bathed in the dulcet tones of The Great One."

"Who?" I am bewildered.

Blue looks at me with what seems to be genuine outrage. "You've just been pulling my leg this whole time, right? You know who Johnny Cash is and you..." he seems to have trouble getting the words out, "... you absolutely have to know, how could anyone *not* know who Frasier Bryson is? You're kidding me, right?"

"I think *maybe* I've heard of him now that you say his name. Isn't he *really* old like, Sixties music or something? I think maybe my mom mentioned him once? Or maybe that was Johnny Cash she was talking about." I shake my head. "I'm just not sure. But, to be honest, if that's what Bryson sounds like," I wrinkle my nose for emphasis, "I'm surprised *anybody* is still listening to him."

Blue grabs his head with both hands as if it is about to explode and keeps his eyes closed for several seconds. I spend the time staring at his flexed biceps and letting my gaze drift down where it shouldn't be going. Blue slides his hands slowly down his face as if in despair and opens his eyes. Then he places his hands on my shoulders, sending my loins leaping out of their assigned areas. I'd read about *loins* in my romance novel phase. They're always flaming or burning or in some stage of combustibility. But mine aren't just on fire; they are also doing calisthenics.

"What has happened to this generation?" Blue is speaking to the ceiling, shaking his head. Then he tightens his grip on my shoulders and peers into my eyes in a way that makes me go weak at the knees.

"It's okay. It's not your fault," he assures me. "Society has failed you. Your parents have failed you. You may have come to the Embassy just in the nick of time. Fortunately for you, I am here to open your eyes."

And hopefully my legs. My damn loins are talking. It sure isn't me.

"I think I need to get all my stuff up to my room. I've got a lot of studying to do." I sound unsteady. Blue's hands are still on my shoulders. I pull away from him.

"Oh, sorry."

He doesn't look sorry, though. The naughty grin is back. He picks up my crates yet again and once more starts up the stairs.

"I got distracted by your appalling musical and cultural ignorance. Not that it's your fault. Right this way, my young pupil."

There's a landing halfway up the stairs and a window that looks out over a back deck. I see more red cups and bottles all over the deck and a couple of lawn chairs. Over the window, a huge Canadian flag hangs on the wall. I pause on the landing and stare up at the flag, then gaze out over the back deck at the weed-choked yard below that holds yet more lawn chairs and dozens more cups and bottles.

"So why is this place called the Canadian Embassy?"

"That's a long and fascinating story that I need to tell you over a couple of beers."

Blue turns to look at me, then spots something that makes him step down to the landing and yell out the open window.

"Max! C'mere boy. Max. Wait. Corey? Man, what the hell are you still doing here?"

I crane my neck to look around Blue in time to see the German Shepherd sniffing around a form in the back yard that slowly rises from the ground. It appears to be a grubby-looking male with wild hair. He's rubbing his eyes and blocking the sun with his hands as if it hurts him.

"Corey," Blue yells again, "go home." He laughs and continues up the stairs. "Still sleeping it off, I guess."

"So is that your dog?"

"Max is kind of the house dog, although I seem to be the one who takes care of him most of the time. He belonged to the Canadians, but they abandoned him when they left town. Long story, remember?"

I nod, realizing how tired I am. I haven't even made it to my room yet. We reach the top of the stairs, and I look from right to left. Three bedrooms, all with their doors closed. And one bathroom, door open. I spot an old-fashioned, claw-foot bathtub and wish I could take a long hot bath.

Blue sets my possessions in front of the door directly across from the bathroom.

"You'll meet Hunter and Kendra later." He wipes his forehead with his arm again. "Damn, I can't believe how hot it is."

"No air-conditioning in the house?"

"Window units in the bedrooms. Yours works the best of all of them, although that's not saying much." He turns the knob. "Here we are."

I step through the door and gasp at the naked couple passed out on my bed.

2

SOME KIND OF SIZZLE

Blue

Keegan almost drops her dentures, as my mother would say, when she sees Hunter and whoever the bleached blonde is sprawled bare-ass and obviously post-fuck (not a word that would ever have come out of Mama's mouth) on what is now Keegan's bed. Not the best introduction to the Embassy, but at least Keegan is getting the full picture up front.

Quite literally "up front," as her new roommate Hunter is lying on his back on the bare mattress, with nothing left to the imagination. The blonde's curled up next to him, snoring softly with her mouth open and a line of drool on her chin. No idea who she is. I can't remember seeing her before, but that's no surprise. The Embassy attracts new people every weekend. And she looks like his type: hot and "breezy"—Hunter slang for an easy broad.

Why Hunter steered the blonde into Keegan's room instead of his own last night, I have no clue. Maybe he already had a girl, or two, passed out in his room. He'll come up with some kind of reason. Dude always has an excuse for everything, especially when it comes time to cough up his part of the rent.

Keegan stands there gawking at them, then looks at me like she wants me to tell her what to do next. There's something quirky and coltish about this girl. She's got legs that go on for days, just the right amount on top to fill out that little black tank and long, glossy hair that I want to bury my face in. Physically, she's definitely my type, although I should have learned my lesson about hooking up with roommates from the whole Kendra drama.

I can tell there's something different about Keegan. She's guarded and kind of innocent; she seems *fragile,* I guess. That's the word that pops into my head, anyway. But there's something else as well, a tender strength that's buried somewhere deep inside, a trait she probably doesn't even yet recognize in herself. I can't quite put my finger on it. But I know it's there. And it actually spooks me, a little.

When Keegan took off her sunglasses in the living room and I saw her eyes, I almost choked. Just like that, I was right back in Afghanistan, looking at the face of a girl with nearly identical eyes. I'd sensed the same quality in that girl that I sense in Keegan. *That* girl probably hates my guts now, for making her life even worse than it was before. Assuming she's still alive.

Spotting the drum stick on the floor gave me a reason to bend over for a moment so I could get my shit together. It's not the first time since I became a civilian that I've suddenly been on the verge of tears. It's happening a lot. And it really pisses me off.

So yeah, I played up my shock at Keegan's musical ignorance and acted like a horny-ass cave man more than was probably necessary. Most of the kids on campus have the same stunted appreciation of the over-processed crap that passes for music nowadays; it's not a surprise that Keegan is just another member of the masses, musically anyway. She does seem to dig the whole 'I need to take you in hand and teach you' routine. Assuming my man radar is in good working order, the attraction between us is mutual, even if she's trying to resist it for some reason. It sure wasn't difficult to let her see my eyes taking a cruise all over her body. I won't mind getting to know Keegan a lot better, in more ways than one.

Kendra will probably want to kill me if I do, but I'm not going to think too far ahead.

I walk to the bed and twist Hunter's big toe hard to wake him up. At the same moment, Max bounds up the stairs, his nails clicking on the wood. He runs right into the room, right toward the bed and sticks his cold nose right into the blonde's nicely toned ass. That's what I love about dogs. There's nothing subtle, nothing complicated about them; they get right to the heart of the matter.

Yowling, Hunter and the blonde both try to sit up at the same time, and the blonde rolls off the bed and hits the floor butt first, which gets Max barking, thinking she wants to play.

"Get that fucking dog away from me," she screams, jumping to her feet while trying—pointlessly—to cover her private parts with her hands. Max keeps barking and rushes toward her playfully. And she kicks him, sending him scrambling behind me like a coward. For a German Shepherd, the dog's certainly no canine cop.

"Hey!" I yell. "Don't kick the dog. He's just trying to play."

She grabs her clothes off the floor and, still cursing, runs into the bathroom, slamming the door behind her.

Hunter cradles his head in his hands. "Jesus, Blue, what the *fuck* do you think you're doing?"

"I could say the same thing to you, dickwad." I pick up Hunter's boxers and throw them at him. "So could Keegan here, who has already paid her share of the rent. Unlike *some* people in this room. And she just had to have the unpleasant experience of walking into *her* room and seeing your nasty bare asses all over her bed. Put on your underwear and get the hell out of here so she can move in."

Hunter squints at the sun pouring through the windows and slowly turns his face toward Keegan. Then, true to form, he gives her a cocky smile as he rolls off the bed clutching his underwear in one hand. He walks toward her, extending the other hand. He is still naked, of course.

"Hi roomie," he says. "Welcome to the Embassy!"

Keegan

I stare at Hunter's outstretched hand, blushing to the roots of my hair. Hunter is hot, no doubt about it, in a bad-boy kind of way. Tall and lean, with shoulder-length dirty blond hair falling into his face and tattoos covering his arms, chest and back, he has a pierced eyebrow and lip. And I'm pretty sure that when he walked toward me, I saw another piercing in a place I didn't even know guys could get pierced. I don't dare look at *that* again though.

I finally manage to shake Hunter's hand and raise my eyes to his face. He puts his hands on his hips and gives me a sarcastic smirk. Something cold and predatory in his eyes makes me shiver, and not in a good way. I turn without a word and rush out the door, hightailing it down the stairs, feeling like a fool. Then I stand on the bottom step, shuddering, wondering what is wrong with me. I hear Blue order Hunter to bring up all the rest of my things as a way to apologize for using my mattress as a "fuck factory."

"Wow, you're sure giving this girl the royal treatment," Hunter sneers. "I assume this mean you're planning to nail her, kind of a Kendra 2.0? Talk about a fuck factory."

There's a shuffle and a thud, then Hunter yelling "Hey! What the…" Then Blue's voice, sounding urgent and angry, but too low for me to hear exactly what he is saying. At the same moment, a cold nose nudges my hand. Max. He whines, and I pet his head to reassure him.

"Easy, soldier boy, get your hands off me!" I hear Hunter snarl. "I'm just kidding around. I don't care who you bang. But if you want *me* to move our new roomie in, I'll need a few more days' leeway on the rent."

Blue snorts. Then I hear the bathroom door open with a loud squeak, and Hunter's voice takes on a wheedling tone. "Hey there, baby. Sorry about what happened earlier. *Some* people around here have no manners. C'mon, we can go another round in my room."

The blonde Hunter was sharing my bed with snarls as she pounds down the stairs. "Don't you 'Hey baby' me, you asshole! You're *both* assholes, and I'm never coming to another party at this loser house and neither are any of my friends."

"Suit yourself." Hunter sounds amused.

The blonde reaches the bottom of the stairs and glares at me. She obviously put her clothes on in a hurry; her shirt's not buttoned up right. "What are you looking at, bitch?"

Max whines again and presses against my leg. The dog really is a wimp. I don't bother to answer, just watch the blonde storm out the front door and slam it as hard as she can. When I turn back toward the stairs, Blue is standing there watching me.

"I'm sorry about all this, Keegan." His shoulders are slumped. "There's always drama around here. I guess you might as well get used to it."

I give him a half-smile and look down at the dog, who is pressing his head into my hand to get me to keep petting him. I really have made a colossal mistake, moving into this place on the spur of the moment. The last thing I need in my life is more drama.

"I see you've made a friend out of Max already," Blue says softly. "He's really picky about who he trusts. Looks like my instincts about you were right on."

I keep my eyes on the dog, feeling kind of sheepish. I assume Blue is joking.

"Yeah, sure," I say. "We just met an hour ago. You know nothing about me, except that I was named after a bar." I look up and roll my eyes. "And that I'm way too easily embarrassed."

But Blue doesn't smile back; he just looks intently into my eyes. "Keegan, before I started my life as a hard partyin' college boy, I did two tours in Afghanistan. One of the things I had to do to stay alive was be able to size people up immediately. And I discovered I'm pretty good at that. I just have instincts about people as soon as I meet them. I'm not saying I'm psychic, exactly, but I've learned to trust my gut. It's not wrong very often."

He takes a couple of steps down so that he's only about an inch away from me, and I swear some kind of sizzle passes between us. I gasp and step back, my eyes drawn to the tattoo on Blue's chest. Some kind of rifle topped by a military helmet and surrounded by the words, *Freedom is Not Free.* I just stand there, my heart pounding.

Blue laughs awkwardly. "So anyway, my gut told me you're cool, and Max just confirmed it. Dogs are never wrong about people."

That's when Hunter comes down the stairs two at a time, stopping short when he sees us standing there staring at each other. He glances from Blue to me and then back to Blue and smirks. "Fuck factory, huh, soldier boy? I'm sure not the only one."

I end up spending most of the afternoon organizing my stuff as well as I can, which is a challenge considering my room has no furniture. Other than the bed, of course. I hadn't even thought to ask Kendra whether the room came with furniture. My room does have the only curtains in the house, made by the girl who'd moved out of it in a hurry. No one seems to know exactly why. Hunter calls her Just Brenna.

"Just Brenna was the only girl I ever met who could sew," he tells me as he carelessly lets the last load of my stuff slide out of his arms and hit the wood floor. "She made those curtains the first day she was here. Too bad she was batshit crazy, not to mention fat and butt ugly. She could have been useful."

I am already starting to dislike Hunter.

One of the first things I do is run out to the nearest drugstore and buy a bottle of disinfectant spray. Then I spray most of the bottle on the bed. And *then* I have to open all the windows and stand out in the hall coughing while the cloud of disinfectant disperses. I lean against the wall, staring into the bathroom at the claw-foot tub that looks like it hasn't been cleaned in a long time, and I can't help thinking about Blue.

Where's he from? What has he seen and done in the military? All kinds of crazy scenarios for how he got the scars on his back run through my mind. How did he end up at Ikana College? How did he come to be living in a house called The Canadian Embassy? What is it about him that seems to fascinate me so friggin' much?

He's promised to tell me the house's history over a couple of beers. Probably not such a good idea. I got really relaxed and way too giggly the few times I've had alcohol. Like just before The PK Penetration.

That's what I'd called it in the journal I've been keeping since I was seven years old. When I was 14, I started giving each date a title that summarizes the day's events, hopefully in a funny and sarcastic way. That's one of the rules I've set for myself. Another is that I have to be brutally honest in the journal about everything that happens each day, everything I do, think and feel. The third rule is that I can't erase or cross out anything I write in the journal, ever. No matter how much I might regret writing it.

So far, I've stuck to my journal rules. Sometimes, it is seriously painful to go back and read certain days' entries. Like what I wrote in the middle of the night after the graduation party attended by pretty much every senior in Fort Peace, Oklahoma, held at the house of Pastor Seth Adams, head honcho at First Baptist Church of Fort Peace. A megachurch led by a megalomaniac. At least that's how his son Tyler once described him.

Seth Adams is a big man with a huge personality, and he can bring thousands shouting to their feet or send them sobbing to their knees with just a few words. People drive from other towns miles away to attend First Baptist. Pastor Seth sure can pack them in. His son, though, is a different matter. Tyler's short and skinny, always strutting around with his arms held away from his body as if he's trying to appear larger than he actually is. He usually tries to act like he owns the town. As Seth Adams' only son, he kind of does. But Tyler is so insecure, so obviously uncomfortable in his own skin, that most people either pity or despise him. Even Pastor Seth seems to find him pathetic.

Tyler goes around insisting that people call him PK. "Preacher's Kid, of course," he said with phony disgust when I asked what PK stood for the day we met. I was one of the few who actually agreed to call him that, for a little while anyway. Poor Tyler. Sometimes, I do feel sorry for him. Other times, I hate his guts.

I try to steer my thoughts back to what matters right now: all the crap I need to do for my job at the paper and my classes. Not to mention figuring out how to deal with the jackhole who'd called my phone last night, obviously disguising his voice. He has called and texted and emailed me over and over in the last few weeks, each time scaring the shit out of me. And I have no idea who it is or why he's doing it.

I do kind of want to have a beer, or two, with Blue while he tells me about the house. And while he tells me about himself. There's something about Blue. I just deny that. But I have other, more important things to take care of. And I sure as hell don't need any more complications or distractions in my life.

I stomp back into my room, irritated that I'm thinking about Blue's loin-tingling grin and rock-hard body. Some of the disinfectant lingers in the air, but I ignore it, coughing as I decide to reorganize the stuff I'd just organized. I move things from one crate to another, and I can't help replaying my first meeting with Blue that morning on the front porch. I can't help smiling. *Dammit.*

I pick up my journal. The Mont Blanc pen my dad worked extra hours for weeks to buy is tucked into the next blank page. I only use the pen for my journal writing. It's the best gift anyone has ever given me.

I fiddle with the pen for a moment, wanting to write down what's happened so far that day as a way to stop it from swirling around in my head. But that would violate my fourth and final journal rule: no writing about a day until it has ended. I want each day's thoughts and feelings to percolate until just before I'm ready to fall asleep. Only then will what pours out of the Mont Blanc be truly ready for the page. At least that's what I decided when I created my journal rules.

Fourteen-year-olds can be overly dramatic. I was no exception. But I've never broken the rules. So I tuck the pen into the page and put the journal back on the floor. My dad doesn't even know I've moved. He's got enough to worry about without knowing some crazy guy is stalking me.

My phone's in the crate that holds my bedding and towels. I turned it off last night, and I haven't touched it since. I pull my sheets out of the crate and stare at the phone: dark, silent and non-threatening. For the moment, anyway.

I quickly tuck the mattress pad into place, then whip the bright pink fitted sheet over the bed, grimacing as it settles into place. Lily Pulitzer sheets, lime green and bright pink. No one but my grandmother would think to buy those for me.

Virginia Cooke Hudson, proud descendant of a family that traces its roots all the way to the Mayflower, doesn't really know me at all. And yet, in her own way, she is attempting to repair the rift that's grown between us. Maybe. Or maybe she's playing another mind game. I wouldn't put it past her. But I'd accepted the sheets anyway and started my sophomore year with a dorm room fit for a prepster. The bedding doesn't really seem to work with the college grunge vibe of my new surroundings, but it is all I have.

I finish making up the bed, then stick the journal and phone under my pillow. I'll have to deal with both of them later.

I step through the open window after dark that night, clutching my phone in one hand, my journal and pen in the other, and shaking my head to get Just Brenna's curtains out of my face. I sit cautiously on the flat roof that extends over the front porch.

I should be grateful to Blue for occupying my thoughts most of the afternoon. He's taken the place of the suffocating sense of panic that's been my constant companion for the last month. Lust—or whatever it is that won't let me stop thinking about Blue—is definitely better than panic.

A huge oak tree with spreading branches stands in front of the house, its massive trunk touching the bricks that have turned the front yard into a parking lot. Several of the branches reach over the roof, with one scraping the tiles near my bedroom windows. The light from my room reveals the deep rust hue of the leaves.

I love the colors of autumn. For years, our family took an annual fall foliage trip around the state, starting at the sprawling Cooke ranch in the northeast corner and driving slowly south through the Ouachita Mountains into what used to be the Choctaw Nation in southeast Oklahoma. I can still remember being awed by the miles of vibrant red, yellow and rust-colored trees.

My Grandpa—my dad's dad, who grew up in Southeast Oklahoma—made it a tradition on the trip to tell us the story of *his* mother Lillian, who at 16 had fallen deeply in love with a tall, handsome Choctaw boy she was forbidden to see. After being caught when they tried to run away together, the Choctaw boy mysteriously left town in a hurry, and my great-grandmother was forced to marry an older man approved by her father.

Lillian lived to be 99 years old and, according to Grandpa, never forgot her lost love. She died when I was six. I have a wispy memory of a frail woman always wrapped in blankets, with melancholy eyes and gnarled hands that would grab hold of me and refuse to let go. The shades of autumn are now seared into my imagination, infused with the story of Lillian's tragic romance. I can never see a tree in its fall glory without thinking about it. I don't even know for sure the story is true. Grandpa was legendary for his tall tales. But he'd always sworn this one was for real.

My phone slips off my leg and comes to rest with a thud on the roof. I shake my head. *Get back to reality. Get yourself together.* Before I can talk myself out of it, I push the power button on the phone. I've been out of contact for almost 24 hours.

The phone seems to take forever to come back to life. I wait to see notifications for missed calls and texts, my stomach knotted. Fifteen calls from *Daily* staff. If I'd turned the phone off on a weekday, it would have been far more. A buttload of texts from staff members too, mainly from Jason, the managing editor. He's probably wondering what the hell's going on, why I haven't responded. I always pick up the phone and answer texts right away.

Five calls from Megan, my former roommate. Not surprising, considering how I bolted out of our dorm room. She's texted me several times as well. *Hey, are you OK?* And an hour later: *Hey, where are you??* Then: *OK, you are freaking me out. I NEED TO FUCKING HEAR FROM YOU, WOMAN!!!!!*

One of the things I love about Megan is that even her texts are grammatically correct. No single letters taking the place of words, no missing punctuation, not even any asterisks replacing letters in her curse words. She loves to read, just like me. She told me once that books were the only thing that kept her sane when she was growing up. She's a word nerd, like me. We only knew each other slightly in high school, but we were the only kids in the school going to Ikana, so we decided to room together freshman year and again sophomore year. And now I've abandoned her.

I'm OK, Megz. I type, feeling guilty. *Sorry to worry you. I miss you already. I'll come by tomorrow and spill all the details.*

Within seconds, my phone buzzes with a reply: *Dear God, you'd better have a damn good explanation for scaring the shit out of me like this!!!!!!!* Then: *Just kidding … sort of. I know why you did it. I'm just glad you're OK. I still don't think moving out in the middle of the fucking night was your only option, but…*

Then: *OK, I'll see you tomorrow. Love you KeeKee.*

I smile as I type. *Love you too Megz...*

There's been no further word from the stalker. That's a minor miracle. I take a deep breath in and let it out slowly, then smile again as I look up at the stars. Maybe it's all going to work out. I open my journal and start to write.

3

BLUE TO THE RESCUE

Blue

I went to bed early. I really need a decent night's sleep. But half an hour later, I'm still staring up at the ceiling, sweating and cursing the house's cheap bastard owner in Toronto. The son-of-a-bitch won't spring for decent air conditioning. Time to remind him yet again who kept his dumbass sons out of jail last year. They'd ended up having to scurry back to Canada to Daddy's protection anyway. But at least, thanks to me, they aren't rotting in prison.

Mr. Money Bags did show his gratitude by letting me stay in the Embassy rent-free. But he's not grateful enough to do much more than that. So we are left to sweat whenever it gets too hot for the decrepit window units in the bedrooms to keep things cool. And when the mercurial Oklahoma weather changes yet again, we'll be freezing. The house has a fireplace that was sealed up long ago, but no central heat.

I sit up and switch on the lamp next to the bed, then grab the guitar leaning against the nightstand. The instrument's dinged wood has almost as many battle scars as I do. That guitar has kept me sane, or at least saner than I would have been without it. No doubt in my mind about that. I'll never get rid of it. Plus, it was the last communication I'll ever have from my old man, his peace offering. Or all the peace offering Bill Danube had been capable of making.

All I have to do is ignore the names scrawled near the bottom. I pull my thumb across the strings, remembering how my hand twitched when I'd stepped toward Keegan that morning. I had to make a fist to keep from reaching up and pulling my thumb across her cheek. She looked scared to death for some reason, and I was barely able to stop myself from folding her into my arms. I can't help feeling protective around women. Mama tells me it's because I am one of the good guys. But that instinct has sure gotten me into plenty of trouble.

Sweat runs down my back. I jump off the bed and head out to the front porch, still holding my guitar. Maybe I can play for a while out where it's cooler. I slump into the squeaking porch swing and bring the guitar to rest on my lap. But a chirping army of cicadas shatters my plans. It sounds like the fucking middle of July outside. Too much damn noise to be able to focus on my music.

The house is quiet, though. Hunter went out around seven and won't be back until very late, if he comes back at all. He usually gets lucky. Hunter can talk most girls into anything, at least until they get to know him better. And even then, a lot of girls are willing to give him a pass. I guess he's that good. Or maybe it's the whole bad-boy shit with the piercings and the treat-'em-like-dirt attitude. It's all so fucking fake. But the girls, at least the ones who are into the bad boys, don't seem to care.

Kendra has apparently not been home since before last night's party, and I didn't even notice. I have no idea where she is. She's gotten quieter, more withdrawn lately, and I'm pretty sure that has something to do with me. I play a couple of chords. *I should just stay away from women altogether.* Then I hear noises from the roof above me. Keegan's light is shining into the tree in the front yard. I slip the guitar over my shoulder and jump off the porch, looking up to see Keegan sitting on the roof with her back against the window.

"Hey, bar girl ... you discovered the best spot in the whole house."

She sniffs a couple of times, then clears her throat. "Hey." It's obvious she's been crying.

"What's wrong?"

A long pause. "Nothing."

"Doesn't sound like nothing."

And that seems to open the floodgates. She starts sobbing. It's too dark to see her face, but I can clearly hear the waterworks and picture her brown eyes, the thick lashes soaked with tears. Just like Aziza's eyes. Just like Aziza's tears. So I do exactly what I just told myself I wasn't going to do anymore. I come to the rescue. Just like with Aziza. And of course, I can't take the stairs to Keegan's room like a normal person. Mr. Blue to the Rescue has to make a big entrance. So I whirl around toward the tree and jump up into the lowest branches, the guitar still on my back.

"What are you doing?" Keegan sounds shocked, but also, I could swear, a little excited. I turn to grin at her as I begin to climb. "I'm coming to see you."

Keegan

It's the most romantic thing any guy's ever done for me, and we aren't even dating. Shirtless and with a guitar slung over his shoulder, Blue scrambles up the tree like Romeo climbing the balcony for Juliet. And then he sits on the branch that extends toward my window, puts his feet on the roof, pulls the guitar to his chest and begins to sing. His voice is like his smile, deep and warm, with a gravelly hint of mischief in it. I've never heard the song before, but it's one of those slow, poignant numbers that should set a loiny lass like me on fire. Instead, I burst into tears. Again.

Blue stops singing. "Not exactly the reaction I was going for." He looks a little hurt. And that makes me cry even harder.

"I'm sorry," I blubber. "I'm really sorry. It's a beautiful song, and you sing it so well. It's just that..." I wipe my nose on my arm. Too late to think about how disgusting that looks. "The song just got to me. It's just that I'm feeling a little overwhelmed right now and..." I snort a couple of times and fight back the urge to wipe my nose again.

I'd just finished writing in my journal, just been writing about how things were looking up, when I received another text from the stalker.

"You want to talk about it?" *Yes.*

"No, no, it's not even your problem. I mean, I know we're living together now. Well, not *living together* but..." I'm stammering. And blushing. There's that unbelievably sexy grin again. I take a deep breath. "Thanks, Blue, I really appreciate your concern. But I'll work through it." I use my editor's tone: controlled, calm, a little distant. Probably too late to pull that out, but it's all I have.

Blue looks down at his guitar for a minute, idly strumming the strings. When he speaks, his voice is soft and soothing. "Do you know who wrote the song I was singing, Keegan?"

I shake my head.

"The Great One himself wrote that song."

For a minute, I have no idea who he's talking about. Then it hits me. "Oh, you mean Frasier whatshisname? The dying cow guy?"

Blue groans. Then he gives me a smile that practically splits his face in two. It's enough to make me stop crying. And definitely enough to light up my damn loins. I've lost control of my own body.

"I can tell you're going to be a challenging pupil, roomie," he says, "but I promise you, I'm up for—"

I scream as he wobbles backwards, grabbing the branch above him just in time. "Oh my God, come up here before you fall off!" I reach one hand toward him while clutching the window frame with the other. "You scared me to death."

He crawls toward me, the guitar hanging off his chest, and I grab one of his arms to help him up, relieved when he finally settles down next to me. My fingertips burn a little where I touched him.

"Mission accomplished." He's still grinning. It takes me a minute to process what he said.

"Wait, did you do that on purpose?" I try to put on a severe expression, but quickly give up the effort. I am too busy just trying to catch my breath now that he's so close to me. I can't help wondering how bad my face looks after all my blubbering. Blue's grin deepens when I punch the rock-hard arm I've just been holding. "I ought to push you off here right now."

"Hey, you're not crying anymore, so I'd say you should be thanking me instead."

Impossible not to smile back at him. "OK, I'll give you that. But don't do it again. I don't think my heart can take it."

"Deal."

We're quiet for a few minutes, listening to the night sounds. The wind has picked up, and Just Brenna's curtains whip in and out of the windows. I finally break the silence. "Why does Hunter call the girl who used to live in my room *Just Brenna*?"

Blue stares at the tree for a moment. His eyes, bathed in the light from my room, glow in a way that's almost eerie. *He's got to be wearing contacts.* "It's the way she always referred to herself." He answers my question with a sigh. "'Hey, it's Just Brenna.' It's like she was always trying to make herself seem as insignificant as possible, like she was apologizing for even existing."

"Oh. That's kind of sad."

"Yeah." He looks down at his arm and traces the tattoo on it with his finger. "Probably some deep psychological issues there. I never got to know her very well. She just moved into the house in August. And then, one day, she packs up and just takes off. No note, nothing. She didn't answer calls or texts." He shrugs. "It was the morning after a party that kind of got out of control. Kendra thinks something happened to Brenna at the party. I don't know. My gut tells me it had something to do with Hunter."

"What do you mean?"

He shrugs again, and his eyes grow hard and angry. "Just the way Hunter acted after she left. *Something* happened. He wouldn't admit to anything, of course. He can be a mean son-of-a-bitch."

"Yeah," I say, "I got that impression the first time I met him. Naked and all."

Blue laughs bitterly and pulls his thumb down the guitar strings. Then he smiles up at me. "But, hey, Brenna leaving meant that Keegan 'Bar Girl' Crenshaw could move in. And that's a good thing." He stares intently at me, the way he did on the stairs. Again, I feel a little freaked out. It's too much, too fast.

"So," I say lightly, needing to change the subject, "the dying cow guy wrote that song, huh? Well, I'll bet you sing it a whole lot better than he ever did."

Blue hangs his head as if he just can't believe what he is hearing. "I sure have my work cut out for me. But like I told you before, bar girl, I'm up for the challenge. In fact, I'm looking forward to it." This time his smile is gradual; it starts at his mouth and climbs his face slowly, finally settling in his eyes. It's unbelievably sensual. And it is completely intentional. Blue Danube is doing his best to seduce me.

"So..." I slap my hands over my eyes without even thinking about it, then pull them away and fasten them to my knees. Now I *really* need to change the subject. "So how did you end up here at Ikana? I mean, you're not in the military anymore, right? You got out?"

He seems startled. "Honorably discharged." His tone has abruptly changed; it's sharp and a little defensive. "I was honorably discharged ... after an injury." He looks away. He seems to be struggling to speak for a moment. I've said something wrong, but I'm not sure why.

"Yeah so, Ikana is the only place I wanted to come," he finally continues, "because of the Great One, obviously."

I must have looked puzzled.

"You really know nothing about Bryson, huh?"

"Like I said before, my mom *might* have mentioned him, but I'm not even certain that's who she was talking about. He's sure not a household name."

Then I add, teasingly, "But I didn't even know who Johnny Cash was, so what do *I* know?"

Blue shakes his head. "Bryson never got the recognition he deserved in the 60s and 70s. He dropped out of the scene for a long time and became kind of a hermit. Then about 20 years ago, he decided he wanted to teach. He's the one that started the music program at Ikana."

I nod. I've heard the college has a great music program and that it is hard to get accepted into it.

"So I wanted to get here before Bryson retired. Or died. He's an old man now." Blue is smiling again. "I had to finagle an audition in front of him because I missed the deadline to apply. Turns out he has a soft spot for soldiers. It was awesome. I'll have to tell you that whole story sometime." His face has softened; for a second, he looks like a little kid.

"Hey," I say playfully, "you should sing at the house parties instead of that guy you said was a douche." I'm thinking I've come up with a great idea. Before I even know what's happening, Blue draws his thumb across my lower lip. And I think that I might have moaned. I am not sure if the sound came out of my mouth or I just heard it in my head. He sits there staring at my lips, and I think he's going to kiss me. I may have even closed my eyes in anticipation.

And then he chuckles. "I was talking about myself, knucklehead," he says. "*I'm* the douche. It was my band playing last night."

You idiot. "Oh." I've barely gotten the word out when he does kiss me. I'd describe it as an exploratory kiss. It's soft, tender, exquisite. And I want more. Oh. Dear. God. Do I want more. But that's not how I react. I pull back, then slap my hands on my thighs in a gesture of dismissal. I'm irritated by how much I want to follow the kissing wherever it might lead. I just met this guy. I do *not* want to end up in bed with him. Well, maybe a part of me does want that. But it's not going to happen.

And really, Blue is out of line. It's way too soon for him to be kissing me. Too much, too fast. I'm mad at him. Sort of. "Okay, well, that's not…" I start, "…this is not what I'm here for and, well, I have to be in the newsroom very early tomorrow so…" I sound harsh, businesslike. That's how I want to sound.

Blue doesn't move, just sits there with his hands draped over his guitar, looking bemused. "Newsroom?"

"Yeah. I'm the editor of the campus newspaper." I'm sort of surprised he doesn't know that. The campus paper and the town's local paper splashed stories about me all over the front page at the beginning of the semester.

"I didn't know we even *had* a campus paper."

Now it is my turn to act outraged. "Really? Ikana's journalism program is known all over the country, and you didn't know we had a newspaper? It's only one of the top college newspapers in the U.S. You mean you *never* read it?"

He puts his hands up. "Whoa, there, bar girl, no need to get upset over it. I try to avoid the news. I don't really want to know what's going on in the world anymore." He looks away, then turns back toward me as I start to inch my way to the window. I've got my journal and phone in one hand, and I'm using the other to steady myself on the roof.

"So you're the top dog at the paper? *How* old are you?"

I pause. "I turn 20 next month." I know what he'll say next.

"Wow, that's pretty impressive. How'd you manage that?"

I've told the whole tale many times before, but I'm not in the mood to go into again now. "It's kind of a long story, but the short version is I had to compete for it at the end of last year against other candidates. It was my first year on the newspaper, and I hadn't even thought of running for editor, but one of my professors really pushed me to do it for my sophomore year. I didn't think I'd get it, but I worked my butt off, and I guess the journalism board liked my presentation. I got it." Then I can't help adding, "I'm the youngest editor ever."

Blue's smile is warm and genuine. "Looks like I underestimated you, Keegan Crenshaw. That's *very* impressive."

I've reached the window. I shrug. "Some people said I got it because of my family, because of who my grandma is." It still stings just to say it. It had never occurred to me when I was competing for the job that people would say I had it handed to me. I start to step inside, speaking over my shoulder. "But that's not true. I earned it." I put my feet on the floor and then lean my head out the window.

Blue's crouched on the roof, staring at me. "I believe you," he says. "But who's your grandma?"

I don't want to talk about Virginia yet with Blue. "Never mind. I'll tell you later."

He stares at me a minute more, then looks over at the tree, and a wry smile plays on his lips. "Um, Keegan, can I go through your room or do I have to go down the way I came up?"

I hesitate. The bed is right there. He's already kissed me, already made clear what he wants. Put all that together with my mutinous body parts, and it could be dangerous. *Maybe dangerous is just what I need.* I can't believe I'm even thinking that.

"Don't worry, Keegan." Blue sounds like he's about to burst out laughing. He can probably tell there's a war going on in my head just from the expression on my face. "I'm going right out the door. You're perfectly safe."

Damn. "Of *course* you can go through my room." The editor's tone again. I need to stick with it. I need to use it every time I'm around Blue Danube. He follows me inside, turning toward me right before he closes the door on his way out.

"Night, bar girl. And, um, sorry if I did something I shouldn't have. The kiss, I mean. I thought … never mind. But I am sorry if I was out of line. Really."

"Night, Blue." I sit down on my bed, trying to ignore the fact that I'm a little disappointed that he's leaving. More than a little, maybe. "Hey Blue?"

The door is almost closed. He sticks his head back inside. "Yeah?"

"Would you maybe sing that song again to me sometime?"

He pauses. Then that slow, impish smile rolls across his face again before he answers. "Count on it, bar girl."

4

BAR GIRL

Keegan

I didn't set the alarm on my phone before I went to bed; I almost never need an alarm in the morning. But I don't sleep well that first night in the Embassy. In fact, it's a terrible night. I wake up the first time with my heart pounding in my chest, staring disoriented into the unfamiliar darkness. No idea, for a few seconds, where I am. Tree branches scrape the roof near my window. When I fall back to sleep, I dream about the awful last days of my mother's life.

In the dream, I'm back at the ranch, in my old room upstairs, with an oak tree just outside the window. I used to sneak out that way when I was younger, until I fell one night and broke my arm in two places. Virginia had her ranch hands shear off the branches near my window and put a stop to what she called my "tree-top adventures."

She always wanted me and my brother, Buick, to call her *Grandmother*. In her mind, *Grandma* was low-class. Buick complied—like he always did—but I called her *Virginia,* or, when I was blaming her for everything that had happened to us, *Granny*. I enjoyed pissing her off, back then.

About a week before my mother died, Virginia swept into the trailer park we'd been living in a few miles from the ranch's southern boundary. She was driving the big SUV emblazoned with the Cooke Ranch logo way too fast along the winding gravel road. I was sitting outside in a lawn chair, swatting at mosquitoes and staring at the setting sun, when she came roaring up. Buick was inside the trailer, trying to figure out what to eat for supper. His choices were pretty much limited to whatever canned food and stale cookies or crackers he could find in there. I'd been meaning to make it to the grocery store, but couldn't seem to get motivated enough to do it.

Buick had the marijuana munchies, but he wasn't getting any sympathy from me. My brother was smart, probably smarter than me, but he'd stopped even trying in middle school. Now a high school dropout, he spent a lot of time sitting around in front of our trailer with his druggie buddies, toking up and making moronic comments about boobs and the girls attached to them.

"Nice job perpetuating the trailer-trash stereotype, Buick," I'd said when I got home from working the noon to 8 PM shift that day, my McDonald's uniform reeking of the French fry machine I'd been operating for hours. "Your mother will be so proud."

He'd told me to fuck off—mainly for his buddies' benefit—and shot me a stricken look that made me feel a little guilty about using our dying mother to taunt him. But only a little. I had to snatch a lighter out of the hand of one of his idiot friends who was hunched over, waving the flame under the loose vinyl straps of the chair he was sitting in.

"Too bad it's fire-resistant, genius," I snapped as the acrid smell of burning plastic reached my nose. Genius just grinned up at me stupidly. Buick was always making dumb choices when it came to his friends.

The druggies were all gone—except for the one I was related to—by the time Virginia walked past me and yanked open the trailer door. She was impeccably dressed, as usual, in wealthy ranch-chic. Her boots alone probably cost more than several months' rent on our little home on wheels, the only thing my dad had been able to afford. Virginia's hair was cut in a sleek bob. She'd never colored it; her natural gray was steely and stylish, just like its owner. But her eyes were puffy, almost invisible without makeup. She looked exhausted. I knew she'd been at the hospital for the last 48 hours.

"Keegan, Buick, pack your things right now." She always spoke like someone used to giving orders. "You're moving back in with me."

I started to resist, just for old times' sake. Virginia and I had a long history of butting heads; it used to make my mother cry and my dad laugh. But they were both beyond that now. And the truth was, I really did want to go back to my big, comfortable room at the ranch. In the cramped trailer, I had to cover my ears every night and pretend not to hear Mom cry out in pain. And when she'd gone to the hospital for the final time, the silence in the trailer at night was even worse. I couldn't wait to get out of there.

In my dream, I'm watching my family from the safety of the canopy bed Virginia bought for me when I was six. Somehow, the trailer, the ranch and the hospital are all mixed together. Mom, Dad, Grandpa, Buick and Virginia are inside the trailer, arguing about something. And then, suddenly, they're standing out in the sunshine at the ranch, laughing together. And then, in another instant, they're sobbing in a waiting room in the hospital. All except for my mother, who starts shrieking as she is wheeled away on a stretcher.

I sit upright in my bed at the Embassy, hearing the screams from my dream for a few seconds even after I'm awake. It's still dark outside. I tussle with the sheets as if they're holding me down, then leap out of bed and run to the other side of the room, resting my hands on the wall and forcing myself to breathe deeply. I cross the room again and pick my phone up off the floor to check the time.

Four o'clock in the morning. I groan and flop back down on the bed. *Shit.* I close my eyes, trying not to think about the *Daily* or the history paper that's due in two days. I especially don't want to think about the stalker. At least there are no new messages from him on my phone.

If I think about any of it, I'm not going to get any more sleep. And so, once more, I allow myself to think about Blue. I close my eyes, hearing the song he sang to me on the roof. My mouth tingles as his thumb moves tenderly across it again in my memory. I can practically taste his lips on mine. I drift to sleep, finally, imagining being pulled to Blue's chest, wrapped up in his strong arms.

Sunlight forces my eyes open, and for a moment, I again don't know where I am. Then I grab my phone in a panic. 8 AM. I should already be in the newsroom. I grab a towel from one bin and my toiletries from another, then race into the bathroom. I throw my stuff in the sink and reach for the handles on the tub, expecting a stream of water from the shower head. Nothing happens. There's no fricking shower head.

"Holy crap!" I stuff the old-fashioned stopper in the drain so I can quickly fill the tub. "What the hell kind of bathroom doesn't have a shower?"

Not sure who I am even talking to. I could just skip the bath altogether, but I worked up a sweat yesterday with all the moving. I don't really want to show up smelly at the newsroom. Ten minutes later, I throw on my clothes and hurriedly brush my teeth, then pull my wet hair into a ponytail. I skip the makeup. The *Daily* staff's seen me barefaced before. At least I am clean. I stuff my laptop and phone into my backpack, along with the books I'll need for my classes.

The smell of freshly brewed coffee wafts into my nostrils just as my feet hit the bottom stair, and I remember the bananas and protein bars I bought the night before. I'm starving and sleep-deprived and already late; a five-minute delay for breakfast won't make much difference. So I run into the kitchen and almost collide with Blue, who is leaning against the counter with his legs crossed, wearing only a pair of plaid boxers and sipping a cup of coffee.

"Whoa there, bar girl." He lifts his mug out of the way just in time. He smells citrusy again and kind of soapy. His dark hair's wet. And there's that stomach, that chest, those arms. Again. I blush.

"Oh, sorry." I step back and hear a yelp. "Oh, sorry, Max, I didn't mean to step on you." The dog wags his tail. I pet his head, then glance at Blue. How bad does my bare, tired face look to him? *Stop it.* Of all the things I should be worried about. I can't stop my eyes from taking in his tanned, muscular legs. Blue sure looks good wearing only a pair of boxers. He probably looks even better wearing nothing at all.

Irritated by my wayward thoughts, I start opening the dilapidated cabinets, searching for another coffee mug, but finding nothing but a motley collection of plastic beer cups, Chinese food soup containers, and weirdly, a set of Hello Kitty plates.

"Sorry," Blue says, "we don't have much in the way of dishes." He opens a corner cabinet and pulls out a package of Styrofoam cups. "I pretty much have the only real mug in the house." He lifts it up for a second. "And I guard it with my life." The cup's oversized, white, with the words UNITED STATES ARMY in gold and an American flag next to some kind of seal. There's a chip on the top of the handle. "But I might consider loaning it to you, when I'm not using it, of course."

He takes another sip, then sets down his mug, fills a cup from the coffee pot and hands it to me. I put my backpack on the linoleum floor and sip with my eyes closed, trying to stifle my panic. When I open my eyes, Blue's holding his mug again and staring at me.

"So how'd you sleep on your first night at The Embassy?"

"Fine" is on the tip of my tongue, but for some reason, I decide to be honest with him. "Not too good. Actually, I had a really rough night." I take another sip. "Bad dreams. And now I'm so effing late."

I open the cabinet that holds my food and tear into the protein bars while also peeling and stuffing most of a banana into my mouth, avoiding Blue's eyes. *I probably look super attractive right now, chewing like a cow.* Did I really need to stuff this much into one bite?

"I know all about bad dreams." Blue speaks barely above a whisper. I regret being honest with him; it just makes me feel more vulnerable. He is staring down into his coffee, and the muscle in his jaw twitches just like when he'd mentioned his father. His lips hover over the cup for a moment. Then he smiles. When he raises his eyes, I see that they're gleaming with amusement. It's a little odd, how quickly he jumps from one emotion to another.

Blue gently tugs my ponytail. "You do know you're allowed to use the word *fuck* here, right?" he drawls. "You don't have to say *effing* at the Embassy, sweet young Keegan. All the F-word derivatives are allowed. No one's going to be shocked or upset if you use them. Nobody's going to punish you." Then he smirks. "Unless you *want* to be punished, of course."

I choke on my protein bar and almost snort coffee out of my nose. My loins are doing a happy dance at the same time that a pretty kinky mental picture of me being "punished" by Blue is setting my brain on fire. *Unbelievable.*

"You OK, bar girl?" There's the grin again.

I shake my head. "You know something, Blue?" I gasp. I can feel my cheeks burning. "I haven't even known you for 24 hours and already I'm wondering what the hell I've gotten myself into." I'm only half-kidding. And I am really late. I take another couple of quick sips of the coffee and look around for the trash. Blue points at a tall, overflowing can on the other side of the fridge. I push the cup into the middle of the pile, then watch it slide off on to the floor.

"Don't worry about it," Blue says. "I guess I'll be doing some cleaning today. Didn't manage to do any yesterday." He sighs. "Kendra and Hunter damn well better show up to help me. We've got a lot to do to get ready for the Halloween party."

I'm bending down to pick up my backpack when he says that, and my stomach lurches. "Halloween party?"

"Yes, ma'am. The Embassy has a reputation to uphold. We always throw a helluva Halloween party."

I must look as queasy as I feel. I have so much work to do. I need to be well-rested and at the top of my game. Trying to sleep in a house with a party reputation to uphold doesn't sound conducive to that.

"Cheer up, Keegan. It'll be a lot of fun. You'll get to hear me play a mean bass. Hey, maybe I'll even sing that song for you at the party."

I give him just a bit of a smile. "I've got to go. Bye, Blue. Um, thanks for the coffee." And I rush out the door.

"Well good morning, Screaming Bad Girl." Jason sticks his head into my office and cracks a smile that's way too wide for a Monday morning. Especially *this* Monday morning. He likes to call me by my blog name, the blog that made me famous before I ever got to college. Or *infamous,* if you believe Virginia. Leaning against the wall in my office, Jason runs a hand through his curly brown hair. He's still holding the thick red marker he uses to edit copy. It's seriously old-school, printing stories out and working them over with proofreading symbols like it's still 1980 or something. But Jason insists he's a much better managing editor doing it that way. And he is definitely a good managing editor. I'm not sure I could do my job without him.

Megz made fun of Jason's long, pointy face and big, "bug eyes" when he came to my dorm room at the beginning of the semester so we could talk about the first issue of the paper. Megz can be mean sometimes, especially about physical imperfections. It's the one thing about her that really bothers me. True, Jason's not the most attractive person. But he's a nice guy, and he's really helped me out with the editor position, pointing out a lot of things I didn't even know. He'd once told me that his grandmother had been the *Daily's* first female associate editor back in the late Sixties. The Parkers were one of Hickory Flat's founding families, and Jason still lives with his parents in the sprawling family home on Main Street.

"So," he asks, "everything okay? You actually moved out of the dorm over this stalker thing?"

"Yeah, I did." I give him a look. I can tell he thinks I overreacted. Of course, so does Megz. "Thanks again for running yesterday's meeting. It really helped me, not having *that* on my plate." It doesn't look good for the editor-in-chief to skip the weekly editorial meetings, but I just had not been up to it. I can't let it happen again, though.

Jason runs his fingers along the bookshelf that holds bound copies of the campus newspaper all the way back to its founding in the 1960s. "No problem at all," he says. "Anytime." There's an awkward pause. Megz is convinced Jason has a crush on me. But he's not my type. Not that I have enough experience to actually have a type.

I look down at my laptop; today's editorial is only partially done. I stare at the blinking cursor for a moment and feel the familiar, skin-crawling anxiety that makes me want to scream. I haven't even started on my history paper yet, and I have a million other things to do. I force myself to take a deep breath. Jason and I start talking over each other.

"Well, anyway, I've got to..."

"So, you moved off campus?"

We both let out slightly uncomfortable laughs, then start talking at the same time again.

"I can't believe you found anyplace to move in the middle..."

"Yeah, I moved into this house that has three other people living there."

He's stopped talking and looks surprised.

"The fourth roommate moved out all of sudden and left them in the lurch," I go on, keeping it short and hoping he'll take the hint, "so it worked out."

The fluorescent lights in my office and the background hum of the newsroom computers—only noticeable when the room isn't filled with *Daily* staff talking, typing, laughing and, occasionally, snoring—have given me a headache. Jason's still fiddling with the bound copies. He turns to look at me. I am trying to be polite, but I don't really care if my face reveals just how much I want to be left alone.

"So, this crazy guy—I'm assuming it's a guy—who is sending you all these messages..." he frowns, "...you *really* have no idea who it is?"

"No, I really don't." I hear the edge in my voice and take another deep breath, trying to control it. "Megz ... you remember Megan, my roommate? She thinks it's this guy I kind of dated in high school. I guess it could be. But I just don't think so. And the detective assigned to my case thinks it's some nut job who's pissed over my editorials or maybe obsessed with me because of the blog and all the publicity it got."

Jason snorts, looking down at my desk, where a copy of last Friday's paper lies open to the editorial page. "Yeah, I can see that," he says. "You're pretty liberal for this state. And a lot of people just don't like your grandma."

I shake my head, feeling a ridiculous prick of tears behind my eyelids. Even though I know it's true, his comment still stings for some reason. "It's so absolutely unbelievable." The frayed-nerves, little-girl-falling-apart tone is back in my voice. So *not* how I need to sound. "I know everyone thinks I'm crazy to have moved," I go on, "but the messages I've been getting are really scary, getting more violent, just like in one of those movies. The guy knows what dorm I live in—lived in—he knows not just the building, but the room number. He knows other stuff about me, personal stuff. And, to tell you the truth, I don't think the police are going to do much about it."

"You haven't changed your number or email or anything?"

I shake my head. Jason frowns again. "That just seems weird they would tell you not to change that stuff," he says. "Why make you have to keep hearing from this asshole?"

"I know, right? I want to change everything *so* much, but the detective told me it might really set the guy off, push him into doing something even worse. And he said leaving everything as it is would help the cops to find the guy faster." I force myself to speak in a stronger, more commanding way. "So anyway, I've moved, and we'll see if that helps the situation. I've got other things to worry about right now than this whack job." I place my hands on the keyboard. "I really have to get back to work now, Jason."

"Yeah, me too." He brandishes his red pen, turns toward the door. "Hang in there, Chief."

"Thanks." I give him a weak smile. "Really, Jason, thanks for everything."

I reach for my old dorm room key and turn it in the lock before I realize I don't really have the right to just walk in anymore. I no longer live here. But I haven't told the RA yet, and I might not tell her. The fewer people who know I've moved out, the better. It's going to be a hard secret to keep though. Megz is Miss Popularity; she practically has groupies. There have probably been at least a couple dozen people in and out of our room just in the last 24 hours.

I sit on the end of my bed and put my feet on my old desk. It is the only clear spot. Megz wasted no time stacking a bunch of her stuff on my side. She's got an expansive personality; she kind of spreads out to fill whatever emptiness—whether concrete or abstract—that she encounters. I love that about her. Most of the time, anyway. My phone buzzes, and I pull it out of my backpack, smiling.

You there, KeeKee?

I'd texted Megz as soon as I got out of my last class and said I'd meet her in the room. I only have about 30 minutes before I have to be back in the newsroom. Things don't really get cranking until about 5 o'clock, so I try to have all my writing done before then. There never seems to be time to even take a breath once the 9 PM deadline is looming.

I'm here, Megz. I type.*Where are you?*

It only takes a moment for her to answer. *Just getting in the elevator. Why the fuck does it always smell like fucking urine in here?*

You'd never know to look at her that Megan Morgan has such a potty mouth. She looks like a China doll. But she can swear with the best of them. The first time I used the phrase *potty mouth* in front of Megz, I thought she'd bust a gut laughing, the way people laugh when a child says something endearing. And then she'd let go with the most amazing string of F-words I'd ever heard. I once told her it was pathetic that someone as smart as her was so addicted to the overused, worn-out, boring old F-word when there's a cornucopia of other fresh and potent words in the language just waiting to come out of her mouth.

"Did you seriously just fucking say *cornucopia*?" That's the only response I got. Thinking about it now, staring at the Pulp Fiction poster on her side of the room, I wish I'd listened to her about moving out. I already miss her. I'm staring at the front page of *The Hickory Herald* tacked up next to the poster when Megz kicks the door open and rushes toward me with open arms. "I've missed you so fucking much, and you've only been gone one day!" She engulfs me in a hug, and for a moment, I think I'm going to cry yet again.

I point at the *Herald*, at the picture of me standing in front of the dorm on move-in day, wearing a *Daily* T-shirt and a goofy grin. "So stupid," I say, "to just tell the world exactly where to find me."

She pulls me over to her bed, orders me to sit, then pulls a couple of beer bottles out of the little fridge under the bed, expertly popping off the tops using the corner of the desk and handing me one before sitting next to me. "Here, drink this and calm down. That newspaper article still wouldn't explain how he got your phone number and email address. But we know that Tyler has both of those."

I sigh, then take a swig. "I guess it's a waste of time to remind you that you could get kicked out for having beer in here. It probably didn't even take you 24 hours to stock up after I moved out. And I can only have a couple of sips. I've still got to put a paper out tonight."

Megz sticks her tongue out, then also takes a swig. "Oh, relax for just a few minutes and tell me about this new place of yours. You said it's a house with three other people? Where's it at? Any guys there? More importantly, any *hot* guys?"

I can't help blushing a little. "Oh. My. God. What the fuck is that?" Megz is pointing at me. "Are you fucking blushing? There must be some sweet piece of—"

"Would you stop?" I take another swig to stop my mouth from spreading out in a smile.

"Tell me now!"

So I tell her about Blue, starting with our meeting on the front porch and ending with his scramble up the tree and his rooftop song and kiss.

"And that's where it ended?" she asks incredulously. "That's all you did with him is kiss? After the tree? And the song?" She smacks me lightly on the side of my head. "No wonder you've only had pity sex."

"I just met the guy," I protest. "And I've got other things to worry about. And you promised you'd stop bringing up the time with Tyler." Megz knows all about my limited romantic history, including the one guy I'd dated freshman year until he dumped me in a text message a week before Christmas. We'd been on the verge of "doing it" more than once, but I'd always called it off at the last minute.

"Hey, what about the other two roommates?"

"One's a guy, one's a girl. I haven't actually met the girl yet."

Megz finishes her beer in one long drink. "So, what about the other guy? Hot?"

I shrug and grimace at the thought of Hunter. "Yeah, I guess, if you like the type. But there's something about him I really don't like. The first time I met him, he was passed out naked in my bed. With some blonde."

"Ooo..." Megz raises her eyebrows, thrusts her lips out and wiggles around on the bed. "Sounds like my kind of challenge." She grins. "What's his name? When can I come over?"

I shake my head and try to look disapproving. "I really don't think he's your type, but his name is Hunter. Actually, there's a big Halloween party on Thursday. They have parties there all the time, with live bands *inside* the house. I sure wish I'd thought more about that before I moved in." I sigh and take another swig. "Blue is in a band that's going to be playing at the party."

"Wait a second." Megz jumps up from the bed, pulling me with her, then grabs my arms. "Are you living in The Canadian Embassy?" She whoops when I nod. "Keegan 'Wouldn't Go to a Party if You Paid Her' Crenshaw is living at the Embassy? Un .... *fucking* ... believable!"

"Oh, stop it. You know why I moved." I'm starting to feel like an idiot.

"Yeah, and it was *so* not necessary, especially in the middle of the fucking night. We both know who's doing this. Tyler's just trying to get your attention, in his own sick way. I always thought there was something wrong with him. Mentally, I mean. And he became obsessed with you after ... you know. Maybe you ought to think about..." She pauses mid-sentence.

"Think about what?"

Megz tosses her wavy blond hair. "Never mind. You can't let him win."

I frown. "Who ...Tyler? Win what? What do you mean?"

She shakes her head. "Nothing, Kee. I was going to say maybe you should lay low, take a semester off, go where Tyler can't find you. But that'd be crazy. I'm sure he's not a *serious* threat or anything."

I walk into the bathroom and pour the remains of my beer down the sink, then toss the bottle in the trash. Her words have given me a chill.

"That's assuming it's Tyler, Megz, and I really don't think it is. And I can't take a semester off, that *would* be crazy. The police are going to figure out who it is very soon. The detective promised me that."

Megz looks out the window toward the center of campus and smirks. "Yeah well, we'll see." Then she starts doing a little jig. "But hey, you moving gives me a reason to go to the Embassy Halloween party. So that's cool."

I pick up my backpack and give Megz a hug. "I probably won't be at the party, Megz. I'll be working. Well, maybe I'll be there later on. But don't let that stop you. You don't need *me* there."

"You know," I add as I open the door, "I worry about you here. The guy, the stalker, knows this was my room."

She scoffs, then walks over and kisses the top of my head. "Tyler wouldn't hurt me," she says. "You're the one he's after."

"That's assuming it's Tyler, and I really don't think it is. It definitely wasn't his voice on the phone."

"You said yourself the voice was distorted. Tyler could have easily bought one of those devices that change your voice." She gives me a little push out the door and blows me a kiss. "*I* know it's Tyler, KeeKee. Which is why you didn't need to move, but *whatever.* Text me the address. I'll see you at the party."

5

THE SWEET SPOT

Blue

The Sweet Spot actually hits the sweet spot as a band about 10 PM on Halloween. Even though we're wearing costumes and that kind of messes up the flow—I throw Corey's stupid Jedi light saber out the window when it smacks me in the shoulder for the third fucking time—we're finally starting to sound decent. Not bad for a band thrown together at the last minute and then slapped with a fucktard name.

Hate doesn't even begin to describe how the four of us feel about being in a band called *The Sweet Spot.* And Bryson knows it; we've begged him to let us change the name. But he just smiles and shakes his head, saying we'll someday thank him for the gravel in our guts. I don't miss the irony: the man I pretty much idolize is not so different from the man I pretty much despise. Or used to despise, until a plane crash wiped out everything but a motherfucking massive load of guilt and regret where my old man was concerned.

Frasier Bryson is applying the Boy Named Sue principle to his cobbled-together band just like Bill Danube had applied it 25 years ago when I was born. Unbelievable.

But after a couple hours playing a seriously random set—everything from The Calling to some Ramones, a bit of Bob Dylan and (to please a really vocal group of girls) some Dave Matthews Band, along with the

Johnny Cash I throw in for Keegan's benefit—we're kind of coming together as a lousy little cover band. I've been on lead vocals most of the night while also playing bass, with Corey taking over vocals for a few songs when we don't need him on keyboard.

By the time I realize I haven't seen Keegan at the party, I've switched to acoustic guitar and told the guys we should go ahead and do the Frasier Bryson mix we planned, even though Bryson himself hasn't showed up. Or if he is here, he's staying out of sight. There's a buttload of people in the house and even more milling around in the back, most of them in costume and quite a few wearing masks. Maybe Bryson is one of them. It would be just like him to try to remain incognito.

We have to stop playing at 11:30 to keep the local cops off our backs. We're running out of time.

I don't need to look at my 12-string Gibson as I start the haunting intro riff of *Comrade in Arms.* That song, like all of Bryson's songs, is embedded in my fingertips. But I look down anyway, staring not at the strings but at the words scrawled in Sharpie on the worn mahogany body. *Monti, Cunny, Hud. Heroes of Hell's Highway. Lameass Singers.* I guess it's some kind of messed-up, masochistic moment. I know better than to look at those names. I know what kind of memories it'll stir up. But I do it anyway.

The guys signed my guitar as a joke after a karaoke contest I won handily. I was pretty much the only one in our unit who wasn't tone deaf. A scene flashes into my mind: four of us from the Hell's Highway Company tossing a football around, lackadaisical in the desert heat but needing some kind of diversion. Cunny's red hair and lopsided grin, with those pearly-white teeth of his that seemed to gleam in the sun. It is seriously weird, the things I remember.

Cunny had fumbled the football, and it knocked off his expensive sunglasses. He accidentally stepped on them, crushing them with his heavy boot, and then furiously unleashed a blue streak of swear words. The rest of us doubled over laughing. If it was someone else, it wouldn't have been funny. But Cunny was one of those people who could make you laugh just by walking into a room. And we were desperate for every chuckle we could get.

I've stopped playing, stopped singing, before the song is over. The band guys are looking at me, uncertain what to do. I shake my head to clear the lingering vision of Cunny, then launch into *Gild the Lily*, the tune I sang in the tree for Keegan. It stings a bit, that she's not around to hear the song, but it's ridiculous to be feeling that way. I've known the girl for all of one week. *Grow a pair, Danube.*

Keegan told me she'd be late to the party; she's worked late every night since she moved in, getting the campus paper out. And every time I've seen her at the house, she's either been on her laptop or phone or with her nose in a textbook. She works a hell of a lot harder than I do. I've started picking up the school paper every morning on campus and reading it front to back, especially the editorials, which are all written by Keegan. Fuck, she's smart. And already getting into my head.

I make myself stare into the crowd. *Do not look down at the guitar again.* And then I see Bryson walk in, wearing his standard denim shirt and jeans and holding a red cup. Not that I'll admit it to anybody, but I am as excited as a little kid who's just spotted Santa. I invited Bryson to the party, but I'm not sure I believed he'd actually show up. I'd asked Kendra to let him into the Embassy without paying the cover we charge everyone else and to make sure he gets a beer. Dressed as some kind of a goth gypsy, Kendra gave me her usual baleful stare. But I knew she would do it.

Bryson finds a spot along the opposite wall to lean on while he sips his beer. The orange lights Kendra strung from the ceiling shine down on his mane of white hair. There are quite a few girls in the music program who claim to have the hots for Bryson, and not just because of his celebrity status. He does look good for his age, fit and tan and always wearing this amused expression on his face. It's hard to read him, impossible most of the time to know what he is thinking. It makes him seem kind of mysterious and cool. To girls, anyway. Hell, who am I kidding? To me, too.

I've slowed down the tempo of *Gild the Lily,* added a weepy guitar flourish in the middle and a keyboard and guitar flourish at the end. The other guys in the band are anxious about making changes to the Great One's work, and Corey hasn't tried to hide the fact he doesn't like what I've done.

"Sounds kind of sugar-coated, if you ask me," he sniffed when I first played it my way for the guys. "Where the hell do you get off thinking you can improve Bryson's stuff?"

As if that bushy-haired maggot Corey would know a good song if it came up and bit him in the ass. I can't figure out how he even got into the Ikana music program.

"Well, that's what Bryson gets for making us call ourselves The Sweet Spot," I'd snarled at Corey, not bothering to argue. "We're gonna sing sappy sweet songs."

I haven't changed the tune out of spite, though. I really like what I've done to the song, and I just can't resist trying it out. *Gild the Lily* sounds more soulful my way. It throbs with this delicate anguish that perfectly suits Bryson's bittersweet lyrics. But I'm sweating bullets as I play it in front of him. I have no idea how he'll react. It really is a ballsy thing to do, messing with his work.

I'm about halfway through the song when I see Hunter stumble in from the kitchen, his whole body draped around some blonde in a skintight Catwoman costume. No doubt he'll be peeling that off her very soon. She's not the uptight blonde from the last party. This one looks classier, even in that costume, but kind of tough at the same time.

"Soldier boy!" Hunter shouts, raising his hand in a sarcastic salute. He's wearing a shit-faced grin. "How about something other than this stupid Sixties bullshit?"

I ignore him and keep singing, not quite daring yet to look over at Bryson again. And that's when I see Catwoman untangle herself from Hunter and turn around. "KeeKee," she yells over the music. "KeeKee, show me around." Then she laughs as Hunter tries to put his arm around her again. "And rescue me from your roommate. He's a little *too* eager." She pats Hunter on the cheek and tugs at his Tarzan loincloth, and damn if the boy doesn't practically slobber all over her. The blonde is hot, no question. But Hunter usually plays it cool with girls, even smoking hot girls. Not with this one, though.

I have no time to think about Hunter because I've noticed Catwoman is talking to Keegan. She comes to a stop alongside the blonde and stares at me with her mouth open. I don't know if she's heard the whole song. But she has such a yearning expression on her face, and she's listening so intently, that I'm sure she understands where I'm trying to go with it. Or at least I want to believe she does. *I'm going to sing that song to you again, bar girl, when it's just the two of us.* Already, in my head, it is Keegan's song.

What a pathetic excuse for a soldier I am. Hell's Highway heroes don't spend time mooning over sappy songs. Or over girls, for that matter. But I'm no hero.

The song is over. And it's already 11:30. "That's it, everybody," Corey yells, holding up his hands as a bunch of people protest. "We gotta keep the cops happy." The guys immediately start breaking down the equipment. I whirl around, suddenly remembering Bryson. But he's gone.

"Hey, did you see where Bryson went?" The guys in the band shake their heads. I look around the living room, then walk through the crowd in the kitchen and stick my head out the back door to scan the deck. No sign of Bryson. I go back to the living room, unsure what his sudden departure means. I'll admit, I'm a little scared. It's a dumbass move, daring to change his song. But then, I have a habit of making dumbass moves.

"KeeKee!" The blonde is still fending off Hunter with one hand while holding a cup full of beer in the other. Some of it splashes on the floor. "KeeKee, where'd Tyler go?"

Keegan points up the stairs. "He said he had to use the bathroom." She's staring at me again, her face tense. Then she turns to the blonde. "Megz, I don't want to see Tyler again. I cannot believe he showed up here! I can't believe he followed you here! We ought to call the police. But he swore to me he's not the stalker. I just don't know what to think." She puts her hands over her face. "Will you just get him out of here?"

Keegan runs her fingers through her hair and stands there with her hands on top of her head. She's wearing a T-shirt and jeans that fit her well enough to almost give me a hard-on just looking at her. For a moment, I forget all about Bryson and my possibly messed-up future in the music program.

"Sure, Kee," the blonde says, stroking Keegan's face reassuringly and kissing her forehead, "sure I will." Then she takes Hunter's arm and smiles beguilingly at him. "My new friend Hunter will help me, won't ya?"

Hunter stumbles, and she catches him. He grins and salutes her. "I'll do anything for Catwoman," he growls, trying to grab her. Boy is beyond wasted.

Someone, probably Kendra, cranks up some Adele, loud enough to be heard but low enough to keep us out of trouble. The party will probably go on for a while, at least out back. But I'm done. I hear Max yelp from my bedroom and scratch on the door. Ever since the night some fool gave him several cups of beer to drink, I've locked Max in there during the parties.

"I'll be right with you, baby." Hunter can barely get the words out, blowing a kiss to Catwoman as he totters toward the kitchen. "But first, I have to get Kendra away from the music. Or the music away from Kendra. I'm not throwing a Halloween party with fucking Adele playing in the background."

I pull the key to my room out of my pocket and am unlocking the door, holding my guitar in my other hand, when Keegan touches my shoulder. Fuck if it doesn't make me shiver. "Can I come in there with you for a while?" she asks, a plea in her voice.

As if I'll say no. "Sure." I almost choke on the word.

Max rears up excitedly when I open the door, first in my face and then in Keegan's. She pets him, and he starts wiggling all over, the way he does when he's happy. "I better get him outside to do his business," I say, watching Max warily as I place my guitar in its usual spot on the chair. Max sometimes gets over-excited and pees on the floor. "Come on, Max, let's go." He follows me into the living room. "I'll be back."

Keegan kind of smiles in return, but she looks uncertain. I wonder if she already regrets asking to come into my room. Shit, this girl's skittish. Like the deer my old man and I used to lie in wait for, sitting for hours like idiots up in a tree in the freezing cold. That was before I pissed him off by deciding I didn't want to hunt anything anymore.

"I'll be here," Keegan says. But she looks ready to bolt.

I could just send Max outside on his own. But there are too many ways for him to get in trouble while the party's still going on. Damn dog has become my responsibility. I push a pathway for Max through all the people still clogging the kitchen, then stand on the deck as the dog finds a spot in the yard. And I keep glancing over at my bedroom window, hoping Keegan will still be in there when I get back.

I've stuck one of the cups of beer in my teeth to free up a hand, and I'm just turning the doorknob when I see Hunter and Catwoman hustling some short, dweeby-looking dude down the stairs and toward the front door. They're gripping his arms like they mean business, and it's obvious Dweeby isn't happy about it. But even drunk, Hunter easily outmatches the kid in size and strength. And the blonde looks like she can hold her own against him as well.

"Don't fight it, Tyler," she's saying. "You had no business following me here. You think I don't know you're the asshole sending KeeKee all those messages? You really think you've got *me* fooled? How about I let your Daddy know what you've been up to?"

Dweeby wrenches free of them. "He already knows," he whines. "The cops came to our house and questioned me. That's why I came up here to find Keegan. She won't answer my calls so I had to come up here. She's *got* to believe it's *not* me. Just let me talk to her."

"No way," the blonde sneers. "Just go home!" They push him out to the front porch.

I open the door to my room and take the cup out of my mouth. Keegan's not standing where I left her. No denying the stab of disappointment in my chest. Then I see her, stretched out on my bed with her arm slung over her face. She sits up quickly as I hand her one of the cups. "I remembered on the way back that I owe you a beer and a story."

Her hair's sticking up in a brown halo of static electricity. She looks puzzled for just a second, then gives me a soft smile as she takes the beer. "Oh, yeah. The story of the house. Why it's called the Canadian Embassy." She takes a sip and closes her eyes, releasing a long breath as if she's been holding it.

"You okay? I just saw Hunter and this blonde throw some kid named Tyler out of the house. Sounded like he wanted to talk to you." I say it casually, not sure I really want to hear about the dweeb. I have other things on my mind. But I do want to know about Keegan. I want to know *everything* about her, including how it would taste to lick off the drop of beer that's glistening on her upper lip. Still standing by the bed, I take a big gulp of my beer.

Keegan sighs. "The blonde is Megz—Megan Morgan—my roommate. Uh, she *used* to be my roommate. Tyler is this guy from high school that I never wanted to see again." She looks down at the bed. "Megz thinks he's the one who's been sending me these horrible messages, calling me and making all these threats. It's the reason I moved in here, the reason I thought I had to get out of the dorm." She takes another sip of beer, then gets off the bed and picks up her backpack. She pulls out a phone and stands there pushing buttons, then thrusts the phone toward me. "You should probably know about it, I mean, I should tell you about it now that I'm living in the same house as you. I guess I should have told you guys about it before I moved in."

Another heavy sigh. "I got a couple more texts today. I try not to even read them, but it's hard not to. The police told me not to delete them." Her lips—these perfect, pillowy lips—are trembling. I take the phone, my fingers brushing her hand. She flinches, and once again, Aziza's face flashes before my eyes. Aziza, who's been hovering at the edge of my memory ever since I met Keegan. They're worlds apart, born into different cultures, with radically different futures. They have nothing in common except for their eyes. But for some reason, one reminds me so much of the other.

I squeeze my eyes shut for an instant. That same old need to protect, to rescue, to be the hero, crawls over me. I've learned to hate that feeling. But I can't stop it.

I open my eyes and start reading what Keegan has pulled up on her phone. And rage absolutely fucking floods me, popping out on my forehead in beads of sweat, running like hot lava down my arms, turning each scar on my back into a smoldering ember. Sometimes, when I'm angry or scared—and I'm angry or scared a lot lately—the scars on my back burn almost as bad as they did when they were fresh.

I sit on the bed, staring at the dozens of ugly text messages, all from Unknown. Each one is addressed either to *Keegan* or *Ms. Crenshaw* or *Hey Bitch* or *You Cunt.* You can track the guy's moods, figure out what the tone of each message is going to be, just by those first words. They're all insulting and threatening, but in some, he seems to be trying to sound sophisticated, while the others are just the lowest, most foul crap. Except for about a dozen of them that are addressed to *Screaming Bad Girl* or *The Famous Screaming Bad Girl* or *The Girl Who Thinks She's Benjamin Franklin.* Those are kind of a mixture of both, and I can't figure them out.

Keegan sits next to me, and I look up at her. Her lips are still quivering.

"What the fuck is this?" I ask. She puts her face in her hands and starts to cry. *Nice, Blue, very comforting.* I put my arm around her shoulders, feeling a little awkward. Panic squeezes my chest. *Get out of this now, before you get in any deeper. Get away from her right now.* It's the same warning some voice in my head gave me a few of years ago, when I sat in a village in Afghanistan, clenching my fists as Aziza cried her eyes out. I hadn't listened to that voice then, and I already know I'm not going to listen this time.

I grind my teeth trying to silence the voice, then force myself to speak calmly. "I'm sorry. What I mean is, it's going to be okay. It's … Have you gone to the police about this? What are they doing about it?" I wave the phone around, then drop it on the bed like it has scorched my hand.

Keegan nods, her face still buried. "They're supposed to be trying to track the guy down," she sniffles. "But I sometimes get the feeling they don't want to be bothered with it. Or with me."

"Well, they're sure as hell going to be bothered with it!" I get up and start pacing, then whirl toward the door. "So you guys think that pasty little guy named Tyler is doing this? And he has the nerve to show up here? I'll kill the son-of-a-bitch right now!"

Keegan lifts her face and puts her hands up. "No! Blue, I don't think it's him. I know Megz thinks it is, but…" She shakes her head. "He doesn't have it in him to do this. He's weird and pathetic, yes, but he's not like *that*." She nods at the phone on the bed. "It's somebody else."

There's a long pause. I stand there, not sure what to do next.

"This is so embarrassing," Keegan finally says, wiping her eyes. "I shouldn't be crying all the time. I'm tougher than this. Or at least I thought I was." She runs her hands down her face, then pats the bed next to her. "I don't want to think about it right now. I'm *not* going to think about it right now. Come on. You still owe me a story. And I'm going to finish this beer." She tilts the cup and drains it, then wipes her mouth and smiles at me.

It takes me a fraction of a second to forget about the dweeby dude and the terrible texts and let my hard-on lead me right back to the bed. Maybe I'm not such a hero after all. Before I can sit next to her, though, Max jumps up in my place. I've forgotten about him. Keegan laughs as Max tries to fit his 80-pound body in her lap.

"Max!" I snap my fingers at him. "Get off her. You have no idea what size you are. Get off." He ignores me and snuggles his head right under Keegan's breasts.

"Aww, Max, you're so cute." I roll my eyes as she scratches his ears. Yeah, I'm jealous. "You know just how to make me feel better," she says in baby talk to the dog. Why do girls always talk to dogs like that?

"Hey," I say, "you only get one chance to hear the story." I try not to think about how pathetic it is that I am competing with a cowardly—not to mention smelly—German Shepherd. And that I'm probably losing. "Max!" I don't mean to sound as sharp as I do, but it gets the dog's attention. I point at the bathroom, and he jumps off the bed and slinks in there, settling down next to the toilet. I close the door on him.

"Aw..." Keegan says again.

"He'll be fine. It's story time." I kneel on the bed and tell Keegan to turn around.

"Huh?"

"Turn around. I'm going to give you a massage while I tell you the story. I give good massages. And you could use one." She lets out this tiny beer belch and giggles kind of nervously as she turns to face the headboard. She's sitting cross-legged with her head tilted back a little. I quickly take off my boots. When I put my hands on her shoulders, a low moan escapes her lips that does nothing to ease the swelling in the front of my fatigues. *Easy, Blue.* To distract myself, I ask the question that's stayed in my mind since I read the text messages.

"So, before I tell you the story of the Canadian Embassy, I just gotta ask something."

She opens her eyes and turns her head to one side. "Yeah?"

"Who's Screaming Bad Girl?" I squeeze her trapezius muscle, wishing I could yank her T-shirt off. "And what the hell does Benjamin Franklin have to do with any of this?"

Her shoulders slump under my hands. "Screaming Bad Girl is the name of my blog." She says it with another sigh. "Or *was* the name of my blog until I shut it down." She turns to look at me. "You haven't heard of it? It was all over the news about a year ago."

"Stop moving." I gently turn her back around. "I told you, I try to avoid the news."

"Oh, yeah. Well, so I started this Screaming Bad Girl blog while I was still in high school to, kind of, *comment* on Oklahoma politics. I mean, I knew about all this stuff going on that was just..." She shook her head, grimacing, "...just disgusting. I wanted to do something about it." I can't help smiling at the outraged idealism in her voice.

"The tagline for my blog," she goes on, "was *A 21st-Century Silence DoGood*." She lets that phrase hang in the air, obviously expecting me to pick up on something.

"Um..." I'm drawing a blank and still thinking about what's under her shirt.

"You know, Benjamin Franklin's pen name, Mrs. Silence DoGood? They talk about it in the first *National Treasure* movie? Franklin wrote letters to the newspaper, pretending to be this woman named Silence DoGood?"

"Oh yeah. Now I get it, I think."

"My idea was that in the 21st century, a woman wouldn't be a silent do-gooder, she'd be a..."

We say it at the same time: "Screaming Bad Girl."

"Exactly." She's rolling her head back against my hands, clearly enjoying the massage. "I got to 100,000 subscribers before some reporter figured out who I was."

"Wow! But why did you shut it down?"

Another sigh. "It caused a huge uproar 'cause of who my grandmother is. Everyone assumed she was behind the blog, when she actually didn't know anything about it. She's the *last* person I'd tell. We don't agree on anything."

"Um ... you lost me again."

"My grandmother is Virginia Hudson, President Pro Tempore of the Oklahoma State Senate. Virginia *Cooke* Hudson. You know, Cooke Ranch and all that. Have you heard of the Cooke Ranch?"

My hands stop moving. "Oh. *Oh.* Yeah, yeah, of course I've heard of the Cooke Ranch. One of the biggest ranches in the country, very powerful family. Huh. Wow. I'm kind of speechless." I move my hands to her neck. "So, Keegan Crenshaw, you're part of Oklahoma royalty. I guess I should be thanking you for allowing me to touch you."

She snorts. "No, I'm not anything of the kind," she says firmly. "Especially not now. Virginia was really, really unhappy with me. I didn't hold back in the blog, and I'm pretty opinionated when it comes to politicians. Or some politicians, anyway. But I ended up shutting down the blog. Virginia said it might make Ikana change their mind about admitting me, but I think she was just trying to scare me. If anything, the journalism board seemed to like the whole blog thing. Virginia was mad because people were saying bad things about her. Quite a few were even calling for her to resign over the whole thing. She got really pissed over that."

"What did you parents say about it?" My question makes her stiffen under my hands.

"My dad thought it was the coolest thing ever."

"And your mom?"

"My mom died of ovarian cancer three years ago." She says it in the same clipped, controlled tone I'd mastered when talking about my old man. My index finger trails down the soft skin on her neck.

"Keegan, I'm so sorry." She bends her head to the side so that it touches my finger.

"Virginia actually said she was glad my mom wasn't around to witness the 'family shame.'" She puts it in air quotes. "Can you imagine, saying you're glad your own daughter is dead? I almost knocked Virginia on her ass for that. My mom died just before the whole thing blew up. I'd started the blog while she was sick. I guess it was kind of distraction for me. Or something like that."

For a few moments, we're silent. Max whines from the bathroom. "Poor Max," Keegan says. She tilts her head all the way back to look at me. "So, Mr. Blue Danube, I've answered your question. Now I really want to hear that story."

"You got it." I'm still working on her neck, which is really tight. Not surprising, given what she's dealing with. In less than a week, Keegan Crenshaw has surprised me more than any girl I've ever known. And I thought I was beyond being surprised.

I move my hands up to her scalp and begin to weave my fingers through her soft, shiny hair. She arches her back like a cat, clearly enjoying it.

"Oh, you've found my sweet spot," she says. I choke back a laugh, but it comes out anyway. She tries to turn her head, but I hold it in place. "What?"

"Nothing. It's just that Sweet Spot is the name of our band, believe it or not."

"Really? Sounds like kind of a, I don't know, *girly* name for a band with four guys."

"Tell me about it. Bryson's making us use that name. He puts all the music students into bands, and *he* gets to name the bands. I think maybe he's trying to toughen us up. So anyway, the story."

She's closed her eyes and is smiling.

"There once were two boys from Canada. Twins, actually, who considered themselves to be musical geniuses. And they decided they really wanted to go to Ikana, so they applied like everyone else, and lo and behold, they got turned down. So they did what any spoiled rotten sons of a very rich man would do. They begged Daddy to buy their way in. And lo and behold, Daddy made a very big donation to the college, and, suddenly, the boys were accepted."

Keegan opens her eyes and interrupts me. "Really? Somebody would bother to bribe their way into the music program here?"

"Hey, the program is a big deal! Of *course* people try to bribe their way in." She closes her eyes again. "Bryson was really steamed about it," I go on, "but he gave the twins a fair shot. Their papa bought this house for them to live in, and they started throwing parties and running up big bills. Actually, Bryson got over being mad about having to let the twins into the program pretty quick 'cause they'd have kids from the program playing at all the parties. One night, one of the twins put up that Canadian flag and announced to everybody that this place would now be called The Canadian Embassy, and it has been ever since."

"But what happened to them?"

"Once their Daddy found out they were failing all their classes, he cut them off. So they started selling drugs." I shake my head. "They were idiots."

"Oh my God."

"Yeah."

"But how did *you* end up living here?"

"I met the twins in the program, and I needed a place to stay and they needed money, so I moved into what's now Kendra's room. Then the twins made some enemies—no big surprise there—and had to hightail it back to Canada or they were probably going to either be arrested or murdered. Who knows. Anyway, their dad decided to keep this house as a rental." I don't go into any further detail. No need to tell Keegan the seedy underbelly of that story. Max whines again and scratches the door.

"And how did Max come into the picture?" she asks. I'm still massaging her scalp.

"Max was taken as partial payment on a drug debt, believe it or not. One of the twins had this girlfriend who begged them to take him. He was a puppy then, all fuzzy and cute. But after a few days, they forgot he existed, could never remember to feed him or anything. *Assholes.* So anyway, Big Daddy up in Toronto lets me live here free in exchange for collecting the rent and keeping things up around here, although he never wants to cough up much money to actually fix anything. But it helps me make ends meet."

As if on cue, Max whines again. Keegan takes hold of one of my hands and looks up at me. "I really admire you, Blue. Growing up poor, serving your country, making it on your own. How old are you, anyway?"

I smile and rub a strand of her hair between my fingers. I can't resist raising it to my nose and inhaling the scent. Coconut and something else I can't quite identify. "I'm 25, practically an old man. And who said I grew up poor?"

"Oh." She turns around to face me, sitting cross-legged on the bed, still holding my hand. "I just assumed. I mean... I *didn't* mean to assume but..." She looks confused. She's probably seen a change in my expression. I am seeing my dad's plane in pieces in a hangar and the body bag they unzipped just long enough for me to identify his body so that Mama wouldn't have to. "I didn't grow up poor. But I'm on my own, and I'm definitely poor *now.*" I'm not going to mention the $5 million trust fund sitting out there in my name. I am never going to touch that blood money. "And we have something in common," I go on, raising her hand and kissing her palm, her wrist and the satiny skin on her forearm. Then I cup her face. "My dad died almost five years ago in a plane crash. I *know* what it feels li—"

And suddenly, before I can even finish, her lips are on mine. She kisses me frantically, greedily. She grabs my face and lays those lips against my mouth, my cheeks, my eyes. She kisses me as if she's been waiting a long time to do it. She kisses me like no other girl has ever kissed me. And I kiss her back, cradling her face in my hands as I drink in the taste of her lips, running my tongue over her teeth and into her mouth, placing soft kisses on her nose and eyes, nuzzling her neck. I tilt her face up into the light and kiss her on the top of her head, her chin, her cheeks, before returning to claim her lips again.

I pull back just long enough to whip off my shirt, and she moans at the sight of my chest, pulling me toward her and running her hands down my arms. Then she takes a deep breath and closes her eyes and puts her tongue on my collarbone, leaving it there for a second, then slowly letting it glide down my chest toward my abs. It's all I can do not to tear off all her clothes and take her right there and then. *Easy. Go slow.* I don't want to spook her and mess things up. But I've never wanted any woman like I want Keegan.

"Blue." She places her cheek against my chest. "I've been wanting to do that since the day I moved in. I can't believe I actually just did it, though."

I pull her to me. "What do you know about that?" I whisper. I swoop down on her mouth, trailing kisses down her throat. Then I lean her back against my arm and lift her shirt to expose her taut stomach, making circles on it with my tongue. She arches her back and sighs, and I swiftly pull the T-shirt over her head. She's wearing a lacy black bra that I want to tear off with my teeth. The swell of her breasts leaves me weak and stupid with desire.

Keegan is staring at me, her lips open slightly, her eyes blazing, her expression a strange mixture of lust and fear. "Blue." She puts a finger on my chest, and something in her voice tells me what she's going to say next. "I can't do this. Not yet. We barely know each other. It's just too quick."

"I think we know each other pretty well already. And I've got some really good suggestions for how we could get to know each other a *lot* better." I give her a *I'm kidding but I'd love to be serious* grin, then raise her palms up and place my lips gently against them one at a time. Then I pull her hands above her head. "But I want you to be ready." I'm still whispering. I slip the shirt back over her head, kissing her once more, feeling pretty damn heroic just for stopping myself.

She sits there, looking miserable. Max whines yet again. I get up and open the bathroom door, wishing I could take a cold shower right then. Max bounds out and jumps into the bed, and Keegan scratches his ears. "Aw, Max." She looks at me, seeming unsure what to do next.

I stretch out on the bed. "So you want to cuddle with me and Max for a while? Nothing else, just cuddling?" *Aw, yes, cuddling.* Girls always go for that. She hesitates. *She's going to say no.*

"Okay." She grins and stretches out next to me.

So we spend about an hour talking. It's one of the best hours I've had in a long time. Almost better than sex. Okay, not really. But it's pretty damn great. I finally have to get up to let Max out, and when I come back to the bed, Keegan is sitting up, looking sad and serious. "Blue," she says slowly, "how'd you get those scars on your back?"

And just like that, the skin on my back again feels seared and torn, an agonizing reminder of a choice I can never take back. I've had plenty of people notice the scars before and ask me what happened. It's not like I never take my shirt off around others. It always makes me catch my breath, though, always feels like someone just punched me in the gut when I hear that mix of horror and fascination in the questions they ask.

Women are usually more subtle, and most of them adopt a maternal tone: *Oh my goodness, what happened? Were you in an accident?* Men are more blunt and coarser: *Jesus, what the fuck happened to you?* I prefer the men's attitude. It's easier to brush it off with a tough-guy shrug, and they never press me for details. With women, I have to let them know I'm not willing to talk about it.

It's a lot worse when someone I care about wants to know what happened. I almost broke down and cried the first time my mother saw my back. I was like reliving that terrible day in Afghanistan all over again. And three years later, the same thing is happening with Keegan.

I sit on the bed, facing away from Keegan, trying not to show how much her simple question gets to me. Her hands carefully touch my shoulders. "I'm sorry, Blue, I'm so sorry. Forget I asked. I'm sorry."

I turn toward her. "It's not your fault. It's a normal question to ask. But I can't tell you about it. I just can't."

"I understand. Shit, I don't know why I asked." She pulls the sheets back. "Come on, lie down with me."

We get in, and I pull her to me and hold her as tightly as I can. We stay like that for a long time. After a while, she speaks again, her voice sleepy. "Blue? I'm sorry I'm not ready. I'm sorry if it seems like I am teasing you. I didn't mean to do that."

I kiss her forehead. Sleep's tugging at me, too. "Don't be sorry. I don't feel like I was teased. I want you to be ready. I want you to be sure. I'll wait for you, Keegan. I'll always wait for you."

Too much, too soon, Danube. Way too much, way too fucking soon. Typical of me, going all in all at once, making big-ass statements like that. But God help me, I mean it.

6

DREAMS

Keegan

For once, it's a good dream. We're floating down the river just like we used to do when we were kids. Buick's ahead of me; the bottom of his pruny feet extend past the air mattress. Buick used to spend all summer outside, on the river or riding his horse, Okie, or just lying around on a bale in the barn, chewing on a piece of sweet hay like a character in a Western. The ranch hands sometimes allowed him to help out, and he'd turned out to be a pretty competent cowboy. But then we moved out of the ranch late one night after a screaming match with Virginia, and Buick had gone quite literally to pot.

The sun in my dream sizzles on my skin, the air pulsing with an itchy mix of 100-degree heat and bugs that feels absolutely real. Mom's on my left, struggling to get comfortable on the under-inflated air mattress. She always insisted on blowing up her own and never quite filled it up enough. She looks young and healthy; her long brown hair hasn't fallen out yet. Her high-pitched guffaw trails behind her. I remember that laugh every time I think of her. Dad is up ahead next to Buick. His teeth flash in the sun as he paddles with his arms. We are happy. We are so happy.

But then it suddenly gets cold, and I look back to see a nest of water moccasins slithering behind, fangs gleaming, eyes venomous slits as they bear down on us. Some of the snakes have human faces, people I know: Tyler, Megz, Hunter, Jason, Blue. Someone is screaming. I grab frantically with one hand at the water, trying to pull my mother toward me, trying to comfort her and silence the screams piercing my dream like punches to the head. But as my hand touches her air mattress and reaches for her face, I see that Mom's still laughing, still happy. Not screaming.

And then I wake up, abruptly; it feels like coming to a sudden stop on a moving roller coaster. Just lying there, I am breathing heavily, staring at the stained ceiling. Beams of sunlight stream around window blinds. Where am I? Then it hits me: Blue's ceiling, Blue's bed. And even though I'm awake, screams still fill my ears. Blue's screams. He sits up next to me, gasping, and crawls to the edge of the bed, then puts his feet on the floor and buries his face in his hands. He's shaking. I watch him for a moment, then sit up and move toward him, placing my hand on the rough and puckered skin of his back.

He flinches at my touch and shoots to his feet, then whirls around and stands there, his eyes wild, unfocused, crazed with pain and anger. He moves toward me, muttering something I can't quite make out between his clenched teeth. Before I can react, he grabs my chin and tilts my face up, then starts to squeeze. It scares the crap out of me. And it hurts. "Blue! Blue! It's me!" I wrap my fingers around his hand. He grips my chin a little tighter. "Blue! It's Keegan."

His hand suddenly relaxes. I watch the madness slowly drain from those cobalt eyes. But the look of shame that fills them and spreads across his face is worse. He stands like that for several moments, clearly struggling to contain his emotions. We stare at each other, two people who in less than a week have become so exposed, so vulnerable, to each other. A part of me wants to take his face in my hands, to smother it with kisses, to soothe and comfort him. But another part of me wants to get *out* of that room. Blue's pain is too real, too raw, too scary for me to deal with.

Maybe he senses my conflicting desires. Maybe they're obvious on my face. Maybe he feels sorry for me. His agonized expression fades, and the warm, amused look he wore when we first met reappears, although it looks a little forced. "Well, I guess that'll teach you to fall asleep in my bed." He says it lightly, trying to be nonchalant, but the ragged edge to his breath gives him away. He sits next to me, raises his index finger as if to stroke my cheek, then puts it back down without touching me.

He raises the finger again, curves it and brings it close to my face. But just before he touches me, I flinch. Don't mean to, but can't help it. I'm totally freaked out, by Blue's intensity and rage, and by the way I'm reacting to him. I'm appalled at the way I've literally thrown myself at him, the way I've opened up to this guy I barely know. It's all too much, too soon.

Blue inhales sharply, and his eyes flood with pain. "Sorry if I scared you." He says it so softly I barely hear him.

I try to smile, try to answer with something reassuring. I want to hug him. But I'm scared and uncertain, and so I just sit there as Blue's eyes search my face. He slumps over a little. I can tell that I've hurt him.

When someone knocks sharply on the door, I bolt off the bed, glad for an excuse to get some distance between us. At some point during the night, I took off my jeans to get more comfortable, and so, when I pull open the door, I'm standing there in front of Kendra wearing only a T-shirt and a thong. Kendra's eyes widen, and a swift rush of emotions—shock, fury, hate, pain—cross her face before it goes blank. She's holding Blue's U.S. Army mug. There's a folded piece of paper inside it.

"I believe this is for you," she snaps, thrusting the mug at me. When I take it, she turns and stalks away without another word.

Somehow, I already know what's written on the paper in Blue's mug. And I know who wrote it. Not his name, maybe, or his face. But I'm beginning to know the nature of this mystery person who seems to hate me beyond reason. So my hand shakes as I set the mug down on Blue's desk, and a single thought pulses in my ears: *It's him. It's him. It's him.*

I pull the folded note out of the mug and stand there looking at it. Blue's eyes on me make my heart beat a little faster. He doesn't say anything. I unfold the paper. It's printed, in all caps, and swimming in exclamation marks.

DID YOU REALLY THINK YOU COULD GET AWAY FROM ME YOU SOCIALIST BITCH?!?!?!!!!! DO YOU REALLY THINK I'M THAT STUPID?!!! I WILL TRACK YOU DOWN, NO MATTER WHERE YOU MOVE, NO MATTER WHO YOU'VE GOT HELPING YOU!!!!! NO MATTER WHO YOUR FAMILY IS!!!! I WILL MAKE YOUR LIFE HELL UNTIL YOU LEAVE THIS TOWN YOU LYING CUNT!!!!!! THAT'S ALL YOU'VE GOT TO DO WHORE. LEAVE!!! WE DON'T WANT YOUR KIND HERE!!

The paper slips out of my hand. I grab the desk to steady myself. How does the stalker know I moved? The room gets wobbly. I feel sick to my stomach, and tears blur my eyes. I blink, trying but failing, to hold them back. The guy wants to turn me into a scared, sobbing mess, and I am playing right into his hands. I turn my head slightly to see Blue standing right behind me, so close he could kiss the tears off my face. The heat from his body singes my over-active nerve endings.

"Keegan." His breath touches my neck, and I close my eyes. "Can I read it?"

I nod, my eyes still closed. Blue brushes against me as he bends down to pick up the paper. It rustles slightly while he reads it, then makes a crinkly sound as he wads it up. Every sound seems magnified.

"I should have kicked the shit out of that slimy little motherfucker while I had the chance. Is he a student here? You know where he lives, right?"

I open my eyes in time to see Blue throw the note on the floor and begin pacing around the room. He's still speaking through clenched teeth. That muscle in his jaw is working overtime.

I shake my head. "Tyler's still living at home in Fort Peace, at least he was last I heard. He didn't actually graduate high school, even though his family pretended he did. Supposedly, he was going to have to repeat his senior year. Or maybe he's getting his GED. I don't know. The police told me they already went to talk to him and don't have any evidence that it's him." My eyes linger on the tattoo on Blue's chest. It's moving up and down as he breathes.

"He works weekends at the church where his dad is the pastor, doing janitorial stuff, I think." I'm not sure he's listening to me. "That's another thing that doesn't make sense," I go on, "if it's Tyler, is he doing all this stalking from Fort Peace? *And* he's able to hide his phone number? Tyler's just not that smart."

"You know where his parents live, right?" Blue demands. "What's the name of the town you're from? Fort Peace? I'm going there today. I'll find the son-of-a-bitch and make him wish he'd never set foot in this house."

Blue's all action now, sliding on a pair of jeans and zipping them while I notice this little line of dark hair that runs from his belly button into his boxers. He slips a plain white T-shirt over his head, and I think about how it felt the night before to curl up next to him and lay my face on that chest. And about how gentle he'd been. Gentle and unbelievably hot, all at the same time. That's all I want to think about. *Stop it.*

He bends down to pick up the note, and I grab his arm. "Blue."

He places the note on the desk. "I shouldn't have crumpled it up like that." He tries to smooth it out.

"Blue." My hand is still on his arm. I can feel the ridges of his muscles under my fingers.

"The police are going to need this. Maybe we should go to the police in your hometown since the local police aren't doing much."

"Blue."

"Or maybe I'll just take care of this on my own." He snorts, then laughs harshly. "I've dealt with characters a hell of a lot worse than this chicken-shit ex of yours."

"Blue!" I punch his arm in frustration. He's talking like he's almost forgotten I'm there. "You're not listening to me. His name is Tyler Adams, but he's *not* my ex. He's just a guy that I..." I don't want to finish that sentence. I wave my hand in front of my face as if to wipe away my words and start again. "He's the son of a pastor in my hometown. But I *still* don't think it's Tyler. That note doesn't sound anything like Tyler. Why would he call me a socialist? I doubt Tyler even knows what a socialist is."

"Keegan, my mug was in the kitchen last night. The note was in the mug. Tyler was here last night. Of *course* it's him."

I start shaking my head before he stops speaking. "There were lots of people here last night," I say, "and a lot of them wore masks. How do we even know who all was here, who might have stuck that note in the mug?"

Blue stares at me. "But if it's somebody else, how did he know you just moved in here?"

I shake my head, tears once again brimming in my eyes. "I don't know." Hard as I try to steady it, my voice comes out shaky. "Who knows, the guy, the stalker, could have seen me leave the dorm in the middle of the night. I'd just gotten a call from him. He knew exactly what dorm I lived in. He could have followed me here."

Blue crosses the space between us in an instant and puts his arms around me. And I try to ignore the alarm bells ringing in my head. My chin throbs where Blue's hand squeezed it only moments ago. I fold myself into my roommate, pressing so hard it's like I want to burrow my way into his skin. He wraps his arms around me tightly and nuzzles my forehead, then my ear, with his lips.

"Don't worry," Blue whispers. "We'll figure this out. No one's going to hurt you. I won't let anyone hurt you."

And for a few moments while we stand there, I'm flooded with sweet relief. I'm flooded with something else too, a warm vibration that flows from Blue's body into mine, making my nipples jump to attention and setting off what feels like at least a three-alarm fire down below. The loins are leaping again. I can't get this close to Blue Danube without facing a mutiny from inside, even at the most inappropriate moments. It's ridiculous. And I want much more of it. At least my body does.

But my head's still analyzing, processing, panicking. And I've just thought of something. I pull back away from Blue a bit. "Hey, how do we know the note was put in your mug last night?" I ask. "I mean, all I know is that Kendra showed up at your door this morning with the note in the mug." I'm thinking of the look on Kendra's face: the anger, the unmistakable jealousy. Blue's face twitches. "You know, Kendra looked really pissed to see me standing herein your room. I mean ... like ... *girlfriend*-pissed." His face twitches a little more, and he looks down. "Blue." I let his name hang there for a few seconds. "Are you and Kendra..."

"No, no." He runs a hand over his head. The other arm is still holding me. "Not anymore. And Kendra wouldn't..." I pull away from him. He frowns. "We weren't ever dating, Keegan. We were just... We just..." He sighs heavily and tries again. "She started using my shower 'cause there's not one upstairs, and things just kind of happened."

I cross my arms. I have absolutely no right to be jealous. I am jealous as hell. And that cautious, cowardly part of me that's been silently screaming since I moved into this house has just spotted an escape hatch. "Oh," I say sarcastically. "I *see*. Roommates with benefits. Is that how it is here at the Embassy? Am I supposed to be part of that too?" My voice is rising; I sound silly. But I can't stop.

"Keegan, come on. You know it's not like that."

"I don't know anything of the kind. Is Hunter in on this? Is he expecting 'benefits' from me too?" I actually do air quotes. A part of me is already embarrassed by my behavior. But the rest of me is just getting started.

Blue takes a deep breath. "Let's get back to what's important here," he says in a low, controlled voice. "We need to figure out who this is and stop him. I can go meet up with this Tyler kid. I'll know if it's him after I spend a few minutes with him. Remember, I told you that I can read people? I can help you, Keegan." He reaches out and puts his hands on my shoulders. "Let me help you."

I stand there, torn between wanting to wipe out the last few minutes and wrap myself around his body again and wanting to tear his eyes out without even really knowing why. I am scared. Scared of that other side of Blue I glimpsed when he first woke up. Scared of my own swift, almost savage desire for him. Scared of the rush of feelings that go with that desire. It's so much more than physical. But it's too much, too soon. So I do what I always do when I don't know how to handle my emotions, when I don't stop to think things through: I run away.

I snatch the note off Blue's desk, grab my jeans off the floor and throw open the door. It hits the wall hard and bounces back. I pause for a fraction of a second, thinking I should turn around and apologize. But instead I turn, with my face set hard against the pleading in Blue's eyes. "Just stay out of it, Blue," I say. "Just leave me *alone*." And I run up the stairs.

7

FORT PEACE

Blue

I hear yoga music coming from Kendra's room as soon as I start up the stairs. That means my conversation with her is probably going to be unpleasant. Anyone else would blast rock or heavy metal or, hell, even estrogen-soaked chick music like Adele or Pink. But when Kendra gets pissed, she cranks up some New Age shit and twists herself into some ridiculous position that would leave me writhing in pain. She claims it makes her feel better.

Keegan's door is closed. So's Hunter's. He is no doubt still asleep, probably wrapped around the blonde Keegan said was her old roommate. I am pretty sure I heard Keegan rush out the front door about an hour after she ran away from me. I can usually tell who's going up or coming down the stairs just by the sound each roomie's feet makes on the wood. Each person has a particular pattern of squeaks and thumps. Hunter's a pounder, always skipping two or three steps at a time. Kendra's feet seem to seek out the squeakiest spot on each stair and then linger there a moment, pulling groans out of the wood like she wants to be sure everyone knows she's there. Keegan hits the stairs at a fast pace, barely skimming them, until she reaches the landing. Then there is always a pause—like she's stopped to look out the window—then another swift series of squeaks as she moves up or down the remaining stairs. No idea what my steps sound like to my roommates, or if they notice things like that.

Kendra doesn't answer when I knock, but the yoga music gets louder. Typical of her to ignore me if she's mad. I open the door and walk into her tiny room. The last of our original group to move in, Kendra was stuck with the smallest bedroom. It has a single window that looks out over the detached garage and is directly above mine. I can always hear her moving around up there.

She has her hands and feet flat on the flowery area rug she bought at a garage sale. Her ass is up in the air, and my eyes automatically slide over it without any instructions from my brain. Kendra keeps herself in good shape, and it's a nice ass to look at. Or to feel, for that matter. I have to admit that. *Jesus, Blue, you are a douche.*

Kendra twists her head to glare up at me through her arms. "Stop looking at my ass, Blue. You gave that up, remember?"

I'm not going to rehash our relationship, if you could call it that, or my clumsy attempts to end it. "Sorry to interrupt your downtown dog or whatever the hell that is," I say, "but I really need to talk to you."

Kendra's knees drop to the floor, and she sits up with a heavy sigh. "It's *downward* dog, you idiot." She runs her fingers through her short hair and gives me a cool stare.

I met Kendra last year while I was playing at this funky coffee shop in the basement of the student union. It's a place frequented by overwrought, angsty grad students. Most of them, like Kendra, are getting masters or doctorates in some kind of literature or something equally pointless, and they spend hours debating some esoteric point no one else cares about. I always like to try out some of my more soulful material on them, stuff I can't get away with playing at Embassy parties. And I always throw in several of Bryson's more philosophical songs, figuring they'll go over well with the bookish crowd.

One evening last semester, I was about halfway through a Bryson set at the coffee shop when this waif of a girl in a sun dress with long, strawberry blond hair walked up and stood right in front of me with her arms folded. That close, I could tell she wasn't really a girl, though. She was in her late 20s and had gone through some hard living in those years, judging by the stony look in her eyes and the bitter twist to her mouth.

When I took a break, she strode over and stood next to me, tapping her sandaled foot impatiently. Then Kendra launched into a tirade about Bryson, skewering his music, his undeserved stature at the college, his political leanings. I spent my entire break arguing with her, and we carried on the discussion for weeks, whenever she'd show up when I was playing. I actually started looking forward to debating her. She was well-informed and whip-smart, even if she was dead wrong about Bryson. When Kendra mentioned one day her apartment lease was up, and she really wanted to move, I told her about the last empty room at the Embassy.

Now, watching her rise from the floor and switch off the music, I realize with a pang of guilt that she probably would have been better off if she'd never met me. She crosses her arms. "What the hell do you want, Blue? You're surely not tired of Miss Mayflower already?"

"Ouch, Kendra. Why the poisonous tone?" I notice the chipped black polish on her fingernails. Right before she moved in, Kendra suddenly chopped off her hair, dyed it jet black and took to wearing black dresses with combat boots. She also got several more piercings, including one in her tongue. Not that I minded that.

She told me once she was running away from a bad marriage and an ex-husband who used her as a punching bag. Maybe the goth-girl transformation is part of her healing process. I've never asked about it. That's the thing. I don't care enough about Kendra to ask, to even think about her much when she isn't right in front of me. I can't figure out exactly why. But I do feel bad about it.

"C'mon Kendra, cut the crap." I don't mean to sound so nasty, but I'm trying to head off more drama. Kendra and I have already had a couple of knock-down, drag-out fights since she moved in, and I don't have time for another one. "Where'd you find that cup this morning? My Army mug, with the note in it?"

"It was sitting on the kitchen table. Why?" Her lip curls. "You sure move fast, Blue. You waited 'til I'd been living here a few months before getting me in bed. Miss Mayflower's only been here a week, and you've already been in her pants. I guess she's better looking than I am."

I clench my teeth, trying not to get mad at her. Truth is, *she'd* put the moves on *me* "You have no idea what we've done or haven't done, Kendra." I scowl as she smirks. "And why do you keep calling her Miss Mayflower?"

She gives me the Kendra look: disgust and amusement mingling in the most annoying way possible. "You *seriously* don't know who she is? Miss Hotshot Editor, Big-time Blogger? Virginia Cooke's granddaughter? The family traces its roots all the way back to the Mayflower and makes a big stinking deal out of that? Her grandmother controls everything that goes on in this state, politically anyway. Don't you ever read a newspaper, Blue?"

For a while after we got together for the first time months ago—after Kendra asked to use my shower and left the bathroom door open so I would just happen to see her standing there naked—I thought I could maybe fall in love with her. She's intelligent and sometimes really funny and not bad-looking, even with the short hair. But it didn't take long for the acid that seems to be eating its way through her soul to surface. It's the same bile that soaked my mother's voice in the last years before my dad died. That was my old man's fault, but it still made me pull away from Mama. And it made me pull away from Kendra.

When she talks about Keegan, it's like listening to someone rake fingernails across a chalkboard. I can't stand it. I take a deep breath, then try to speak softly. "Look, Kendra, I'm sorry it didn't work out between us. I really am." Kendra snorts, then sneers and throws her head back. But she's not a good enough actress to mask the hurt in her eyes every time she looks at me. I try again. "Keegan … She's in trouble. She needs my help. She needs *our* help."

Kendra's mouth trembles, and her eyes narrow. "Keegan's got some crazy guy stalking her," I go on.

"Yeah, I read the note." She pauses for a moment, working her lips like she's battling with herself over what else to say. "What the hell is *that* all about?"

"There's this douche from her hometown who might be the one doing it. He was here at the party last night. Short, skinny guy. Nerdy looking. He had an Oklahoma Dodgers cap on backwards, but no costume."

Kendra raises a penciled-in black eyebrow.

"Keegan doesn't think it's him," I say quickly, impatient to get on the road, "but I want to have a talk with him anyway. I'm leaving for Fort Peace in a minute. But I wanted to find out if you saw him put the note in the mug or if you saw anybody carrying around my mug or putting a piece of paper in it last night."

Kendra's eyes search mine with a look of bitter resignation. "No, I didn't see anybody with your mug, Blue. I was busy." She flops down on her bed. "Does Keegan know you're planning to track down Stalker Boy? And why are you going to Fort Peace? Doesn't he live here?"

"No. Keegan said he lives in Fort Peace. She doesn't know I'm going. She doesn't want me to get involved. But I need to do *something*. I thought maybe I could track him down there."

"So Mr. War Hero wants to rescue the damsel in distress, even if she doesn't want to be rescued, huh?" After too many drinks one night, I'd told Kendra more than I should have about my past, and now she's using it against me. I haven't told her the terrible truth, though, that could get me thrown into a military prison. I haven't told *anyone* that.

Kendra is still staring at me. "So now you're going to go confront this guy who *might* be the one stalking our cute new roomie, but also might not be, and then what are you going to do, huh, Blue? You going to beat the shit out of him just in case?"

I've already turned toward the door, but pause to answer. "I'm just going to talk to him, try to figure out if he's really the guy."

"Oh, yes. You're going to use your famous gut instinct."

I ignore her sarcasm, but turn around just as I step out into the hall. "Keegan's not like her grandmother, you know. You'd like her, if you got to know her."

I see the smirk on her face and then, that flash of pain again. "And which of your heads is telling you that? Hmm, Blue? Which head is in charge?" Then she laughs. "Maybe you *are* using your brain after all. Keegan's filthy rich. I'd take *her* over me, too."

I'm already heading for the stairs, but I can't let that go by unanswered. "You don't know what the fuck you're talking about, Kendra. You just never know when to keep your mouth shut, do you?"

I hear her door slam as I reach the living room. I run out the front door, pulling my car keys out of my pocket. Fort Peace is about 90 minutes away. There's no Embassy party tonight since we had the Halloween party last night. So I have plenty of time to find Tyler Adams.

I turn the key in the Coupe's ignition, wishing for the thousandth time that I hadn't agreed to take my old man's car after he died. His prize Mercedes is an embarrassment, even if it is a guaranteed chick magnet. Just pulling into a parking spot on campus seems to make certain girls want to straddle me right on the car's shiny black hood. But I'm not really interested in girls like that.

Hunter, on the other hand, is very interested in girls like that, and he's asked a couple of times to borrow the Coupe as a "great pussy procurement vehicle." But I always refuse. There's no fucking way I'm letting Hunter drive my car; no telling what he'd do with it. Besides, he sure doesn't need any help with pussy procurement.

Hunter is an asshole. But he usually doesn't pretend to be anything else. I, on the other hand, reek of hypocrisy every time I pull the Benz out of the driveway.

"Your dad would want you take it." We'd been sitting at the kitchen table after the funeral when Mama pushed the keys toward me. The kitchen was one of the few rooms I felt comfortable in. It was intended to be just for servants, but I never willingly ate anywhere else in the ridiculously large mansion my dad built when I was a little kid.

I'd pushed the keys right back to her. "I don't want it, Mama, and considering Bill hadn't spoken to me for six months when he managed to get himself killed, I seriously doubt he'd want me to have it." I hated myself all over again every time I thought of my cold, sarcastic tone that day and the anguish it practically carved into my mother's face. I hadn't apologized to her, not then anyway. But I did take the Coupe. All I had at the time was this rattletrap car I'd spent every penny I had to buy. It was always breaking down; I needed a more reliable vehicle. I told myself I took the Benz to make Mama feel better, but who was I kidding? And five years later, I'm still driving it.

Maybe I'm feeling bad about Kendra or the Coupe, or maybe I want to punish myself, but for whatever reason, I plug the Hell's Highway playlist from my phone into the car's audio system just as the Coupe starts eating up the miles on the highway to Fort Peace. I haven't been able to listen to the bad-ass songs we blasted as we rumbled down roads in Helmand province in Afghanistan, trying to find IEDs before they blew up a comrade or an innocent civilian. Bands like Mystic Prophecy, Laaz Rockit, Metalium. Not the kind of stuff I'd listen to with my mother or even want to hear by myself now that I am out of the service. But it helped make us feel invincible, and we needed that. Even though *invincible* turned out to be the last thing we were.

Predictably, the songs stir up memories, especially of Cunny. He was the only one still alive when I reached the site of the attack, and he died in my arms, managing to grin faintly at me at the end as if to console me. The son-of-a-bitch died grinning. That's what I was dreaming about when I scared the shit out of Keegan. It was Cunny's name I was saying when I grabbed Keegan's chin like a lunatic; Cunny's face I was searching as the life drained out of it. We were best friends, me and Richie Cunningham. Yeah, that was his full name, just like the character on that old TV show *Happy Days*. Cunny's parents must have been almost as twisted as mine. Maybe that's why we bonded so quickly. I would have done anything for Cunny, and he would have done anything for me. And he did everything, gave everything, for me.

Cunny regularly gave all of us these slaps to the side of the head. He called them 'Pull Your Head Out of Your Ass Pats.' As I'm driving, my head suddenly jerks like Cunny just gave me one of his best. The Coupe surges ahead; my foot's pressing the gas pedal to the floor. My hands grip the steering wheel so tightly my knuckles are white. *Shit. Get yourself under control.* It's Cunny's voice in my head. I take my foot off the gas and rub the wheel with my hands. *Think of something else before you get arrested or manage to kill yourself.*

So I set the cruise control at the speed limit and start thinking about my music, about my upcoming class with Bryson, about the encouragement he unexpectedly gave me after hearing us play at the Embassy. Encouragement from The Great One is like water in the desert: rare and precious. I lapped it up. I'm working on a couple of new songs I am eager to try out for Bryson; both songs have been inspired by Keegan, this girl I can't seem to get out of my head. It's not just that Keegan's eyes are so much like Aziza's eyes. Or that I can sense the same goodness in Keegan that had been so obvious in Aziza. I'd wanted to protect Aziza, rescue her from the fate that awaited her. But she was only 14 years old. I thought of her like a little sister.

My feelings for Keegan are definitely *not* sisterly. I've already had a couple of hot dreams in which Keegan plays the starring role. I can still smell her, taste her lips, feel her skin under my fingers. I'm not even sure if those sensations are from our brief makeout session or from my dreams, or maybe some delicious mixture of both. It's more than just lust, though. Even for men—well, a lot of men—lust by itself is kind of empty, cold, unfulfilling. I'd never have said that, though, in front of my guys; I'd have been laughed out of the platoon.

It's not that I haven't had my share of one-night stands and a few months-long relationships. But I always knew it wasn't the real thing.

Man, you sound like a girl. I can almost hear Cunny saying it and feel one of his head pats. But it doesn't change anything. I know I want more of Keegan. Much more. Of her body, yeah. But also of her mind, soul, spirit, everything that I can feel inside her that seems to have connected instantly with whatever's inside me. If I can only manage to stop scaring her away.

I have to swerve across three lanes to keep from missing the Fort Peace exit, which seems to pop up out of nowhere. *Holy crap, get it together.* I slow down when I see the massive marble sign with the elaborate stone base at the town's entrance: WELCOME TO FORT PEACE, Population 25,433. It sure isn't your typical roadside sign. Someone's paid a lot of money for it. And what catches my eye, besides the picture of a smiling but stern-looking woman, are the words carved next to her in all caps:

HOME OF THE WORLD-FAMOUS COOKE RANCH AND VIRGINIA COOKE HUDSON, PRESIDENT PRO TEMPORE OF THE OKLAHOMA STATE SENATE AND DESCENDANT OF JOHN COOKE, A PASSENGER ON THE MAYFLOWER.

I pull off the road, park near the sign and get out. Virginia Cooke Hudson's eyes seem to glare at me as I approach. My imagination, of course. I study the Oklahoma map carved under her picture, with a star for the town's location in the northeast corner of the state, and next to it what I assume is the ranch's brand: a topsail with a large, fancy C inside it.

"So," I say to Virginia, crossing my arms and feeling foolish. "*You're* the dreaded grandmother."

Again, it's obviously just my imagination, but as I walk back to the car and slide my hypocritical ass into the soft leather seat, I'm sure I can feel Virginia Cooke's eyes burning into my back. And it hits me just as I turn the key in the ignition that I've seen her face before. If you take away the gray hair and the wrinkles and soften the steel in the brown eyes, you're looking at Keegan's sweet, heart-shaped face: same eyes, same nose, same mouth. Keegan looks just like the grandmother she despises. *Yeah, I should probably keep that observation to myself.*

The town of Fort Peace was named after an actual fort built in the 1880s to keep the peace between the settlers streaming into Oklahoma Territory and the Indian tribes already living there. That fact from my fourth grade Oklahoma History class suddenly pops into my head. I still remember watching a video with grainy pictures of grim-faced tribal leaders signing treaties almost immediately broken by the American government. I am one-quarter Choctaw on my mother's side. I still feel a trace of the outrage that made my 10-year-old self tremble with indignation on behalf of my Indian ancestors, who lost their land and way of life. It's funny, the things that stay with you.

I drive slowly down Main Street, looking for the First Baptist Church of Fort Peace. During the drive, I'd done a quick search for *Tyler Adams Fort Peace Oklahoma.* Dozens of links popped up on my phone about Seth Adams, "The People's Pastor" and "The Force in Fort Peace" and lots of other shit like that. There was even a story in *The New York Times* about "Oklahoma's own Pied Piper."

Keegan said Tyler was a preacher's kid, and I can't find any other reference to a pastor in Fort Peace with the last name Adams. It has to be this guy. She also said Tyler works weekends at his dad's church, so I figure I'll find the church and then just show up and ask for him. What I'm going to do once I'm face to face with the dweeb, I have no idea. I'm kind of rolling along on adrenaline and the urge to do *something* to help Keegan.

And all at once, there it is in front of me: First Baptist itself, a complex of buildings dominated by a sprawling structure that's topped by this massive glass-enclosed steeple that shines so brightly in the sun I can barely stand to look at it. Acres and acres of parking lots surround the complex, and as I turn into the church's sweeping driveway, I spot a half-dozen of those trams like you see at Disney World. "Wouldn't want the faithful to have to walk too far," I mutter as I pull into a spot not far from the main building. It's a Saturday, and there's only a smattering of cars.

I have a bias against these huge churches. I've never actually gone to one, so maybe I am being unfair. For years, Mama and I attended this tiny, dirt-poor country church 20 miles away from where we lived, just because of the pastor there. He's the most humble, godly man I've ever met; anything I know about faith and compassion and decency, I've learned from Brother Philip. Bill would never come with us to services. He always said it was a bunch of hokum, and I think he was embarrassed to be seen at such a ramshackle place. Good old Bill Danube, always worried about his image.

I read online that Seth Adams' church has thousands of members. He can influence people and events way beyond his home state, and if you believe all his press, his influence is growing by the day. Something about that sets loose my inner cynic. I just don't trust power or those who have it. I grew up watching my father accumulate it, along with a huge fortune, from his natural gas company. Politicians of every stripe, hats in hand and favors at the ready, were always trooping out to see my old man. And the richer and more powerful Bill became, the more of a grade-A asshole he turned into.

Then, when I enlisted, I found out quickly that power's the only thing that really seems to matter to so many people. Almost everyone who gets good at holding on to power, wielding it and building up more, is left tainted by it. Big church, big company, mighty military, it doesn't matter. Power corrupts even those who try hard to stand against it. At least from my perspective. I want nothing to do with any of it.

I shut off the Coupe and roll down the windows. It's warm again, too warm for November. I press against the headrest and close my eyes, feeling the hot wind roll over my face and waiting for the sick feeling in my stomach to go away. I hate thinking about Bill, but I've done it a lot lately. It usually gives me a headache. And sometimes, like now, I get that old feeling of panic that used to roil my insides and claw its way up into my throat when I was a kid and had done something I knew would piss Bill off. *You're still just a scared little kid. Pathetic. Absolutely pathetic.*

I have no fucking clue what to do next. Go into the church and demand to see the preacher's kid? Or just go straight up to the Big Man himself and ask if he knows what the hell his son has been up to. Or maybe I should just get the hell out of here. This is a crazy idea. I don't even know if Tyler is really the guy.

A loud bang jolts my eyes open in time to see a side door in the largest building bounce off the wall and slam shut again just as the dweeb I saw at the Embassy storms away from the building. *Too convenient.* I don't even have to go into the church. Stalker Boy is coming to me.

And then the door is thrown open again, and two thick-necked goons in suits rush out after him. "Just leave me alone," I hear Tyler yell back at the sunglass-wearing suits. They look like fucking Secret Service agents. The suits stop running, put their hands on their hips in unison and stand there staring as Tyler walks rapidly across the parking lot, straight toward me. It looks like he's muttering to himself; he's still wearing the backward baseball cap. He has on torn jeans and a grubby-looking T-shirt. He doesn't look like the son of a rich and famous man. Keegan said he's the weekend janitor at the church; he sure looks the part.

I get out of the Coupe and lean against it, my arms folded. Tyler lurches toward me, still muttering. He seems to be lost in an argument with himself; I'm not even sure he sees me. I try to imagine what there is about him that would make Keegan want to...

Ugh, don't even go there. But there it comes again: the thought of this weirdo putting his hands all over Keegan. My teeth grind into my jaw; my hands tighten into fists. *Don't do something stupid.* I relax my hands, but can't quite unclench my jaw. I want to bust this kid's ass. I'm just waiting for him to give me an excuse. But all he does is stop about 10 feet away, as if he's just become aware of me leaning against the Coupe giving him a death stare behind my sunglasses.

"Can I help you with something?" His voice is unexpectedly soft and polite. He looks like he's been crying. When I keep staring at him, he looks nervously back at the suits, who are watching us. Then he tries again. "Um … I'm Tyler Adams, my dad's the pastor here." He waves a hand back toward the buildings. "Do you need some help? There are lots of people inside who can help you." Not what I expected. The little moron is messing everything up.

"I'm here to talk to you about Keegan," I say stonily, crossing my arms. "About what *you* are doing to Keegan. I think maybe we need to go in and talk to your old man about that. Then *you're* the one who's going to need help."

Tyler gasps and steps back. He looks scared. "Are you a cop?" His voice is actually trembling. "I've already told you guys, I'm not the one who's stalking her!" He covers his face with his hands and sinks down onto the pavement. "I love Keegan." He speaks through his fingers. "I wouldn't do anything to scare her."

The suits walk toward us, and one of them pulls out his cell. I walk quickly over to Tyler and yank him to his feet. "Look, I'm not a cop," I say impatiently. "I'm Keegan's roommate, and I just want to talk to you."

Tyler's mouth falls open.

"Hey, who the hell are the goons?"

Tyler sighs. "My dad's security. They keep an eye on me, too. Whether I want them to or not." His voice is bitter.

"A Baptist preacher needs a security team?"

Tyler's staring at my car. He nods. "You'd be surprised at all the threats he gets."

“Everything okay, kid?” one of the goons calls out as they slowly approach. It’s obvious to me they are both packing. Why they need to be armed in a Baptist church parking lot in a podunk town in Oklahoma is beyond me, but I’m not making any sudden moves.

“Just talking to Tyler about a mutual friend of ours.” I smile as I say it.

The suits don’t smile back. “That true, Tyler?”

And this is where he could nail me, make sure I never bother him again. But he doesn’t. “Yeah, it’s true,” Tyler says, trying to be nonchalant. “We’re just about to go for a ride.” He pulls open the Coupe’s passenger door and plops down in it like he’s done it a hundred times.

I grin at the goons as I get in on the driver’s side. “Later.” I have no idea how things are going to turn out, but my gut’s telling me to go. So we pull back on to Main Street. “Where are we going?” I ask.

Tyler slides his cap around so he’s wearing it the right way. Then he points at a Sonic restaurant up ahead. “You’re going to buy me lunch.”

We certainly don’t end up as friends. But after I buy the manipulative little moocher a large order of onion rings and a peanut butter and bacon shake, then threaten to shove it all where the sun doesn’t shine if he lies to me, I’m pretty sure he is giving me honest answers. Actually, I’m certain he’s telling me the truth. And I’m certain of what my gut told me the moment he asked if I needed help in the parking lot. Tyler’s not the guy.

So I drop him off at the church about an hour later. It still repulses me to think of him with Keegan. That just doesn’t make any sense. But I can’t hate him. In fact, I feel kind of sorry for the kid.

“So...” He gets out of the car and leans into the passenger window. He’s turned his cap back around and again looks like a goofball.

"...when you figure out who's sending Keegan those messages, when you catch him ... you'll let me know?" His voice squeaks a bit.

I shake my head. I still don't want to get too buddy-buddy with Tyler. "I don't know, maybe. Probably not." I point my finger at him. "But you stay away from Keegan. No contact. You freak her out."

His face wilts. I've hurt his feelings, but I had to say it. "Okay, then. I'll stay away from her." He turns and walks away, his shoulders hunched.

I raise the windows and crank up my Bryson playlist, the best stuff from the Seventies, his golden years. I need to hear it. I'm glad I came to Fort Peace. But I still have no idea who is making life so unpleasant for my Keegan. *My Keegan. Shit, man, you've got it bad.*

Just before I shift into drive, my phone buzzes on the seat next to me. A text from Keegan. *Kendra just told me what you're doing.* I grip the phone and curse Kendra, debating how to answer. But before I can, another text comes in. *Why are you doing this?* I type quickly. *u can b mad at me if u want but I had 2 do it*

A long pause. I can't stand it so I keep typing. *i told u i would help u i need 2 help u*

Another long pause. Then, from Keegan. *I'm not mad at you.* I smile, debate what to type next. My phone buzzes again. *Thank you. Really. Thank you. But why are you doing this? Why are being so nice to me? This isn't your problem.* Now it's getting easier. My thumbs fly over the tiny keys. *cuz ur cute & u have a great ass & the rest of u aint bad either*

Yeah, I'm being a smartass. But I can't just go all Romeo and start declaring my undying love. *& cuz I have not forgotten about those music lessons it would be a disservice 2 society 2 let u go around being so ignorant*

Another long pause. I turn Bryson down and the A/C up. I am sweating. Another buzz. *How is it that someone who uses phrases like 'disservice to society' is unable to spell out words like 'you' and 'to' and use appropriate punctuation?* Now I'm grinning. We're flirting. I type as quickly as I can. *Sorry, Madam Editor, I forgot with whom I was communicating.*

This time the pause seems to go on forever. Finally, the phone buzzes again. I am still in the fucking parking lot. *So what happened with Tyler?* A few flirtatious texts, and I've already almost forgotten about him. *You were right,* I type, making sure to use good English. *It's not Tyler. At least I don't think it is. But I will find out who it is and I will stop him. I promise you that.*

No answer. I wait, nervous for some reason. Finally, my phone buzzes. *Blue?*

Yeah?

Meet me on the roof tonight. At 9. Bring your guitar.

8

ON THE ROOF

Keegan

I guess I'm expecting Blue to do the Romeo thing again and climb the tree. So when he knocks on my bedroom door instead, it startles the crap out of me. I am already out on the roof, waiting for Blue in the dark. Even though I'm just sitting here, my heart's pounding. I am excited about what I've decided to do, but nervous about it too.

The only light in my room is coming from the glow of my phone on the bed, plugged into the wall and charging. The phone has behaved itself all day, not displaying any threatening emails or vulgar texts from the stalker to spoil my giddy mood. There's been a flurry of *Daily* emails and a couple of texts from Megz, the first one raving about the "hot, hilarious, horny hunk" that is my new roommate Hunter. About an hour later, a second text ranted about the "absolutely arrogant asshole" that is my new roommate Hunter. Megz is big on alliteration. And it's really easy to piss her off. I've twice typed out a reply to her texts. *I can't believe you actually hooked up with Hunter.* And twice I've deleted it. I'm not quite sure how Megz will take it.

When Kendra texted me that afternoon to tell me Blue had raced toward Fort Peace like a knight charging into battle to defend his lady's honor, it sent a thrill all the way through me. I think Kendra meant to cause trouble between me and Blue, but it had the opposite effect. No one's ever gone to bat like that for me. Well, except for my dad. He tries, anyway, although he doesn't always succeed. But that's part of the Dad job description. Blue did it because he wanted to. And that really turns me on.

I spent most of the day in the newsroom, catching up on emails, preparing for tomorrow's editorial meeting, just trying to get my brain to focus on the job at hand. We only put a paper out on weekdays, so Saturday's usually my time to catch up and plan for the following week. And today, I realized that I was also using the newsroom to hide out. I just didn't want to face Blue at the Embassy. But by the time I got Kendra's text, I was wishing I hadn't run away from him. So I'd impulsively invited him to meet me on the roof. Then I'd stayed at the newspaper until almost 8 o'clock, wondering what the hell I'd been thinking. When I finally got up the nerve to go home to the Embassy, Blue wasn't there. It did not feel good, wondering if he'd changed his mind about meeting me.

I'd been so tempted to write in my journal before creeping out on the roof. I'm itching to get it all down, work through the last two days' events in writing like I always do. Megz has made fun of my journal habit more than once. "Goddamn, Kee Kee," she'll say while I scribble away, "you writing a fucking novel over there in that stupid diary? 'I woke up, I went to school, I came home, I'm going to bed.' What more is there to say? Turn off the fucking light!"

I know Megz thinks my journal writing is stupid. But it's like a close friend to me. I can't end my day without spilling everything into it. I slept in Blue's room last night, so I haven't had a chance to write in the journal for Friday. I want to stick to my rules and wait until Saturday is completely over before catching up with it. And I'm hoping I'll have some really juicy details from the rooftop to add.

So here I am, waiting for my knight in shining armor. I want to reward him. And I want to wipe away the memory of Tyler.

I twist around to stick my head in the window and call "Come in" just as Blue opens the door. The light from the upstairs landing cuts into the darkened room and illuminates Blue's white T-shirt. He's carrying his guitar. He grins when he sees me. His face is in shadow, but I can see his teeth gleaming. I smile back at him, hoping I look alluring in my cami and cutoffs. It's been another hot day. At 9 o'clock at night, it is still warm, even though it's the first of November.

"Hey there," I say, scooting away from the window so Blue will have room to climb out. "I've been waiting for you."

He crosses the room quickly, and I watch him stick one muscular leg out the window. He's wearing gym shorts. I swallow hard and look away for a second. When I look back, the arm clutching his guitar is outside, and he's just pulling the rest of his body through the window. He settles down next to me, still grinning, just as lightning lights up the horizon, followed several seconds later by the distant rumble of thunder.

"You do realize," Blue drawls, "that sitting outside under a tree in a thunderstorm might be considered kinda crazy." He plays a few chords on his guitar and begins to sing.

Come listen to the story of Keegan and Blue
Struck by lightning, left behind just a shoe.
Old folks said they were crazy in the head
And all it got 'em was good and dead.

I bust out laughing. "Yeah, okay. I guess it *is* pretty crazy. But I don't care. Crazy is what I want to be right now."

"All right, bar girl. I'm in. We'll ride the crazy train together." His smile deepens and melts into those unbelievable eyes, and another flash of lightning makes them glow. I swallow again. I want to be playful and seductive, but I don't really have a clue how to do that. Blue is pulling at the sleeve of his T-shirt and seems to be trying to subtly sniff it. He looks sheepish when he realizes I've noticed.

"I went to work out after I got back from Fort Peace." He runs a hand over his close-cropped hair. "I showered at the gym, but I didn't have any other clothes with me so I had to put these back on. And when I got back here, I was, um, kind of distracted by the thought of what might happen up here on the roof tonight. You weren't back yet, so I went for a run to kind of calm myself down." That big, wide grin again. "And then, when I got back from running, I forgot to change. And I forgot to shower again. Sorry if I'm smelly." He rips his shirt off in one movement and sends it sailing into the air. "There, takes care of that. Well, at least it takes care of the stinky shirt."

"You smell just fine to me." I try to put a little growl in my voice and allow myself to openly ogle Blue's chest and abs. He seems to like that. He gets up on his knees and slowly pulls at the waistband of his shorts. "I could take these off too, if you'd like?" He's teasing me.

I close my eyes, wondering if I have the nerve to tell him to take it all off. That's the point of our rooftop rendezvous, after all. But I can't quite do that. "Do you know," I say to cover up my nervousness, "that the first time I met you I thought you were wearing contacts to make your eyes match your name?"

The last part of my sentence is drowned out by the sound of thunder that's a little closer now. Blue sits back down on the roof and leans in toward me. "Say that again. I don't think I heard you right." He looks amused.

"I thought you were wearing contacts to make your eyes match your name." This time, I say it too loudly.

Now it's Blue's turn to laugh. "That's what I thought you said. Seriously? You seriously thought I was wearing those colored contacts?"

I nod, a little embarrassed. "It just seemed too much of a coincidence: your name is Blue and you've got these unbelievably blue eyes. I wondered if they were fake."

Blue slaps a hand to his forehead. "Ouch, bar girl, that hurts. You really thought I was that kind of phony? These eyes are natural, I promise. They are the same color as my mother's." His mouth twitches up on one side. "But I'm glad to know you like my eyes."

I blush, then trail a finger down his face, feeling very brave. Blue stops smiling and holds my gaze with an intense look that's hard to read. But then he looks down at the slate roof tiles. "So," he says a moment later, still looking down, "you know that I look like my mother. Who do *you* look like?" He glances up at me with a knowing half-smile.

I sigh and stare at the tree. Then I shrug. "Everybody always says I look just like Virginia, but *I* don't see it."

He nods, still smiling. "Yeah. Actually, I already knew that."

I turn to stare at him. He drags his thumb just under my bottom lip. That's all it takes to get the loins leaping yet again. I close my eyes for a second.

"I saw that big-ass sign in Fort Peace, the one with your grandma's picture on it. Don't go and knock me off this roof for saying so, but you *do* look like her. A *lot* like her."

I groan. "I forgot about that stupid sign. I don't even notice it anymore when I go home. I think I'm blocking it out. Such a waste of effing…" I remember our conversation in the kitchen the day before. "...such a waste of *fucking* money!" I shout the last two words. It feels kind of liberating, using the F-word like a little kid getting a thrill out of breaking the rules. It's not that I am such a prude I've never said that word before. I don't say it very often. It does make me kind of uncomfortable. But mostly, it's because I'm just really tired of hearing it. The word is *way* overused.

Blue starts laughing. "There you go, bar girl. Let it out."

"I think I'm done for now." I have Virginia's disapproving face in my mind. Not what I was aiming for. "But seriously, it's just like my grandmother to make everyone who drives into Fort Peace look at her face, as if she's taking credit for the whole *fucking* town, the whole *motherfucking* state." I'm fumbling to find a different F-word variant to use, but I've run through my entire arsenal. And I sound like an idiot. "Now I am definitely good for a while on my F-word usage," I add, lamely.

Blue's face softens. He purses his lips, shakes his head slightly and looks down at his guitar. "I shouldn't have goaded you into using the word, Keegan. It doesn't really suit you. You're too classy. You're too sweet." He looks up at me. "Too *innocent.* I love that about you. It makes you so different."

No tears. No. Tears. Seriously. No. Effing. Tears.

Naturally, tears are swamping my eyes. Everything Blue Danube says, everything he does, seems to turn me into a weepy, goose-pimply mess. It's mortifying and utterly wonderful all at the same time. So I do the only thing I can think of. I throw my arms around him and start kissing him, urgently, wildly, passionately. I'll show him I'm not so innocent. Even though, technically, I pretty much am.

Blue gasps and moans as he kisses me back. My eyes are closed, but I feel him shift the guitar out of the way. Then he grabs my face with both hands and devours my lips with his, thrusting his tongue inside my mouth and running it along the insides of my cheeks. Blue kisses my lips again, then my chin, my nose, my forehead, and then swoops down once more on my mouth as he presses his body against mine, pinning me to the roof.

I can hear myself moaning. My hands find their way down his shoulders, over his arms and then along his back. It's crazy-train kissing, up on the roof, out in a storm. I want it to go on forever. I open my eyes in time to see lightning blazing above me, and Blue's eyes lit up with lust. He trails kisses down my neck and chest as thunder answers the lightning. Blue's hand cups my breast, and his mouth swiftly follows, his tongue tracing a pattern along the top of my cami until I surprise myself by frantically yanking the cami off with both hands. I throw it in the direction of the tree. I'm panting and arching my back, pulling Blue closer and closer, driven by a sensation I've never experienced before. It's as if my entire body is on fire, and only Blue Danube can quench the flames.

Blue's hand is behind me, unlatching my bra with one practiced move. I look down in wonder at my newly freed breasts as another flash of lightning tears across the sky, then cry out and arch my back again as Blue's dark head blocks my view and his tongue finds my nipples. I'm deep into the romance novel arena now, and I think I'm beginning to understand, finally, just what all those books were trying to tell me.

I open my eyes again just as Blue lifts his mouth to mine. His kisses are harder this time, rougher, more insistent. After a few moments, he stops kissing me and holds his body just above me, his arm muscles flexing as I trail my fingertips over them. My lips are burning. I moisten them with my tongue, then lift my face toward Blue. I want him to kiss me some more. A lot more.

But Blue breaks into a soft smile, still holding his body slightly away from mine. He's breathing heavily, the guitar still on his back. "You okay, bar girl?"

I nod. I don't really want to talk. I want him to press his body hard against me, plunge into me, consume me. I want to find out, right there on the roof, what I've been missing all this time. But then a bolt of lightning, followed by an ear-splitting crack of thunder, seems to explode right above us. I scream, and Blue scrambles to grab the windowsill, reaching out for me with his other hand just as the sky opens up, and it begins to pour.

"Keegan, take my hand!" he shouts. "We gotta get inside."

I sit up, looking around in vain for my cami before remembering I flung it off the roof. And my bra is nowhere to be seen. I take Blue's hand, screaming again as another lightning bolt and its corresponding thunder threaten to put us in the news: *Topless lovers on a rooftop fried to a crisp by lightning. Details at 11.*

Blue helps me through the window, then climbs in as well. He's bending down to tenderly kiss my wet breasts when my bedroom door is flung open. The hallway light shines on us like a spotlight. Hunter stands there, his eyes adjusting to the darkness. I can see Kendra right behind him, peering over his shoulder.

Before I even think to grab another shirt, Hunter fixes his eyes on my boobs and smiles sarcastically. "We heard a scream and thought our new roomie needed help," he drawls. "But I guess it's just the fuck factory getting cranked up, huh, soldier boy?"

Before Blue can answer, Max pushes his way past Kendra and Hunter and makes a beeline for Blue, pressing against his leg and whining. The dog is shaking. Blue puts his hand on Max's head. "He's afraid of thunder," he says. When Max whines again, Blue squats down next to the dog and puts both hands on his body. "It's okay, boy, it's okay."

A gust of wind blows rain through the window, and I look down at the drops on my skin as if I'm watching someone else. Then I come to my senses with a jolt and lunge toward the crate that holds my clothes. Grabbing a pajama top, I struggle to put it on; it's like I've never done that before. My face and neck are burning with embarrassment.

"Need any help there, Keegan?" Hunter leers.

I intend to give him a withering stare, but then I'm distracted by the fury on Kendra's face. If she could have killed me right then and there, I think she would have. She spins around on her heel and stalks away. I hear her heavy steps on the wooden floor even over the storm. A moment later, her bedroom door slams shut.

Blue is next to Hunter now, shoving him out the door. "Get the fuck out of here, Hunter." His tone is low and level, but with that same flat, dangerous note I heard before when he was talking to our obnoxious roommate. It doesn't seem to faze Hunter, though.

"'Night, Keegan," he calls out mockingly, pushing back against Blue's hands. Then his voice changes. "Get your goddamn hands off me, Blue! I'm tired of telling you that!"

The hall light throws a harsh glare on Blue's face, and I see his jaw tense as he gives Hunter a final push and closes the bedroom door. The room's suddenly dark again. I hear Blue take a deep breath and blow it out slowly. The door rattles as he leans against it. "That douchebag has no idea how close I've come to killing him on more than one occasion," he says quietly. His words make me shiver.

Another flash of lightning illuminates the room for a second, and the dark outline of Blue's guitar reminds me he still has it on his back. "Oh, crap, did your guitar get wet?" I move toward him. "I'm sorry. I wanted you to play that song for me again, the one you sang to me on the roof before, but then I, um, kind of jumped the gun. Things didn't exactly go according to plan."

The guitar jangles as Blue sets it against the wall; then I hear his footsteps. The next flash of lightning shows him walking toward me. "There was a plan?" He puts an arm around my waist and runs his fingers through my wet hair with his other hand. I turn my face into his palm.

"Oh yeah," I say, enjoying the feel of his fingers on my scalp. "There was a plan. But I'm not very good at this kind of thing."

He cups my face with his hands. I can feel his breath on my cheek. "What kind of thing, Keegan?" His voice is soft, seductive. My lips had parted, waiting for his kiss. I reluctantly put them back together to answer his question.

"The seduction thing. That's what I was trying to do. I mean, I know I'm not very good at it, but that's what I was, that's what I wanted to do. Seduce you, I mean." I am babbling now, my cheeks tingling with the touch of Blue's hands, my lips still waiting.

"Not very good at it? Are you *kidding* me? You're a natural." His lips finally find mine, and I wrap my arms tightly around his neck, pulling him against me as he kisses me over and over. But he's not quite done talking.

"So..." Another kiss. "Wait a second." Kiss. Kiss. "What I want to know is..." Kiss. Kiss. Kiss. "Why, Keegan?" Now he pulls back out of kissing range. "Why now? What changed your mind? And why on the roof?"

My lips are still open, waiting for him to start kissing me again. "Because," I sigh, "I wanted to thank you for going to Fort Peace, for trying to find the stalker, for wanting to be my hero." I feel a little silly saying it, but it's true. "No one's ever done anything like that for me before, Blue. And the roof is kind of our spot. It's where you climbed up the tree to find me, like, like Romeo coming to get Juliet."

Blue's face crinkles into the warm, flirtatious smile that made my insides flop around the first time I met him. "I hope I'm the only one you try to thank like that, Keegan," he whispers fiercely, grabbing my face again and covering it with his kisses. "And I hope I'm your *only* Romeo, your *only* hero."

That's crazy-train talk, coming from a guy I've only known for about a week. Cautious Keegan would shut that down right away. But I don't want to be Cautious Keegan right now.

Suddenly, Blue pulls my pajama top over my head and starts setting my breasts on fire with his lips. But then it is *me* who can't stop talking. There is something else I want him to know. I speak to the back of his head and try to finish a sentence while he brings the girls to grateful attention. "And, also, because I wanted..." I'm panting, "... because I wanted to make a new memory. I wanted to wipe away the memory of Tyler, and I wanted to do that with *you*."

Blue's head snaps up. *You are so stupid.* Why couldn't I just keep my mouth shut?

"Yeah, you know, I wasn't going to say anything..." He looks out the window a moment. The rain has stopped, and the storm's moving on. I see a flash of lightning behind the tree, miles away now. "...but what the *hell* were you thinking? I just can't see you with that dweeb."

I close my eyes a second, embarrassed. "It was pity sex," I finally blurt out, using Megz' term without thinking until a second too late how stupid it sounds.

"Huh?"

"It's a long story, but I did something in high school that really hurt Tyler, and even though he's a dork, he's not a bad guy, and I felt terrible about what I'd done, and then we were at this graduation party at his house, and I'd had alcohol for the first time, and he was upstairs with me, kind of taking care of me 'cause I didn't feel good, and so there was, like, sympathy sex." I sound even more pathetic than before, if that's possible.

Blue's mouth forms an O. He just stands there, not saying anything, so I ramble on. "At least I *think* it was sex. It was over so fast, I'm not even sure what it was." I bury my face in my hands. "I feel so stupid right now."

Blue pulls my hands away from my face and kisses my fingertips, then my forearms, nuzzling his way up to my shoulders and then down along the curve of one breast before moving over to the other one. "Don't feel stupid," he breathes between kisses. Then he chuckles. "You've got a generous heart, bar girl. And *dear God,* you've got a beautiful body."

Very good answer. I take a deep breath. I want to reward him and do something I've never done before. I want to be wild, at least the Cautious Keegan version of wild. So I peel off my cutoffs, tossing them on the bed.

"Keegan," Blue whispers, his breathing scattered and staccato. I place my hands on the waistband of his shorts and pull them down his legs, using my bare foot to send them all the way to the floor. Then I press my naked body against his, reeling at the volcanic feel of skin scorching skin. The desire inflaming his eyes sends my loins into overdrive. "Oh God, Keegan." His voice sounds almost dreamy.

I'm in uncharted territory now, and I'm nervous as hell. I so want to do this right. But reading about it and actually doing it are two different things. Book blow jobs used to make me blush, but I'd read every word slowly, sometimes more than once, with a kind of fascinated revulsion. Now, as I move slowly downward, never taking my gaze away from Blue's, my skin sliding against his 'til my knees reach the floor, I'm not repulsed—only amazed, empowered—by the look of awe on his face.

I stand up, sweeping my palms from Blue's abdomen to his shoulders as his breathing finally begins to slow.

"Wow," he pants.

"I assume that's a compliment?" I'm being playful. I can tell I performed satisfactorily.

My eyes have adjusted to the darkness, and I can see Blue nodding, then breaking into a wide grin. "I'll say it is. What else do you think you're not any good at?"

I put my arms around his neck. "Let's find out."

With a growl, Blue sweeps me up into his arms and carries me to the bed. "I've been wanting to do this since you first pulled up to the Embassy," he says, standing above me as his eyes travel from my chest to my stomach and further down. "God, Keegan, you are just stunning."

He stretches out next to me, propped up on his elbow, close enough for me to feel the heat from his skin, but not touching me. I wriggle a little, desperate with desire, just like all the characters in those romance novels. Blue flutters his fingers across my abdomen, dips down a little further, then drags his hand back up. Then he does that several more times, each time getting a little closer to the spot I really want him to touch. He seems to be thinking. Either that, or he's the world's biggest tease.

"Blue," I finally say, impatiently. I'm in agony. "Touch me."

And then my phone buzzes. We both looked over at it, not moving. He sits up. "Just leave it," I say, noticing how desperate I sound. When I'm with Blue, I can almost forget about the scary part of my life, the part that would normally have turned me into a complete basket case. "Please, Blue. Just ignore it."

But he shakes his head and slowly stands up. "I need to see if it's him." He crosses the room and picks up the phone, his face bathed in its glow. I see his mouth tighten. "Motherfucker." Even though he is whispering, I can hear the fury in his voice. "You motherfucker, I'm going to find you."

For a moment, I just lay there, staring at Blue. I don't want to see what's on the phone. But I have to. I get off the bed and walk over to Blue with my hand out. He hesitates, staring at me. Then he hands me the phone. I close my eyes for a second. I can feel myself starting to shake. But I open my eyes and start to read.

DID YOU LIKE MY NOTE? HUH SCREAMING BAD BITCH? HOW'D YOU LIKE IT?!!! DID YOU REALLY THINK YOU COULD GET AWAY FROM ME BY MOVING?!?! DID YOU REALLY THINK I WOULDN'T KNOW WHERE YOU WENT YOU STUPID WHORE?! YOU THINK I DON'T KNOW WHERE YOU ARE, WHAT YOU'RE DOING, ALL THE TIME? I'M EVERYWHERE!!

"Oh, God!" I let the phone slip out of my hand, but Blue catches it before it hits the floor and sets it down carefully. "Blue." I put my face into my hands. "Blue, what am I going to do? This guy is scaring me."

He folds me into his arms and holds me tightly. "Shhh." His breath flutters my hair. "Shhh. It's going to be okay, Keegan." I burrow into his body, wanting to believe that, and he strokes my hair. "We're going to figure this out. I'm going to take care of this sonofabitch. I'm going to make this stop. I promise you that."

He pulls me over to the bed, and I curl up on his chest while he runs his fingers up and down my back. For a long time, there's no sound except the rain against the windows. After a while, Blue gets off the bed and slips his shorts back on.

"What are you doing?" I can't help sounding a little upset. I want to pick back up where we left off. I want to forget about everything else.

He comes back to the bed with my shorts and the pajama top he threw off earlier. I sit up and take them, reluctantly. "Listen to me, Keegan." He sits on the bed and puts his hands on my face. "You want to make a good memory with me, right?"

All I can do is nod.

"And I want this memory, our first time, to be *really* special. Somewhere away from here. Away from your phone. Where this asshole can't reach us. Somewhere special. So, let's wait one more day." He holds up his hand as my mouth falls open. I probably look bewildered because I am. "I've just had a great idea. I know how to make it special. Much more special than it will be here at the Embassy, on this bed, where..." He doesn't finish the sentence. "You'll be glad we waited one more day, I promise you."

I rub my eyes. Blue is always surprising me. He stands up and walks toward the door, then turns around. "Here's the thing, though. You have to be ready to go at 8 o'clock in the morning."

"Huh?" I've finally found my voice.

"Do you have any hiking boots?"

"*What?*"

"Never mind, sneakers will do. I'm going to get out of here before I change my mind and take you back out on that roof." He walks toward the bed, then trips over Max lying a couple of feet away. We've both forgotten the dog is still in the room. "Sorry, Max." The dog wags his tail.

I put my hands up and shake my head. "Blue, I can't go hiking tomorrow. I have the editorial meeting. I can't miss it! And we have a sponsor visit on Monday that I have to get ready for. There's just no way I can go anywhere right now."

Blue gives me a long, lingering kiss and brings my hands together, enveloping them in his. "The meeting's at 5, right?" I nod, and Blue goes on in rush of words. "I'll have you back by 4. I promise. Bar girl, you need this." He kisses me again. "You need to get away. Trust me, you'll be glad you went. There's a special place I want to take you. Please. Say you'll go with me."

I can't help smiling. I close my eyes. I can't think straight when I'm this close to him. "Blue." Just saying his name feels so good.

His lips brush my fingertips. "Please, Keegan, just say you'll go."

How can I refuse him? I open my eyes, and he's staring at me with such a tender expression that my arms of their own accord just throw themselves around him. "Okay. I'll go. I'll go."

He gives me a huge, loin-lighting grin and kisses me one more time. "It's going to be great," he says. "I promise."

And then he is gone.

9

MAKE A MEMORY

Blue

I'm wide awake by 5 AM, and for once it's not because of a nightmare. I wake up with the image of Keegan's beautiful tits floating in my mind and a painful case of blue balls. And I can hear Cunny's voice in my ears, so real I think, for a split second, it's actually him ordering me to hand over my man card.

"No red-blooded, testicle-totin' *man* would have walked away from a sweet, warm, willing piece of ass like that. Especially not so he could *'make it special'*." Here the voice in my head turns seriously sarcastic. "You wanted to *'make a memory'*? Are you fucking kidding me, Danube? What the hell is wrong with you? Strap on a pair and nail the girl to the wall like she wanted you to!"

Yeah, Cunny would be ashamed of me. But there's no point in denying that I want to make the first time with Keegan something different. Something, yeah, special. Even if it means tearing a few holes in my man card. And I want to get her away from her phone, away from this fucking nut-job who somehow knows she moved to the Embassy. Did he follow her that night she left the dorm? Has he been following her all week?

The old, familiar panic rises in my throat; it tastes like battery acid or something. Sometimes, I feel like someone's hands are around my neck, squeezing. It happens every time I think about the guys, about

Afghanistan. And now it's happening because I feel so fucking powerless to protect Keegan. I have to figure out a plan of action. I throw off the covers and sit up, forcing myself to take a few deep breaths.

There's one more reason I hesitated last night in Keegan's bedroom. I was scared to fall asleep again with her, and that's what would have happened if we'd gone at it on her bed. I still can't control my dreams, can't quite regulate my actions in that brief waking-up phase when the dreams are still holding on to me. Better to be making love in the daytime, when I'm just carefree Boy-in-the-Band Blue, fully in command of myself.

I check my phone. Still only 5:30. *Shit. Think of something besides what a dumbass you are.* I try to distract myself by focusing on the technical details of the day: All rappelling equipment needed? Check, already stowed on the ROTC bus. Transportation method secured? Check, aforementioned ROTC bus already reserved with a driver lined up, assuming he shows up sober. Enough qualified personnel to ensure a safe and effective exercise? Check, as long as you assume a bunch of hung-over undergrads looking to complete their Adventure Training hours fits the bill.

Plenty of the ROTC guys and girls have brought dates along on our unit's weekend rock-climbing trips, but today will be the first time for me. I've never wanted to bring along a girl before Keegan, and I'm not exactly sure how she'll react to the whole climb-down-a-sheer-cliff-on-a-rope thing. *Rappelling as foreplay. Brilliant, Blue. She'll probably hate it.*

It was a spur-of-the-moment thing, to suggest Keegan come along on the training exercise I was already scheduled to assist with as a ROTC adviser. But the rappelling isn't the memory-making part. That will hopefully happen *after* rappelling, when we slip away from the group and hike downriver to this pretty little spot I stumbled across last year, a secluded, lushly green alcove where the river tumbles over the rocks into a deep, clear pool. And above the pool, behind the waterfall, is a cave just big enough for a blanket and a campfire. Seriously romantic stuff. At least I hope so.

"You are beyond saving, Double D." Cunny's voice again. I can't seem to shake it. Double D, short for Dancin' Danube. The guys started calling me that after I was fool enough one night to tell them the whole Boy Named Sue story. None of them had ever heard of *The Blue Danube.* "It's a waltz," I said, regretting it as soon as the words left my mouth. "Well, actually, it was a song written by this Austrian dude, and they used to dance the waltz to it, like, a long-ass time ago, back when women wore long gowns all the time."

I'd even played an audio clip of *The Blue Danube* I had on my phone for the guys. The phone's crappy speaker couldn't do justice to the song. Mama took me to Oklahoma City once when I was 10 to hear it performed by a live orchestra, and I was transfixed. Some things are just better done the old way. Of course, Bill had given her hell for taking me, when he found out. Mama never told him about the dancing lessons she signed me up for, so I'd know how to do a waltz. He'd have killed her.

"A Walt?" Monti's Southern accent had stretched the word out over a couple of syllables. "Isn't that a man's name? Like, an *old* man's name?"

"Not *Walt,* you dumb motherfucker," I'd said, irritated. "*Waltz.* Don't you guys know *anything*?"

Cunny had been staring intently at me; for once, he wasn't grinning. "Your old man named you after some girlie ballroom dance, Danube?" he asked. "That's some seriously messed up shit. 'Let's see, how can I totally fuck up my own kid?'" He'd slapped me on the back in a show of support. That was about the most sympathetic gesture we could give each other and still hold on to those man cards. From then on, I'd been Dancin' Danube, or more often, Double D. The guys got a big kick out of saying it. Tit references were always good for a laugh.

Jesus. Think of something else. And so my mind goes back, blessedly, to Keegan's body. I picture her cute little ass in those short, tight cut-offs, strapped into the rappelling harness. I can see those long legs pushing off the rock face with the rope sliding between them as she slowly descends to the bottom, where I am waiting to catch her and carry her downriver to the cave. *I sure hope she wears those cutoffs again today.* I keep on thinking about Keegan, and my hand moves down my chest, my stomach and further down, and then it does what I need it to do.

❧

A few minutes later, I look at my phone again. 6 AM. *Fuck.* I sit up and grab my laptop off my desk, open it, then wait impatiently to get online, vowing to call the cable company to complain yet again about the "lightning speed" Internet connection I'm supposedly getting. That reminds me that Hunter hasn't reimbursed me for the last three months of cable bills. Every time I bring it up, he makes some excuse and promises to get it to me the next day. And then, just like with the rent, he always manages to forget.

Hamilton, you cheap ass motherfucker. He is using me like he uses everyone else. *That's about to stop, dickwad.* It's not really the cable bill or the rent on my mind, though, as I picture myself wiping the smug look off Hunter's face with my fists. It's the way his eyes had flickered contemptuously over Keegan and then stared brazenly at her breasts. I'd almost gone all Army on him. If I ever do, the soft, spoiled college boy who thinks he's some tough shit won't know what hit him. One of these days, I'm going to stop holding myself back.

It seems to take forever to pull up what I'm searching for: *keegan crenshaw blog.* But then the links start popping up, one after another: "Cooke Ranch Heiress Revealed as Bad Girl Blogger;" "Virginia Cooke's Granddaughter Has Legislature in Uproar;" "Cooke Family Embroiled in Blogger Scandal;" "Screaming Bad Girl's Gone Silent." I read about a half dozen of the articles. They all describe an unknown blogger who for months ripped apart Oklahoma politicians in a "savagely funny, brutally honest way," according to one of the stories I read. Then someone figures out the blogger is a high school senior from a family long involved in state politics.

"Heir to the Cooke family fortune and raised on the sprawling Cooke Ranch in northeastern Oklahoma," I read out loud, "18-year-old Keegan Crenshaw has instigated a firestorm, with some suggesting she was being used by her powerful grandmother to improperly influence legislation."

"Whoa." I blow out a breath, reading on about how the blog had abruptly shut down, and Keegan had "gone into hiding." There are newer links about her appointment as editor of the Ikana College newspaper: "Bad Girl Blogger Now Big-Time Editor;" and "Cooke Granddaughter Back in the Spotlight as Youngest Editor of College Newspaper;" and "Do Rich Girls Always Get What They Want?" I click on a link headlined: "Ikana College Defends Cooke Heiress Choice" and scan through the interview with the head of the journalism school. A couple of sentences catch my eye: "Keegan's appointment had nothing to do with her family connections. It was based on her demonstrated talent, drive and passion. Even as a freshman, her work on our award-winning student newspaper stood out. We are confident that, as a sophomore, she'll make an outstanding editor in chief."

"Good for you, Screaming Bad Girl," I mutter. I try to click on links to the blog itself, but get an error message each time. Keegan said the blog was shut down; I really want to read what she wrote, but it seems to have been scrubbed off the Internet.

I put the laptop back on the desk, then stretch out on the bed with my hands folded behind my head. What I read leaves me breathless. Keegan is *so* much more than a hot chick who can rock a pair of cutoffs. She's so much more than a small-town innocent who's never experienced anything but "pity sex" with a dork. And she is more than a rich girl apparently raised with a silver ranch in her mouth. I've never met anyone quite like her. Even before I knew all this extra stuff about her, I sensed she was something special. I'd pretty much fallen for her the first time I met her.

And what happens when she finds out what you are? What you did? I roll off the bed, shaking my head like I can banish the thoughts that way. But they're bouncing around in my brain now and shouting into my ears: *She's too good for you.* I think of the phrase used to describe Keegan's blog: "brutally honest." Brutally honest people don't like liars.

I start pacing around the room, trying to avoid the conclusion that's staring me in the face. I can't get any more deeply involved with Keegan. Not unless she knows the truth about me. And I *cannot* tell her. I don't have it in me, Purple Heart notwithstanding. I'll have to end it with her. Now. But that's not going to be easy to do, not when I've just told her I want to be her only Romeo, her only fucking hero. What in the hell had I been thinking? I didn't think; that's the thing. The words just came spilling out on their own. And now I have to take them back.

I sit down on the bed again and put my face in my hands. Hot tears sting my eyes. *That's it, son. Cry like a little girl.* Bill's voice, this time. I grab my guitar and start playing one of Bryson's songs. I'm singing softly, wallowing in self-pity.

Truth can be a liar
As twisted as they come
She'll set your soul on fire
And laugh when you try to run.

She'll lead you down the primrose path
She'll let you think you've fooled her
Then sacrifice you to Heaven's wrath
Just when you think you rule her.
Truth lies, baby, truth lies
Cause when truth gets honest, baby
Everything else just dies.

I put the guitar on the floor and slump back on my bed again, staring at the ceiling. I should just leave before Keegan gets up, blow her off, then be a total dick to her when I get back to the house. *That's the breaks, baby, I changed my mind. Get over it.* It's the only way.

I must have fallen asleep because the next thing I know, Keegan's standing over me, wearing those cutoffs. She's smiling. I'm naked. "I knocked, but you didn't answer so…" She lets her eyes travel down my body, and I see her chest rise as she inhales. Her lips part, and I have to jump up and run to the bathroom. Otherwise my hard-on is going to take control of the situation.

I hear Keegan laugh. "You OK there, Mr. Waltz?" I slip on my boxers and come out of the bathroom feeling like an idiot. The boxers do nothing to hide my interest. "Actually, the guys in my platoon called me Double D, short for Dancin' Danube. After I was dumb enough to tell them that the Blue Danube is a dance." No idea why I'm telling her that. I'm supposed to be breaking it off with her, not sharing more personal stuff.

"Dancin' Danube, huh?" She grins. "I like that." She'd pulled her hair back into a ponytail, but a couple of soft tendrils are hanging down in the front. I think of the day she moved in, when I couldn't resist reaching out and tucking a strand of her hair behind her ear. She's had me from the very beginning.

She's in a good mood. "I'm looking forward to getting away from here. I'm glad you thought of it, Blue. As long as you're sure we can be back by 4."

I hate the tremor in my voice when I respond. "I'm sure. And it will be awesome. At least I think it will be. I hope you'll like it. I mean, I think you will?" *Do it now, you fool.*

Keegan's grin fades. She tilts her head to the side, looking puzzled. "You okay, Blue?" The sweet concern in her voice dissolves any strength I have left. I can't do it. I can't break it off with her. I pull her to me and kiss her so hard, so long, that, she finally breaks away, gasping. "Wow! That's a good start."

She snuggles against my chest. I put my arms around her and rest my lips on her hair. It smells like coconuts again. I breathe in and close my eyes, willing all the voices out of my head. The hell with it.

I only want to hear from Keegan. She needs me. And God help us both, I need her. We'll make it work, somehow.

"Let me get dressed, and we'll go," I whisper against her head, then pull her chin up and kiss her lips again. "It *will be* awesome."

10

CAUTION TO THE WIND

Blue

I set my guitar in the back seat of the Coupe and place the blanket—with the ax wrapped inside—into the trunk, along with a cooler full of water bottles and snacks. Just as I pull open the passenger door for Keegan, Max comes bounding out of the backyard. Someone yet again failed to latch the gate. He heads right for the car and jumps into the seat.

"Maxie!"

Keegan puts her lips together in an air smooch at the dog, then lifts her smiling face into the morning sun as she leans against the car. It's going to be a warm day again, with just a light wind, perfect weather for rappelling. And for other things, I hope.

"Not today, buddy," I say to Max, snapping my fingers to get him out of the car. Naturally, he ignores me. "Max!" He looks away as if he has no idea I am talking to him. Little bastard. Or big bastard, considering he's about 90 pounds.

"Okay, buddy, we'll do this the hard way." I reach in and grab his collar, then try to pull him out. He hunches down into the seat, determined to put up a fight.

"Max! Get out of there, right now." I pull a little harder, and he finally gives up, jumping to the ground and, I swear, giving me a 'Go to hell' look as he walks dejectedly over to Keegan. And of course, she falls for it hook, line and sinker.

"Aw, Maxie," she says. "If I didn't have my hands full, I'd give you a big hug. You kept me company last night after I was "."

She throws me a teasing smile, and I return it, suddenly nervous about my plan. *What if she hates the whole thing?* I take the champagne bottle and package of plastic glasses out of Keegan's hands and set them in the back seat. She crouches down and cradles Max's manipulative head.

"Aw," she says again, stroking his ears, "you sure we can't we bring him along?"

"Positive. We wouldn't be able to take him where we're going."

"And when are you going to tell me where that is?" Keegan asks, still smiling as she rises to her feet and adjusts the backpack she's got slung over her shoulder. I've closed the back door and am about to close the trunk when Keegan puts her hand on my arm.

"Hey, why not wrap the champagne in the blanket, to help keep it cold?"

I kiss her lightly on the lips. "You're so smart." I pull the bottle out of the back seat. I'd noticed the champagne in the fridge and plastic stemware in the cabinet a couple of weeks ago. It is a perfect addition to my romantic cave scenario. So I grabbed both items just as we were leaving. I have no idea who they belong to. Yeah, it's pretty shitty to just take them, but I do it anyway. All's fair in love and war. Or something like that.

The ax clatters to the bottom of the trunk as I yank the blanket out and wrap it tightly around the bottle.

"Um, we're taking an ax?" Keegan voice is a little uncertain, and her eyes have widened.

"Oh yeah." I try to look serious. "It's the latest thing in foreplay. Really makes things interesting. You didn't know that?"

I turn away so she won't see me grinning and put the rolled blanket in the backseat. When I look at Keegan again, she's still wide-eyed, her mouth kind of halfway between a smile and a scream. I can't help laughing. "Just kidding." I kiss her again. "It's to chop wood. For a campfire."

She punches my arm. "You're going to pay for that, Double D." She puts the backpack on the passenger seat and reaches into it, pulling out her sunglasses. Then she slips them on and tries to stare me down.

"Nice shades," I say, flashing another grin at her as I grab Max's collar and start tugging him toward the back yard. "They make you look very glamorous, Madam Editor."

"Flattery *will* help you. Keep it up." She slides into the Coupe's passenger seat and closes her door just as I secure the gate and head back to the car. I can hear Max whining on the other side of the fence. *Give it up, you damn dog. You're not coming with us.* I can't help feeling bad, though. Max has both of us wrapped around his hairy paw.

"Nice car." Keegan inspects the Coupe as I pull out of the driveway.

"Thanks. It was my dad's." She must hear something in my voice because she puts her hand on my arm and rubs it with her thumb.

"I'm sorry, Blue."

"Hey, no apologies, bar girl," I say briskly, sliding on my own sunglasses. I nod at the backpack on the floor by her feet. "Your phone's not in there, right?"

She slants her eyes at me above the shades and answers with a kittenish smile.

"Right, Keegan? Do I have to search you?"

"The phone is on my bed, sir." She salutes me. "Just as you ordered."

"Good girl."

She pulls up the sunglasses and shoots me a warning look. "Just don't get used to it. I don't usually follow orders."

I smile and plug in *my* phone, cranking up my Sixties playlist. Bryson's first, of course. We're on the highway in a matter of minutes, headed west toward Red Rock Canyon. I set the cruise control at 70 and let out the breath I hadn't realized I was holding. It feels so good to be driving along with Keegan by my side, watching farmhouses and fields, tree-studded hills and dying, one-horse towns slide by in a blur. Even in November, with the grass brown and the trees bare, it's beautiful. At least it is to me.

I thought about Oklahoma a lot when I was confined to a tank rolling through the parched landscape of Afghanistan. When I finally set foot in my home state again, I understood the stories I'd heard about POWs who would kiss the ground when they returned to American soil. I'd gone weak-kneed when I stepped off the chartered DC-10 at Fort Sill, home for good. And as soon as I could get off by myself, I'd cried like a little girl. Good thing Bill wasn't alive to see that.

Keegan's staring out the window, seemingly lost in thought. "I can't believe how hot it's been all week," she muses. "So weird for November."

"Yeah, the weather's just getting weird everywhere." I take my eyes off the road for a minute and let them linger on Keegan's bare thighs. "Of course, any weather that lets you wear those cutoffs is fine with me."

She punches me playfully in the side. Then she runs her hands down her thighs, leans forward, leans back, puts her hands behind her head for a moment and then clasps them in her lap.

"You nervous, bar girl?"

She puffs out her cheeks and then takes a deep breath and blows it out slowly. "It's just so weird not to have my phone with me," she says after a moment, her hands fluttering. "I hope nothing big happens. It really doesn't look good for me not to answer calls and emails."

I put my hand on top of hers. "It's Sunday. It's only for a few hours. You need the break." I squeeze her fingers. "You're addicted to that phone, you know."

Again she cuts her eyes at me. "It's what I signed up for, Blue. It's part of the editor job." She turns her hand up and interlaces her fingers with mine. "You should come into the newsroom sometime and watch us put out an issue. It's really cool."

I bring her hand up to my lips and kiss it. "I'll make you a deal. I'll come see you in the newsroom if you'll come meet Bryson and watch us play together. I reworked some of his songs, and I was nervous as hell that he'd be mad, but he really likes them. He wants to record together." I sound like an excited little kid. I *am* an excited little kid, when it comes to Bryon and my music, anyway.

"That's awesome! You've got yourself a deal, Blue Danube."

We drive in silence for a while. Bryson gives way to Leonard Cohen, The Doors, The Grateful Dead, Zappa. There's a lot of great music still waiting to be listened to when my pupil revolts.

"Okay, I can't stand it anymore!" Keegan throws up her hands. "No more Sixties music. How about *something* from the 21st century?"

I make a face, but decide to indulge her. "What would you like to listen to?"

"I don't know, Taylor Swift maybe?"

I jerk the steering wheel with one hand, just enough for a safe swerve, and clutch at my chest as if I'm having a heart attack. "I will pretend you didn't just say that. Have you learned nothing in the time you've been around me?"

"Oh, *please.* You're being dramatic." She hits the radio button and starts looking for a station that suits her. Finally, she settles on a country song. "There. Happy?" I stick a finger down my throat. "*Fine,* Blue. Have it your way." She hits the AUX button, and Hendrix blessedly pours forth.

I offer her an overly sweet smile. "Much better, thank you, bar girl." She shakes her head. I think I see her eyes rolling behind the glasses.

The landscape changes as we get closer to Red Rock Canyon. The iron-rich soil has turned red, and the rolling prairie grass seems to go on forever. Keegan's staring out the window, tapping it with her fingers. I'm worried she's going to hate the whole rappelling idea and feel pressured into doing it anyway. So I decide to go ahead and tell her my plan, give her time to back out if she wants to before we meet up with the rest of the group. I've just opened my mouth to speak when she says something that stops me cold.

"He called again last night. At three o'clock in the morning." She's still tapping the window. "I had the phone on vibrate and didn't hear it, fortunately."

I grip the steering wheel, vowing to torture the sonofabitch, assuming I ever find out who in the hell he is.

Keegan looks over at me. "He left a voicemail," she adds, her voice somber. "I deleted it without listening to it."

"Good." I stare at the road for a minute. "Hey, I've been meaning to ask you. Why don't you get a new number and new email address? That would seem like the first thing you'd want to do."

Keegan shifts around in her seat as if she's uncomfortable. "Because the police told me not to. They said it might really set him off, whatever that means. And they said it would be easier to find him if I didn't change anything. I've stopped using Facebook and Twitter, though. He was harassing me there too." Her voice quivers, then hardens. I glance over in time to see her lift her chin.

"Besides I don't want to have to change everything," she says defiantly. "I shouldn't have to. I don't want to change my life any more than I already have. This motherfucker is *not* going to break me."

"That's right, Screaming Bad Girl. He's not." I can't help grinning. It's cute, the way she curls her tongue around curse words, giving them a slightly different sound as they come out of her mouth. Keegan is this irresistible mixture of innocence and worldliness.

"Why are you smiling?"

"I was just thinking what an amazing person you are."

"Oh." One side of her mouth lifts up in a sly grin. "You know you're getting laid today, right, Double D? You don't have to keep flattering me. Although I don't mind if you want to keep on doing it."

"Thanks for that clarification. It sure is good to hear." I raise my eyebrows suggestively. "But I'm *not* flattering you. I mean it." I should probably just stop there, but I really want to say more. "I don't want to creep you out, but..." She's staring at me "...I couldn't sleep early this morning so I looked you up on my phone." Keegan's eyebrows shoot up. "And I read about the blog, about your family, about what happened when they gave you the editor job here." Her eyes get big, and she looks alarmed, but she doesn't say a word. "And I just want to tell you that I think you're *exceptional,* Keegan Crenshaw. I'm not just blowing smoke up your ass, either." Now I detect a bit of a smile from her. "I mean it. What you did, what you're doing. Do you know how special you are?"

For a second, her lips trembles. Keegan looks down at our hands, still clasped together. She opens her mouth as if to reply, then closes it again and turns her face away. We sit there in silence for a few moments. I stare at the road, trying to focus on driving.

Through the Coupe's speakers, Bryson's bourbon-soaked voice begins crooning the slow, agonized opening refrain of *Gild the Lily.* I've sung it so many times that the words come out of my mouth of their own volition. Keegan turns toward me, listening.

"Hey, I know that song," she says. "You sang it at the Halloween party, didn't you?"

I nod and keep singing, slowing down as I get close to an 18-wheeler ahead of us. In the left lane, preventing me from passing, some geezer in a Cadillac who's never learned the Keep Right Rule. Or maybe he forgot it. I sing a little louder:

Perfumed violets, painted gold
To a garnished Heaven, my soul's been sold.
Love's perfection, it once was mine
But I couldn't see, I missed the signs.
Gild the lily, twist the knife
Blind ambition, sh...

I hear a choking sound and glance over at Keegan, seeing the streak of tears below her sunglasses. "Keegan..." I turn down the music. "What's wrong?"

She pulls off the shades and wipes her eyes. "I'm sorry. I have no idea what the hell my problem is." She smiles ruefully and shakes her head. "I think your song got to me, that's all."

"Hey, I already told you, no apologies."

"Oh, yeah." She runs a finger down the side of my face. It makes me shiver. I turn the music back up.

A few minutes go by, and neither one of us says anything. We're getting close to the exit for Red Rock. So I open my mouth to tell her what I've got planned, but she cuts me off again.

"So I got, like, a dozen texts yesterday from Megz, all of them about Hunter." She laughs softly. "She goes from being crazy about Hunter to being furious with him to telling me he's probably the guy she's meant to marry to swearing she's going to kill him. And she really means it. I mean, she *really* means every single crazy text she sends. At the moment she sends it, anyway." She shakes her head. "Classic Megz. She's pretty volatile."

I remember the look on Hunter's face when he was staring at the good-looking blonde in the sexy Catwoman costume. "So's Hunter. Maybe they'll be a good match for each other." I shrug, not wanting to talk about Hunter. "Or maybe they'll burn the house down around each other."

Keegan frowns, two lines creasing her brow. "Yeah, but Megz is really strong, really tough. She grew up in foster homes, with almost nothing she could call her own. She's had to claw her way up from the worst conditions. She's not a spoiled brat like Hunter. I think she's too *good* for him."

She pauses as I tap the brakes when I see a cop parked behind a stand of trees in the median. "Crap," I mutter, looking in the rear view mirror after we pass him. "I hope he doesn't decide to ruin my day." The cruiser stays put, and after a few minutes, I speed up again.

"The thing I really like about Megz," Keegan continues, "is that she's not afraid of anything. I mean not *anything*." She bites her lip. "I don't think I've ever gone through a single day without being afraid of something. I'm a coward."

I grimace, studying her face between glances at the road. "How can you even say that? The girl who published the blog, who held all these powerful politicians' feet to the fire, who had the whole state paying attention to what these slick assholes in Oklahoma City were doing? There's no fucking way *that* girl is a coward. Just don't even say that about yourself, Keegan. I mean it!"

She sighs and shakes her head, but her eyes light up with gratitude. "The thing is, Blue, I could only do it *anonymously*. As soon as they found out who I was, as soon as my family put some pressure on me, I folded like a house of cards."

"You were just a high school kid, Keegan. Why are you so hard on yourself?"

"Even in high school, Megz would've told everybody to go fuck themselves, and she would have kept right on going with the blog. 'Throw caution to the wind.' That's what she's always telling me. Well, actually, she says 'throw caution to the *fucking* wind.' But I can never do it."

I don't know what else to say to her. My playlist is about halfway through a long Bob Dylan set, and after a few minutes of silence, Keegan starts singing along. "Now *these* songs I know, at least some of them I do," she says.

"Yeah, everybody knows Dylan." I tilt my head at an upcoming sign hanging above the highway: Red Rock Canyon Exit 53B. "That's our exit." I start talking in a hurry then, before she can interrupt me again. I describe my whole plan—rappelling with the ROTC group, then the river hike to the waterfall and cave, the whole campfire and blanket thing—and I've just finished when we pull up next to an old school bus with *Reserve Officer Training Corps* painted on both sides. In front of us loom the red sandstone cliffs that gave the canyon its name.

Keegan's face alternates between delight and uncertainty. The whole ROTC group is standing outside the bus, near the river, sorting the gear. They turn as one to stare at us as we sit in the Coupe. I've never brought anyone along with me, and I expect some smart-ass comments from the guys. They're incapable of being subtle. Or well-mannered, for that matter.

"You don't have to do the rappelling," I assure Keegan. "You can just watch me. I have to participate with the group, but then we can get away and…" I let my voice trail off and run my fingers down her throat, then let them linger on her collarbone. She takes a sharp breath and closes her eyes.

"No, I want to do this, Blue." She opens her eyes. "I want to throw caution to the wind. What better place to do that than at the top of a cliff?" She laughs. "I know I sound stupid, but I really want to do this. *All of it.* With you."

I can feel my face stretching as I give her one big-ass grin. "That's my girl." I shut off the car and pop open the trunk. "You're going to be great at it. At all of it. And I can't fucking wait to get you downriver."

11

DANGLING

Keegan

I am about to be dangling off a cliff with only a lousy rope between me and certain death. Not only am I not about to throw caution to the wind, I couldn't have hauled caution out of my feet—where it has settled like a big, heavy pile of rocks—or out of my hands—which are shaking like lily-livered leaves—even if I wanted to. I am frozen with fear. And everybody's looking at me.

The wind, that thing I was going to toss my lamely prudent personality into, seems a lot stronger on top than it did below. I followed Blue and the ROTC members a couple of miles along a winding path that curved up and around, through trees and around boulders, until suddenly we were standing on top of the sandstone cliffs, looking down at the river. The guys, all clad in fatigues, jumped into action, anchoring rappelling ropes to two wide trees that stood about 10 feet from the edge. Then they quickly wrapped other ropes around their rear ends, creating harnesses with an elaborate system of knots.

And then, almost before I realized what was happening, they clipped themselves to the rappelling ropes and, one by one, they simply walked off the cliff. Headfirst. Hollering and howling and whooping as if it was the greatest moment of their lives. They're young and brave and free. And they're completely insane.

Blue stood near the edge with a beat-up iPad in his hands, reading out what sounded like a safety checklist before each team member stepped off the cliff. He looked deadly serious and sounded very business-like. But now that the last guy has seemingly disappeared into thin air, he looks over at me. I'm sure I look scared to death because I am.

No fucking way. The F-word comes very easily to me this time. And after I think it, I say it. "No. Fucking. Way." I start to back up, turning to head down the path I just came up. "No way, Blue! Are you kidding me?"

He's instantly at my side, the same expression on his face—warm, reassuring, sob-inducing—as the day I moved into the Embassy, when he reached out to me as I crouched next to my car. I could get used to that expression. I could get addicted to it.

"Keegan." He sticks the iPad under his arm and puts both hands on my shoulders. "You're not going down like that." He chuckles and pulls me to him. "I should have warned you. That's the advanced way to do it. They call it Aussie Style. These guys have been trained on how to do that. You're going down butt first, slowly, with me right there next to you."

He laughs again and kisses my forehead, and I stand there feeling foolish. "Oh." That's all I can manage.

"And remember, you don't have to do this at all. No one's going to think badly of you. None of those guys down there will, I guarantee you. The only thing *they're* thinking about is how to get you away from me."

I'd seen the way all the ROTC guys looked at me. I'd be a liar if I said it doesn't make me feel good. But I do not want to back out in front of those guys. In front of Blue. *Caution to the wind, you wuss.* "I'm doing this, Blue." I walk back toward the edge to a pile of rope and start wrapping a length of it around my waist and through my legs, then try to tie it the way I'd seen the others doing.

"Hang on, hang on." Blue tucks the iPad into the backpack on the ground nearby; then his hands gently take the rope away from me. "You gotta know what you're doing with the seat; otherwise you could get yourself killed. Besides, I brought a harness for you. It's safer, especially for a tiny butt like yours." He grins and holds up a contraption with what looks like a waistband and two leg loops. Then he bends over a little and holds the harness out in front of me. "Step into these leg loops, gorgeous."

I put my hands on Blue's shoulders and my legs into each of the loops. Blue pulls the harness up above my waist and cinches the loops just above the edge of my cutoffs. His hands linger a little longer on my thighs than is probably necessary. Not that I mind. Then he pulls me against his body, his hands on my hips. "Just part of the safety check," he says as my loins begin to flutter. "I have to make sure the waistband is above your hip bones."

Being pressed against Blue like that is enough to make my heart beat faster and my lungs feel like they can't get enough air. For some strange reason, a memory flashes into my mind just then.

I was sitting next to my mother's hospital bed, holding her pale, bruised hand. They'd given her more pain medication, and she was floating in and out of consciousness. I'd been reading one of my romance novels, but I looked up and let the book close when she squeezed my hand. "You okay, Mom?" I could barely keep my voice from shaking. She was near the end, according to the doctors. She stared at the book in my lap. Its cover showed the usual torrid embrace of an impossibly beautiful couple. When she gave me a weary smile, I noticed how dry and flaky her lips were. I was looking around for the salve I'd brought in a few days earlier when she clutched my arm. Her bony fingers felt like a claw.

"I used to read those." She was only in her late 40s, but her voice sounded so much older. It was painful to hear. "Then I met your dad. He was my real-life love story." I smirked. Or maybe I rolled my eyes. I was still just a smart-ass high school kid, after all. But I remember that Mom held up her hand. "I know it sounds cheesy," she went on, "but I still get that feeling around him, like I can't quite catch my breath, like I just jumped off the Empire State Building or something. But

I'm not afraid. I'm just fully alive for the first time. It's this unbelievable rush that has never gone away. I get it every time the man walks in the door, even after all these years. I know there are lots of women who will never feel like that about anyone, not even once. I've been very lucky that way."

Hot tears had filled my eyes then, and my mother gently stroked my arm. "Oh, I didn't mean to make you cry," she said. *Gah, why am I thinking about my mother at a time like this?*

Blue pulls back a little. "You still with me, Keegan?"

"Yeah, sorry, I was just remembering something."

"You can still say 'No' you know."

I grab the gloves Blue set on a boulder for me and quickly put them on. "I said I'm doing this, Blue. Now let's go!" I sound way more confident than I feel. He snaps to attention, feet together, chest out, hand to his brow in a mock salute. He's wearing a pair of faded jeans and a flannel shirt with the sleeves rolled up, and when he salutes, I catch a glimpse of those marvelously muscular abs. *He. Is. So. Unbelievably. Hot.*

"Ma'am, yes, ma'am! Your wish is my command."

I give him what I hope is a seductive smile and run my gloved finger down the front of his shirt, then do a playful loop around the zipper of his jeans. "Remember that later on, Mr. Danube, when we're in the cave."

He growls as he yanks me toward him and uses some kind of metal clips to attach me to the rappelling ropes that stretch out over the cliff. "Keep that up, sweetheart," he whispers, "and we'll just go find a place over there behind those boulders. We could have some fun with these ropes." He pulls my head back and kisses me urgently, hungrily. And I pretty much forget all about rappelling. I am more than ready to head over to those rocks. But then Blue lets go of me. "Nah, you're right," he says. "You've come this far. You've got to do it now. I can wait a little longer."

Blue grabs some more rope from the pile and is wrapping it around himself like the other guys did when we hear a voice calling from down below. "You kids still coming down, still need someone on belay? Or should we just give you two some *alone* time up there?" Whoever's speaking stretches the word *alone* out over two or three syllables. A bunch of guffaws reach our ears.

"Hey, Henderson?" Blue walks over to the edge and yells. "I have the ability to make you scrub every toilet on campus with your toothbrush! Would you like to rephrase that question?"

Instantly, we hear the chastened reply. "Yes, sir, I just wanted to let you know I am here available to belay for the lovely lady on your command. No disrespect intended, sir!"

Blue grins, still tying knots. "Technically, I don't have any power over them as I'm a civilian. But they don't seem to know that," he says in a low tone. He swiftly creates a seat out of the rope like the others did and then starts cinching himself to a second set of ropes tied around a tree and hanging over the edge. "This is called a Swiss Seat, bar girl," he tells me. "I'm going down right next to you."

"What did Henderson mean when he said he was available to *belay* me?"

Blue is checking my harness and the clips, making sure everything is tight. "It means he's going to be holding on to your rope. And that he will catch you if you fall." I draw a quick, sharp breath. "But you're not going to fall, Keegan. I'd never let that happen." He yells over the edge to Henderson. "On belay, grunt?" And the answer comes right back: "Yes, sir, on belay."

He puts the other rappelling rope in my hands and tells me to turn around and place my feet on the edge of the cliff. "Grab the rope with your right hand and put it behind your back. That's your brake. And put your left hand in front of you on the rope. That's your guide."

I do as he says. My heart is racing. A part of me wishes I could back out. But another part of me—I guess it's the stronger part—is determined to see this through. "I was never very strong, but *you're* just like my mother." I'm hearing Mom again. I'd been kind of angry at her for saying that, considering how I felt about Virginia. But I tried hard not to show it. You can't get mad at someone on death's doorstep. And I couldn't tell Mom she didn't know what she was talking about. But I am nothing like Virginia Cooke. She's steel without any trace of a magnolia. I'm more like an overripe banana, nothing but mush inside. Or not much else. *Why the hell am I thinking about this right now?*

Blue is talking to me. "Now just step out over the edge, Keegan. Keep your feet up high on the rock. Make an L shape with your body." *Sure. Just step out over the edge.* The wind suddenly picks up, and a cloud of dust settles over my face. "Aagh!" I am shaking my head, trying to clear my vision without letting go of the rope. I can't seem to move my legs. I am panicking.

And then Blue is next to me, hanging casually on his rope, his face full of concern. I feel the tears coursing down my face. "I got a bunch of dust in my eyes, and I can't let go to wipe them!" I hope he believes that's the reason for my ridiculous tears.

"Your right hand is braking you, Keegan. Just keep it in the small of your back. Use your left hand to clear your eyes."

"Oh." *I totally hate myself right now.* I wipe my eyes with my glove and then notice Blue is sliding over, his boots scraping the rocks until his body is covering mine.

"We're going to go down together, bar girl." His lips are right next to my ear, and his voice is calm and soothing. "When I say 'Right hand out,' you're going to stick your right hand out to the side. That will allow you to move down the rope. And at the same time, you'll push off with your feet. Just go a few feet down, then bring your right hand in tight to the small of your back again to stop yourself. Understand?"

I nod. Having his body pressed up against me, moving with me, makes all the difference, even if it does make me look like a big baby.

"You ready?"

I nod again. Then, at the last minute, I think of something. "Hey!" I turn my head to the side. He's so close his lips skim my jaw. "What about our backpacks? Won't we need them?"

"Oh, we'll get them when we go back up. You didn't think you were only going down once, did you? Next time, you're going down by yourself."

Before I can protest, he calls "Right hand out," and we put our right hands out in unison, pushing off the rock with his feet straddling mine. We slide down the rope a few feet and then plunge toward the cliff again. "You do realize," Blue whispers into my ear as our feet push off again, "the real reason I wanted to go down with you was so I could thrust into you just like this." He pushes his crotch against me each time we touch the rocks again.

I can't help laughing. And, yeah, I'm turned on. Just as we reach the bottom, I turn my face into the wind to shout. "You are unbelievable!"

He puts his mouth right next to my ear again. I can feel his warm breath against my face. "That's what they all say, bar girl."

12

CAVE MAN

Keegan

We've hiked for about an hour, following the river, most of the time in companionable silence. The fall foliage envelopes us in blazing shades of orange, red and yellow.

"Those are the only native Caddo maple trees left," Blue points out when we finally stop and pull water bottles out of our backpacks. "The Plains Indians used this canyon as a winter camp. Then the settlers going west used it as a stop on the California Road to get fresh water and fix their covered wagons. You can still see the wagon ruts along the trail." He takes a swig of water as I search the ground for signs of the long-ago settlers. "I used to come camping here when I was in Scouts so I know the place pretty well."

"You were a Boy Scout?"

"Yep." He sticks his water bottle in the outside pocket of his backpack. "I made it all the way to Eagle Scout." He grimaces. "It was the only thing I ever did that my old man approved of."

I stand there, awkwardly staring at the trail while gulping water. His words make me uneasy. Between the two of us, we sure have a crapload of baggage to carry around. But Blue has it worse. I have a problem with my power-tripping grandmother. But at least I know my parents love me unconditionally. Or loved me, in the case of my mother. Blue apparently has major Daddy issues. And then there's the whole war thing that I can't even begin to figure out. It's probably insane to think we can make this work. Whatever *this* really is.

Blue steps toward me and lifts my chin with his finger, then places the finger on his lips and shakes his head, staring into my eyes. It's as if he has read my mind. *Stop thinking so much. You always over think things. Just be in the moment. Just enjoy right now.*

Blue moves back a little, watching me as a slow, naughty smile creeps over his face. "Being a Boy Scout really comes in handy when I need to tie ropes around hot college girls. I do good knots." He runs his eyes over me, and my skin cells skitter up and down my body as if they're being swept up by his spiky black eyelashes. I grin and slap his arm. I am determined to ignore the shivery sense of danger, of foreboding, that keeps trying to surface. I want to be happy. I want to forget about everything except Blue.

I lift my face toward the sky and take a deep breath of the pure air. It's a bit more brisk than it had been that morning, with just a hint of a chill. "I can't believe I went down the cliff six times by myself!" I know I sound like a boastful little girl, but I can't help it. I'm seriously proud of myself. "I'm feeling pretty bad-ass right about now."

Blue throws his head back and laughs. "You never fail to surprise me, bar girl. And I'll tell you something." He pulls me to him. "You *are* bad-ass. Don't ever forget it. I was so fucking proud, watching you bounce down that rope. I felt like an expectant father or something."

"Okay, that's kind of weird, but I get what you're saying." I tilt my smiling face up, and his lips find mine.

We stand there for several moments before Blue finally pulls back. "We've got to get to that cave, bar girl. Let's hit the trail." He hoists the heavy backpack onto his shoulders and picks up the guitar that he'd leaned against a nearby tree.

The ROTC guys had tried to hide their sly grins when Blue pulled the guitar out of the car after we finished rappelling. He'd already stuck the ax, matches, blanket, champagne bottle and glasses, extra water bottles and snacks into his backpack. It was bulging, but he wouldn't let me carry anything in my own backpack except one water bottle and the sweats he'd told me to bring.

Henderson had stood by Blue's car, eyeing the guitar. "Wow, looks like you've got quite a romantic afternoon planned, Mr. Danube." Blue just glared at him. When we said goodbye to the group, Henderson kissed my hand. "Great meeting you, beautiful. If Danube doesn't treat you right, you can always give *me* a call." The murderous look he got from Blue wiped the grin off Henderson's face. Then Blue turned without a word and stalked down the trail so fast I had to run to catch up.

He didn't speak again for several minutes, at least not to me. But I could hear him mumbling. "…fool is just a glutton for punishment. Well, he's going to get it…"

"You're not *really* going to make Henderson scrub toilets, are you?" I'd asked when he turned to help me over some boulders. Blue being jealous over me was kind of cute.

"That smart-ass will be lucky if that's all that happens to him."

By the time Blue extends his hand to help me cross the river on several slippery, moss-covered rocks, I'm really hot and sweaty, even though the air has turned much cooler. Blue pulls me to the other side and tells me to watch my head as we duck under a bluff. He's smiling; he looks excited.

There's barely enough room in front of us to scramble single-file around a curve. As I make my way carefully around the rocks, I gasp at what I see. The river tumbles down the bluff right in front of me and cascades into a dark pool below that's surrounded by moss-covered rocks. And just beyond the rocks, a ring of fiery maple trees encircles the pool. The trees are reflected in the water, and the sun lights up the whole scene as if it has all been deliberately arranged. It's like stepping into a vibrantly-colored oil painting.

"Oh, Blue! This is so beautiful."

A smile of pure pleasure creases his face and warms his eyes. "I knew you'd like it," he says. He takes my hand, and we make our way down one side of the bluff until we are standing next to the waterfall, looking down into the pool. A cool mist settles on my face and arms. Blue slips his backpack off. "Come on, I'll show you the cave."

Carrying the backpack in one hand and the guitar in the other, he presses his back against the rocks and inches his way behind the waterfall, with me following. A few feet in, the rocks curve away, and we find ourselves standing in a cave that's about 10 feet deep and maybe seven or eight feet wide. Blue leans the guitar against the back wall of rock and sets the backpack on the ground. I set my backpack down too.

"Blue, this is amazing. *Really*." I am teary-eyed and touched by his thoughtfulness. "It's perfect," I whisper.

Blue cups my face with his hands. "No, *you're* perfect." He kisses me. "Now let's open that champagne." He pulls the bottle out and tears open the plastic package of glasses with his teeth, then hands the package to me. I pull out two glasses and hold them as Blue twists the top off the bottle. He whoops when it goes off with a loud pop, then fills our glasses and raises his in my direction. "To us, bar girl."

"To us." I take a long sip. "To making kickass memories."

Blue downs his drink, refills his glass and downs it again, then throws the plastic glass against the wall. Then he pulls off his boots and socks. "Drink up, woman, and let's go put our feet in the water."

I tilt my glass up and finish the champagne, then bend down and remove my sneakers and socks, wriggling my painted toes in the dust. Blue takes my hand. I expect him to lead me back toward the side of the pool. Instead, he pulls me right into the waterfall.

I shriek as the cold water courses over my head and down my body. But before I can say a word, Blue is heating me up with his mouth, with his hands, with his hunger. He hooks one arm around my neck, steadying me against his body, and kisses me over and over again. His tongue explores my mouth, then makes its way down my throat, sliding down my chest, over each shoulder and down each arm. I can feel the delicious contrast between the warmth from his mouth and the icy water moving down my body. I am gasping, panting, wanting his lips, his tongue, to move to my breasts and further down where, despite the cold, I'm on fire.

As if he read my mind, Blue pulls his arm away from my neck and slowly sinks to his knees in front of me. I run my fingers through his wet hair, over his face, as he leaves a trail of kisses on my stomach. His hands reach up and find my breasts, and his thumbs circle my nipples. I cry out and grip Blue's hands with my own, amazed and almost frightened by the urgent ache that is spreading throughout my body.

Blue brings his hands down to my hips and rolls his face against my abdomen, his eyes closed. Then he reaches for my shorts zipper and very slowly begins to pull it down, kissing each newly revealed bit of skin on my stomach as he goes. "Blue!" I pull my hands across my face, clearing the water from my eyes, and look down at him with my lips parted. He is torturing me; it's exquisite, spine-tingling torture.

He tugs on my shorts; they slide about halfway down my hips, and he glides his tongue along the waistband of my panties. I inhale and close my eyes for a moment. I'm starting to shudder, from desire or cold or maybe a bit of both. I look down in time to meet Blue's eyes as he gazes up, his face crinkling into that mischievous grin I fell for the first day I met him. And then he tightens his grip around my thighs and falls sideways, plunging us both into the ice cold pool below.

I'm wrapped in the blanket and huddled in front of the pile of wood Blue hurriedly chopped and is now trying to turn into a roaring fire. I stripped off my clothes as soon as we got back to the cave and had to dry off with my sweatpants as we have no towel. I can't stop shivering.

"I didn't think to bring a towel. Sorry about that," Blue says sheepishly, his teeth chattering. He is still in his wet clothes. The scorching look I shoot him should have warmed him up. He smiles a little hesitantly at me as the flame finally takes hold and the kindling he placed under the logs starts to crackle. "Aw, come on, Keegan. It was fun. You gotta admit it was fun."

I scowl, doing my best to stay mad. "It was fun up until you dumped us into the water." I'm irritated by the smile that's breaking through on my face. "What the hell made you do that?"

He shrugs as he strips off his clothes. "I don't know. Just seemed like the thing to do." That wicked smile again. "You could have woken the dead the way you screamed." He's standing there nude in front of me, practically daring me to look him up and down. I've never just brazenly stared at a naked man before. With Tyler, it was dark, and he'd shucked his pants off at the last minute. And that had turned out to be a blessing. Much, much better that it is Blue Danube initiating my virgin eyes.

"Like what you see, Keegan?" He's obviously noticed me staring. He shakes his hips, smiling playfully at me, and again, I can't help blushing. But I definitely like what I see.

"I'll say it again, Blue Danube. You are unbelievable."

I stand up and pull the blanket off my shoulders, then spread it on the ground near the fire. Then, keeping my eyes pinned on Blue's, I pull the sweatshirt over my head and slowly take off my sweatpants, using my foot to kick them aside with what I hope is wanton disregard. And then I'm standing there naked too. Blue's eyes roam over me greedily, and he shakes his head slightly while a long, ragged breath escapes his lips. "Like what you see, Blue?" I shake my hips, smiling playfully.

But Blue doesn't blush. He crosses the space between us faster than I would have thought possible and pulls my head back so that I'm staring directly into his eyes. "Let me show you how much."

"I love the way you growl at me," I say. "Keep on doing it."

He dips an arm under my knees, picks me up and slowly lowers me to the blanket. Then he stretches my wrists above my head and holds them there with one of his hands. He says nothing for several moments, just purses his lips and blows softly, agonizingly, along my jaw line, down my throat, over my breasts. Finally, squirming and feeling as if the flames have leapt onto my body and are racing along my nerve endings, I find my breath long enough to quip, "It's actually going to happen this time, right, Blue? You're not about to leave me high and dry again, are you? Well, not exactly dry."

He laughs. "I love your sense of humor. And yes, it's actually going to happen." He kisses my lips and run his fingers down my stomach. "Now. Right. Now. Are you ready, Keegan?"

"Absolutely. And unless that's a piece of firewood poking into my leg, so are you." *Clever, Keegan.*

"Wait, that reminds me." Blue turns, still holding my wrists, and stretches out his arm, barely able to reach his pants and pull something out of the pocket. He holds it up before my eyes. A small blue square. "Gotta have this."

At first, I'm bewildered, but then I realize what it is. I close my eyes for a second, embarrassed. *A condom, you idiot.* "I'm such a newbie. I didn't even think about that."

Blue releases my wrists and turn aside to put on the condom. Then he stretches out next to me, his skin melting into mine. "Never fear, young pupil." He kisses me, tenderly at first, then harder, more urgently as I pull him to me. "I'm here to teach you *everything*."

But that first time with Blue, it's almost like *I* am the teacher and he the student, he the eager explorer and my shuddering, twisting body the tangled terrain he's trying to conquer. A totally cliched, romance-novelish metaphor, yes. But entirely, deliciously, true.

Blue takes his slow, sweet time, his hands and mouth bringing me along with him, making my fingers and toes curl and then spring open, sending my hands over his back, around his ass, down his arms, chest and abs. My eyelids are fluttering, and every part of me tingling and burning at the same time when he finally thrusts into me. Then it's a steady, scorching ride until we cry out together, and an electric storm of sensation passes between us. Blue holds my lip between his teeth for an instant, then kisses my mouth, pressing his face against mine before moving to my side with a heavy, satisfied sigh.

I'm lying on his chest afterward, watching the flames dance and listening to the soft thud of Blue's heart. He strokes my back, his fingers sending an electric buzz through my skin. The wind is much stronger now; we can hear it rustling through the trees, and every once in a while, drops from the waterfall land on my back. I shiver, then take a deep breath.

"You okay, bar girl?" He squeezes me against his body, and I rub my face against him in a nod, then draw circles down his chest, across his stomach, with my finger. He kisses the top of my head. "So, was it better than with Tyler?"

I raise up to look at him, then press my lips to his. "You really have to ask? No comparison. But I don't want to talk about Tyler right now." I run my lips down his neck, then softly kiss his shoulder, lingering on the dog tags tattoo. "What about for you?" I prop on my elbow next to him. With my other hand, I trace the tattoo with my finger. "I mean, I'm not experienced. I assume for you there's been a lot of others?" I don't really want to know the answer to that. Or maybe I do.

Blue lifts my hand up and kisses my fingers. "It was perfect," he whispers, running his hand down my back and making me shiver again. "*You* are perfect." He pulls me back onto his chest. "And yeah, there have been others, but..."

I look up at him after a few seconds of silence. He has one arm behind his head, and he's staring at the rocks that form the top of the cave. "But what, Blue?"

He closes his eyes for a moment. "I was trying to figure out how to say this without it sounding like a cheap line, but I can't, so I'm just going to say it." He stares into the fire, and then his eyes latch on to mine again. "Even though there have been others," he says carefully, "I've never felt with anyone else the way I feel with you, Keegan. I've never had this kind of connection with someone, this kind of ... God, I hate to use the word *chemistry,* but I guess that's what it is. We have this bond, bar girl, that's special. At least *I* think we do."

I'm fighting the stupid tears gathering in my eyes and the ridiculous sense of panic fluttering my heart. "I'll bet you say that to all the girls." I bury my face in his neck. *Say something better than that. Tell him you feel the same way.* I can sense the tension in Blue's body: the moment he goes from breath-holding expectation to deflated disappointment. That moment shudders right through my skin. But I still don't say what he wants to hear. Still can't quite do it.

After a few more moments, Blue rolls me onto my back and gives me a long, passionate kiss. Then he smiles. It's a rueful smile edged, for just a second, in pain. I've hurt him. But I seem to be unable at that moment to do anything to fix it.

"Sorry to lay all that heavy emotional shit on you," Blue whispers. "Leave it to me to ruin a perfectly good cave romp. Sometimes I just don't know when to keep my big mouth shut." He starts sliding his body down mine, leaving a trail of kisses as he goes. "But now I'm going to make it up to you, bar girl. I'm going to show you what *else* I can do with my mouth."

The fire's almost died by the time I notice the long afternoon shadows on the cave walls. "Not that I wouldn't like to stay like this forever," I say, "but I can't miss that meeting. Shouldn't we head back?"

"Yeah, I suppose we should." Blue doesn't move, though. "Plus, there's no telling what critters might want to use this cave, especially later in the day."

I sit up suddenly. I hadn't thought about critters. Blue laughs at the look on my face. "For a girl raised on a ranch, you sure aren't all that outdoorsy."

I reach for my sweats and quickly put them on. It's starting to get cold, even with the fire still glowing. "My brother Buick got the ranching genes." I brush leaves and dirt off my sweatpants. "He'd stay outside on a horse 24/7 if you'd let him."

"*Buick*? Another cool name."

I sigh. "As in the back of, where he was conceived. My parents." I try to act like I found them ridiculous, but actually, I loved my parents together. It was obvious to everyone they were crazy about each other. They always gave off this *aura,* I guess you'd call it. It made me feel good, even if I sometimes didn't want to admit it. But that was over now.

I notice the guitar still leaning against the back wall of the cave. I need to change the subject. The last thing I want to talk about is my parents. Or my unlucky brother. "Hey! You never sang to me." I do my best girlfriend pout. "I can't leave here 'til you sing. But you've got to do it, like, right now."

Blue raises his eyebrows and gives me an arch look. "Well, I was planning to when we first got to the cave, but *somehow* I got distracted." He grabs my wrist and pulls me down on top of him. "Can I help it if you make me sex-crazed? I'm the victim here."

I kiss him, our tongues interlocking. He tastes smoky. "I want my song, music man." I giggle as he nuzzles my neck. He kisses me again, then pulls himself away and slips on his jeans.

"Yikes," he says, walking in a circle and pulling at his jeans. "They're still wet."

I stretch out on the blanket, my hands behind my head. "So why'd you put them back on?"

"It seems weird to be playing naked." He grabs the guitar. "Besides, as much as I'd like to continue this, we do need to get out of these woods. And if I stay naked…" He doesn't need to finish the sentence. For a moment, I am so tempted to just blow off the editorial meeting. But that cannot happen.

"Okay, then, Double D." I can hear the regret in my voice. "Start singing."

He leans against the cave wall, one foot propped up, tuning the guitar. "This is a song that Bryson wrote about his wife, after she died of an overdose."

I rise up on my elbows and give him a look.

"Yeah, I know, that sounds like a downer." Blue is playing softly. "But it's a stunning song. It's all about his love for her."

And then he starts singing. I lay back and close my eyes. Blue's voice washes over me, full of sadness and longing, but at the same time packed with sweetness. It sounds like childhood. *My* childhood anyway. The song's about a life cut short. But it's also about a love that can never be extinguished. And Blue's voice envelopes every word, first with a harsh edge that somehow bursts open each syllable and then melts away like overheated candy. Like the Tootsie Pops my Grandpa used to slip into the pockets of my jeans. That's the picture that forms in my mind: Grandpa's sun-spotted hand clutching a fistful of Tootsie Pops.

Tears slide down my cheeks. Probably not what Blue is hoping for, me thinking about my dead grandfather. Every time I hear Blue sing, I can't seem to stop the tears. Or the memories.

When Blue finishes the song, he walks over and crouches down next to me, still holding his guitar. "I didn't mean to make you cry. But I wanted to sing that song to you. Because it's the song that popped into my head the first day I met you. I know that sounds like a line too, but it's not." He strokes my cheek.

I wrap my hand around his fingers and sit up, wiping my eyes. "You're right, it's a beautiful song. And a sad one. I guess that's why I'm crying." Then my gaze falls on the words scribbled on Blue's guitar. I tilt my head and read out loud: *Monti, Cunny, Hud. Heroes of Hell's Highway. Lameass Singers.* I look at Blue. "Friends of yours?"

Blue doesn't return my smile. Instead, he stiffens and stands up quickly, setting the guitar against the wall and picking up his backpack. "We really do need to get back, Keegan. Like you said, you can't miss that meeting." He places the ax inside the backpack and has just picked up his shirt when I reach him. I'm confused by the sudden change in his demeanor. A little bit of panic courses through my bloodstream and pounds behind my eyes. I've screwed something good up by staying silent about my feelings, by being afraid. By asking the wrong question.

I touch Blue's bare back, pressing my lips into the puckered skin of his scars and feeling desperate. "Blue, talk to me." I put my arms around him and squeeze. "You said we have this amazing connection, and..." I close my eyes. *Say it now.* "...and I feel that way too. I *do.* But it kind of scares me."

He turns part way, looking over his shoulder at me.

"I want to know everything about you," I say. "I *need* to know everything about you, especially the hard stuff, the bad stuff, the stuff that gives you bad dreams and..." I shake my head. I don't want to start crying. "Don't you understand that? I tell you mine. You tell me yours. That's how it has to be if..."

He looks down while one of his hands curves into a fist on the cave wall. "What does the writing on the guitar mean?" I keep talking. "What happened to you over there? *Tell me.*" But he just stands there, not saying a word. "Blue?" Finally, I drop my arms and step away from him, picking up the blanket and trying to stuff it into my backpack. I can barely see through the stinging tears in my eyes. It spooks me, how quickly he can push me away.

And then I feel his arms around me, and for a fraction of a second, I want to jerk my body out of his grasp. But I turn into his embrace, and he hugs me so tightly I can barely breathe.

"Don't give up on me, Keegan," he whispers. He sounds frightened. He sounds *so* unlike the Blue I think I know. *You practically just met. What do you really know about him?* Not a thought I want to even acknowledge. It's true that it's all happening ridiculously fast. But I've never felt such a connection with anyone before either. It is a lot more than sexual. It's more, even, than standard boyfriend-girlfriend stuff, at least from my limited perspective it is. We're already at romance-novel intensity. Blue is my knight, my hero, my Romeo. Silly as that sounds in my own head, it feels totally real, absolutely all-consuming. It scares me to death. But I never want to let it go.

If only I could silence this nagging alarm bell that keeps clanging somewhere in my brain.

"I need you, Keegan." Blue is still crushing me into his body. "It's kind of crazy, how much I suddenly need you. But you've got to give me more time. There are some things I just can't tell you, not yet."

An icy blast of wind blows right through the falling water and into the cave, cutting off my response and putting out what's left of the fire. And at the same time, Blue's phone, zipped into an inner pocket of his backpack, begins playing its *Boy Named Sue* ringtone.

13

P. I. G.

Blue

I guess men really are pigs. Human history has plenty of examples already, but if you need another one, take a look at me. I'm standing there in the cave, staring at Keegan's trembling lips and frightened face, and I'm thinking about my dick. About how it felt to have those soft lips all over said dick. About how long I'll have to wait 'til I can feel them there again. So yeah. P.I.G. I'm ashamed of myself. But when I force those dickhead thoughts out of my shallow brain and focus again on the lovely person in front of me, I kind of wish I could just keep rutting around in the pig pen. Because it's a lot less painful.

Because if I'm going to be a good guy, I'm going to have to pay attention to the rage building somewhere in my chest. Could be it's in my heart, seeping like blood from a bullet-sized hole and then oozing out, thick and coagulated, until I feel like I'm drowning. It's not a new sensation. I've carried that coiled clot around ever since the day the guys died. I've learned how to manage since then, papering over and diluting whatever it is—rage, shame, fear, or some nasty combination of all three—with the everyday fluff of my college-boy life.

It's only at night, in my dreams, that it explodes inside my head. Or maybe that's my soul. Hard to tell. And the only time that suffocating feeling seems to go away? When I'm with Keegan. Something about her forces air into my lungs, plugs up the hole in my chest, staunches the bleeding. Why Keegan instead of other girls I've come across since I left the service? Not a clue. How could someone possibly become so important, so oxygen-ish to me in such a short time? I don't know. But this thing I have with her is as real as anything I've ever experienced. As real as life. As real as death. I'm not going to let anybody get in the way of it.

But Keegan, *my* Keegan, is scared. I've just watched the color drain out of her face when I handed her my phone. Kendra called a few minutes ago.

"Hey, Blue, is Keegan with you? Yes, of *course* she is … stupid me." I'd sighed, making it loud enough for Kendra to hear. She's just never going to let it go. "Tell Keegan somebody's done a number on her car," Kendra went on. "This weird shit is painted all over it, same kind of stuff that was written on that note in your mug. I don't know when it was done, maybe in the middle of the night. I hadn't been outside until just now."

I hadn't even looked over at Keegan's car when we pulled out of the driveway that morning.

"And right after I noticed the car," Kendra continued, "this girl named Megan shows up, says she's Keegan's old roommate, says she's been trying to get hold of her. She's standing here next to me right now. Put Keegan on the phone."

So now, Keegan is listening to Megz. "We're at this state park, I can't remember the name. We went rappelling." Keegan gives me a look as she speaks. "No, I didn't take my phone with me. I was just … never mind. I can't believe this." She runs a hand through her hair. "Okay, I'll call Jason right now. Send me the pictures."

She hits the End Call button, then stands there staring at the cave's moist walls. A couple seconds later, my text notification sounds. Keegan bends her head toward the screen, her thumb flipping through what must be pictures. "Oh my God! Oh. My. God."

"Let me see." I look at the phone. Pictures of Ikana's student union. All across the lower exterior of one side of the building are the same spray-painted words the sick son-of-a-bitch has been using all along:

KEEGAN CRENSHAW IS A WHORE!!! A LYING SOCIALIST CUNT!!! DON'T READ HER NEWSPAPER!!

One picture shows a newspaper page stuck to the wall, right under the word painted word *WHORE.* And taking up most of the page is a picture of Keegan's smiling face, with the words *DIE BITCH* scribbled in marker across it. I'm trying not to show how worried I am. The guy is getting bolder. And crazier.

Keegan reaches for the phone. "I have to call Jason. Megz said the guy did something at the newsroom too." She swallows back tears, and I want to pull her into my arms. But she's already got the phone to her ear.

Keegan barely said a word when we hurriedly left the cave and hiked to the Coupe. I'd driven back to town like a bat out of hell, and we'd been mostly silent, each of us wrapped up in our own grim thoughts. Mine were centered on how I could find the fucker who was doing this. And on how I could protect Keegan. We made it to the newsroom just as the sun was dipping behind Walker Hall, the tallest building on campus. The newspaper offices took up most of the building's ground floor.

And now we're standing in the newsroom with Jason, the paper's managing editor. He runs a hand through the fingerprint powder covering the desks, then rubs his fingers together as he watches Keegan's eyes flit around the room, taking in the now familiar, ugly words painted on every computer and desk. The broken window has already been boarded up, and there's police tape cordoning off the scene of the crime. Keegan's got her arms folded; her shoulders are hunched. I know her well enough now to read her body language: she's scared and trying not to show it.

"Maybe campus police will finally be able to figure out who this asshole is," Jason says, putting his dusty hand on Keegan's arm and using his thumb to rub her skin like he has a right to do it. "How you holding up?" The fucking thumb is still moving up and down on her arm. I want to break that thumb Two seconds. That's all the time it would take me to wrench it right out of its socket.

Keegan gives Jason a stiff-upper-lip kind of smile. "I'm fine. I just wish they could figure out who the hell is doing this. It's such a distraction. And it's embarrassing."

"I know." His hand finally drops away from Keegan, but not before he shoots me this brief, but unmistakably challenging look. It sends some kind of weird spike right though me. And he's obviously sensed my instant hostility. I stare him down. I'm crazy ass jealous over anybody touching Keegan. Even with one stupid thumb.

"I wanted to be sure everything was ready for the editorial meeting." He speaks only to her, his tone all-business. "I, um, wasn't sure if you'd be here or not. I know things have been rough for you lately."

I wish Keegan *had* forgotten about the meeting. We were having such a good time in the cave, at least until I went all weird when she asked about the names on the guitar. I can't seem to stop pissing all over things, just when they get good.

"I'd have let you know if I wasn't going to be here," Keegan says, a little sharply. She's responding to the slight note of condescension in Mr. Thumb's voice. *Good for you, bar girl. Let him have it.* My gut's going off over this guy. At least I think it's my gut. But I don't know if I can trust my gut when it comes to Keegan.

"I called campus police as soon as I found this," Jason goes on, "and they said for you to call … I can't remember his name. It's the detective who's working on this case?"

"Lugner," Keegan says flatly. I can tell she's not crazy about the detective.

"Lugner, yeah. They said for you to call him in the morning. But, um, the problem is, they said not to touch anything until Lugner and his team look it over tomorrow." Jason looks down at his loafers and sighs heavily. "And we've got the sponsor visit tomorrow."

Keegan inhales and then blows out a long, slow breath, looking around the room. "The sponsor visit. *Shit.* This is going to look really bad."

I step closer to her and put my arm around her shoulders. Jason stiffens and speaks to the ceiling. "Yeah. I guess it is." When I glare at him, he lets his gaze slide over me and focus again on Keegan. "But," he adds brightly, "we'll just have to make the best of it."

"Campus police is handling this?" I say to Keegan. "Why not Hickory Flat PD?"

Both Keegan and Thumbs start to answer. I glare at him again, and his mouth snaps shut. "Campus police started out with it," Keegan says, "but then they passed it to the town cops."

There's a moment of awkward, heavy silence. "Well," Jason says, turning slowly on his heel, "I've got to get ready for the staff meeting." He heads for one of the offices on the other side of the room. Keegan stands there for a few seconds, a range of emotions crossing her face. Then she silently pulls me into the office next to Jason's and closes the door.

She flings her arms around me and buries her face in my neck. I can feel her chest heaving. And yeah, that puts a picture of her tits front and center in my pig's mind. "Blue, what am I going to do?" Her voice is muffled, but I can still hear the anxiety in it. "This whole group of big-wig donors who give to the journalism department every year is coming in tomorrow morning. The president of Ikana is going to be with them. What are they going to think when they see what's all over the newsroom? All this stuff about me, the editor of the paper?"

I pull her face up gently. "This is not your fault, Keegan. You don't have anything to be ashamed of. You just tell them the truth. You can handle this."

She nods, covering my hands with hers, then dips her forehead to my chin for a second. "You're right." She kisses me softly and smiles.

"You make me feel strong, Blue. You make me feel like I can do anything." She steps over to the desk and sits down, spreading her hands in front of the keyboard. "I'll just explain the situation and assure them it's being investigated and will be taken care of soon. And I'll tell them the paper is operating normally."

"Speaking of the investigation," I say, sitting on the edge of the desk, "I want to meet this Detective Lugner. I want to hear what exactly is being done about this."

Keegan nods. "I'm supposed to call him tomorrow morning. I'll tell him I want to meet with him. He wanted me to bring the note we found in your mug in anyway." She looks up at me and smiles again. "But right now, I need to get ready for the editorial meeting. Pick me up at 7:30?"

I'm being gently dismissed. I stand up and run my hand over one of the award plaques on the wall. "I don't really like leaving you here alone."

"I'm not alone. Jason's here, and the rest of the editorial staff will be here any minute."

"Yeah ... *Jason*." I can't keep the sourness out of my voice.

"What?" Keegan looks surprised. I move my finger to another plaque. I want to tell Keegan that her managing editor makes my gut go haywire. But I'm not sure where my gut instinct ends and plain old male jealousy takes over. If I turn out to be wrong, I'll look like some kind of Neanderthal. Being a pig is bad enough.

I shrug. "I didn't like him putting his hand on you." I run my thumb over her bottom lip. "I guess I'm just jealous." I lean down and pour my heart into kissing her. Her breath is sweet. "I wish this day had ended differently, but it was still one of the best days of my life."

She comes out of the chair in a rush and hugs me, then kisses me full force the way she'd done on the roof. "It was for me too, Blue."

"Careful, bar girl," I chuckle, trying to tamp down my hard-on. "You're going to make me have to walk out of here with..." I gesture down at my jeans. No mistaking that I am turned on.

Keegan's mouth curves up. "No matter how bad things get, you can always make me laugh, Blue." She looks at my crotch. "Do you want to wait in here a few minutes?"

I kiss her one more time. "Nah, you've got work to do." I grab a newspaper from the stack in the corner. "I'll just hold this in front of me." I turn back to her as I slip out the door. "I'll be here at 7:30 sharp. Bye, beautiful."

14

THE WALTZ

Keegan

A wringer washer. Climbing the stairs to my room that night, I feel as if I've been put through one of those old-fashioned washing machines like the one that sat in my dad's parents' old farmhouse for decades. Grammy insisted on using it, said it didn't waste power like the washers everyone else used. She said it reminded her of her childhood. When I was a kid, she'd let me feed the water-swollen clothes into the machine's rollers, and I used to marvel at how the clothes would emerge so flat and half-dry.

That is me, all wrung out, the day's emotions squeezed out of me. Or so I thought. Blue is right behind me, his hands on my hips, his thoughts somewhere in that area too. It's funny how easy it is to sense exactly what guys are thinking, to know exactly what they want. Not that I mind. I want to be just a physical being right now too, wild and fearless and unthinking. I want to let my body just act on its own.

But I'm not done with the emotional roller coaster. And it's all because of Blue. He pulls me against him as I reach to turn my doorknob. His lips tickle my ear. "Hey, close your eyes. There's a surprise inside for you."

I turn to look into his face. I'm pretty sure I've had enough surprises for one day. But there's that irresistible grin. It moves through my skin and lights up every nerve ending in my body. And his eyes are twinkling, Santa Claus-style. I close *my* eyes and feel him reach past me to push open the door. Then I hear the light switch click on.

When I open my eyes, I gasp as Blue sweeps his hand around the room. It's full of furniture that wasn't there when I left this morning. "I got to the used furniture place only 15 minutes before it closed," Blue says, "so I had to choose fast." He points at a funky-looking chair, covered in light yellow fabric printed with seashells and fish, and with a circular base and no arms. "Coastal print, designer ... or so they told me, probably to justify what they charged me." His grin turns into something softer as he searches my face, then he walks to an antiqued white dresser, puts his hand on it and turns toward me.

I stare at his backside in the dresser's mirror. Damn, he looks good in those jeans. And even better out of them. "There's also a *distressed* dresser and nightstand, although what the fuck a *distressed* dresser is, I don't even..." He lets out an "Oomph" when I throw myself against him.

"Blue." My voice is muffled because my blubbering face is buried in his neck. He wraps his arms tightly around me, and his chest heaves against mine. I raise my face and kiss him. "I don't even know what to say."

"You don't have to say anything." He dips an arm under my knees, then lifts me off the ground. "But I know just how you can thank me." He walks over to the bed and collapses onto it, flipping over and pinning me underneath him so fast it leaves me breathless. Not that I mind.

Blue pulls my hands above my head, then slowly runs his fingers down the exquisitely sensitive skin of my inner arms. I've just closed my eyes, reveling in the sensation, when his lips touch mine. After a few delicious minutes of kissing, he pauses, pressing into me, just letting his exhaled breath caress my cheek. He is still holding my hands above my head, and after a minute or two, I can't help squirming, desperate for him to do more.

Everything about this guy—his smile, his voice, his eyes, his breath, and of course, the rest of his beautiful body—makes me feel as if I can never get enough of him. And I'm pretty sure Blue Danube's well aware of that.

"You know," he says with a languid smile, running his free hand over my lime-green sheets, "I probably lost a ton of testosterone just making up this bed. These are some *seriously* girlie sheets."

I smile, a little embarrassed. "Virginia gave them to me." *I so don't want to talk about my sheets, or my grandmother, right now.* I outline the razor stubble along his jaw with my finger. "I don't know why I accepted them, but I did. My relationship with her is so weird, beyond complicated."

He pulls away a little to give me a look I can't quite interpret. And then I stop being able to think at all because he lets go of me, sits up and pulls off his shirt, then stretches out next to me with his smiling face propped on his hand. He's obviously enjoying the way my mouth falls open as I stare at his bare torso. His sculpted muscles and smooth, tanned skin are practically tugging my tongue out of my mouth. He still smells like the woods and the fire and the cave. It's earthy and indescribably erotic.

My lips zero in on Blue's belly button and start slowly making their way up, saying "thank you" between each kiss. Blue moans, then catches my face in his hands and pulls my mouth toward his.

"If you *really* want to thank me, bar girl," he whispers, "you should have gone *south* of the belly button." I just manage to whisper back, "all in good time, Double D, all in good time," before it feels like he's feasting on me, searing my lips with his, probing my mouth with his tongue, chomping lightly on my chin while his hands set all the other parts of my body on fire.

With all that going on, it takes my fogged brain a few minutes to process what he'd said about making up my bed. "Wait," I say when we finally come up for air. I sit up and bend over Blue's legs to pull the sheets up. It's not the same mattress. "Did you buy me a new bed too?" I hadn't even noticed the mattress and box springs are now held by a new frame or the new wooden headboard at one end. "Oh Blue, you didn't need to do that."

"Yeah, I did. I couldn't stand the thought of you sleeping another night on the same bed where Hunter was."

I caress his face. "You *really* don't like him, huh?"

He shrugs. "It's his *type* I don't like, I guess. Slick and manipulative. Phony. I grew up with one like that. I can't stand the way Hunter uses people." His face darkens. "Just like my old man."

I've just had an idea. I surprise Blue by rolling off the bed and jumping to my feet, then hold out my hand to him. "There's something I want to do right now, Mr. Blue Danube." He's wearing a bemused smile. "I want to do your dance. I want you to teach me how to do *The Blue Danube*."

His smile gets deeper. "Did you say you want to *do* Blue Danube? He's right here, baby, ready and waiting." Blue sits up and gestures toward the front of his jeans, where the proof of his interest is obvious.

I twirl around, preposterously happy. I was terrified a few hours ago, and that fear is still with me. But I'm feeling stronger, more upbeat. The editorial meeting went well. We have a lot of great stories ready for the coming week's issues. I addressed the whole stalker thing with the staff in a way that made me sound confident and in control. I am still nervous as hell about the sponsor meeting. But just being around Blue makes me feel better.

"You heard me, Double D." I shake a finger at him, then beckon him with my hand. I love the way we tease each other. "I want to dance to *The Blue Danube*. Do you know how to do it?" He doesn't admit that he knows how, but the smile playing on his lips confirms it. "Come on, Blue, teach me how to waltz. You do know how, don't you? It'll be fun."

He falls back on the bed, groaning, hands on his face. "Bar girl, you always keep me guessing." And then he's on his feet before I know it, yanking me against his body with a growl. "Fine, I'll teach you to do *The Blue Danube*. But it ain't gonna be your grandmother's waltz."

He's grinding his crotch into mine, and my loins have reached five-alarm status. I take hold of his shoulders, running my hands down his arms and grinding my hips right back into him. "I'm counting on that."

Blue slowly leans my head back, then stands there without saying anything, his eyes blazing into mine, his chest rising and falling rapidly, his breath ragged. I think for a moment he's about to throw me on the bed and make me forget all about the dance lesson. But then a classic Blue Danube smile creeps over his face. He lets go of me, stepping back to pick up his phone off the dresser.

"Okay, Keegan Crenshaw, I hope you're ready for this." He pushes buttons on his phone, and a tinny-sounding song begins to play. Disgusted, Blue throws the phone on the bed. "The speakers on this thing *suck*" he says, heading out the door. "I'll be right back."

I hear him pounding down the stairs. I move to the window and pull it up, inhaling the cold, clean-smelling air and catching a glimpse of the full moon through the bare branches of the oak tree just before I hear Blue's feet clunking back up the steps.

He shuts the door with a swift kick and turns off the light, then moves to my new dresser, using the light from the moon and the streetlight beyond the tree to plug the external speaker he's holding into his phone. Then I hear a much better-sounding version of the song. Blue pulls me to him, then gently pushes me back a few inches, clasping his right hand in my left and holding it at shoulder's height. Then he cups my right shoulder blade with his left hand, and I place my right hand on his shoulder, our elbows up. Blue stands straight, a sad little smile on his lips as the song's shimmering violin introduction flows over us.

"Just think of a box, bar girl," he says. "Our feet will make a box on the floor." He pushes his left foot forward while I step back with my right. Then he steps diagonally with his right foot. "Okay, now you." He nods at my left, and I slide it out. Then he brings his left foot to his right, so that both feet are together again, and I do the same.

"Okay, now we go the opposite way. 1, 2, 3… 1, 2, 3…"

Blue's right foot steps back while my left foot goes forward, and so on. We do it over and over again there in my room in the Canadian Embassy, while *The Blue Danube*, set on *repeat*, just keeps on playing.

It has to be one of the most memorable days of my life, and it's not even over yet.

I'm doing really well with the steps until Blue tries to do a turn. Then I clumsily get tangled up in his legs. I would have fallen if he hadn't caught me. He dips me back until my head almost touches the floor. My whole body tingles as his lips graze my neck. Then he pulls me up hard against him.

"You're a natural. *Almost*." He grins and releases me, then runs his hands down the front of my shirt. And I go from tingling to throbbing, especially when Blue starts to unbutton his jeans.

"I guess the dance lesson's over," I drawl. Not that I mind.

"Oh no." Blue tosses his jeans aside. "You're not getting off *that* easy. I'm just making myself more comfortable." Will I ever stop melting when he grins the way he does then? "Without the jeans on, I can waltz like a wild man."

He twirls me around and around, counting out the steps as I follow and try to focus, while my loins, pressed up against Blue, are scalding me from the inside out. Finally, I stop and step back from him, my fingers slowly unzipping my shorts while I watch Blue's face. I figure turnabout is fair play. I inch the cutoffs down my thighs. His eyes widen; in the dim light, the whites of his eyes seem to glow. His lips part.

"I need to get more comfortable too," I tease, sliding the cutoffs over one foot, then lifting the other foot off the floor. The shorts catch on my heel as I pull them off, and I stumble a little, stepping on something hard. My journal, on the floor by the bed. I pick it up and slip it under my pillow.

"I noticed that today when I brought in the furniture." Blue's voice is husky. "Your diary?"

Oh God, I hope he didn't read it. He is, of course, all over the last week's entries. I'm not ready for him to find out how pathetically infatuated I sound when writing about him. Or about how just plain pathetic I sound about everything else. How scared I really am about the stalker, about what might happen to me. How insecure I am about whether I'll be able to handle the editor job and my class load. About whether I am screwing everything up.

"Journal." I always feel foolish correcting people, but I can't stand to hear it called a *diary*. The curtains flutter as cold air blows into the room, and I can't help shivering. I'd left the window open.

Blue pulls me to him. "Am I in the journal?" he asks.

"What do *you* think?"

We're both panting even though we are not moving. We're just standing there half-naked, pressed against each other. Blue suddenly looks very serious. His hands grab my face, and his thumbs caress my cheeks. "Do you have any idea what you've done to me, Keegan?" His voice is choked, almost frightened. "What you're doing to me?"

I put my arms around his neck and press my mouth against first one of his eyes and then the other. I taste a salty tear. "Blue."

It's all I can bring myself to say. We stand like that for a few minutes. I close my eyes, buzzing from the intensity, the raw need, that has flowed like an electric current between us from the first time we met. I never want it to end.

But Blue finally breaks the moment with a flash of the humor that's so much a part of him. "If that fucking song plays one more time, I'm going to have to throw the phone out the window." We both laugh, and he steps over to the dresser, stopping the song. When he turns back to me, I can't help chuckling at the way he gasps and lets his mouth hang open as he stares. I've whipped off my shirt and bra and I'm standing there in only my thong, amazed at my new-found confidence.

Blue crosses the space between us in an instant and takes me in his arms. "I am so *unbelievably* turned on right now, Keegan," he whispers. I barely recognize myself as I push him down on the bed and say in a seductive voice, "Then do something about it." And he does.

"You *will* marry me, won't you?"

For the second time that day, I'm lying on Blue's chest, tracing his chest tattoo with my finger, every exhausted cell in my body purring with bone-deep satisfaction. Does it matter that some lunatic has me in his sights? Or that, because of me, the newspaper probably looks bad in front of the whole school? Sure, it still matters. But I'm not panicked about it, not at the moment, anyway. I am safe, strong, calm Keegan. I am throw-caution-to-the-wind Keegan. I'm a girl, a *woman*, who's been expertly laid twice in one day. And in spite of everything, I'm feeling playful. So I come out with a quip from my mother's favorite movie. And then I laugh at Blue's loud gulp.

"Um. What?" His Adam's apple bounces up and down like the bobber my dad always put on my fishing pole when I was a kid.

Time to put him out of his misery. "It's just a joke, Blue. Have you ever seen the movie *Somewhere in Time*? With Jane Seymour and Christopher Reeve? After they make love, they're sitting on the floor eating, and she says to him 'You *will* marry me, won't you?' That line just popped into my head." *Do people actually say 'make love' anymore or do I sound like a naive little fool?*

"When my mom was sick," I tell him, "she'd beg me to watch movies with her, and we'd watch all her favorites over and over again." I pull the covers over us and settle into Blue's warm body to fight the chill. I can't bring myself to get up to close the window. "*Somewhere in Time, Romeo and Juliet, Titanic, Casablanca, Legends of the Fall.*" He tightens his arms around me. "Now that I think about it, all of those movies were about doomed lovers. How could I never have noticed that before?"

The realization gives me an odd fluttering in the stomach. I'm seeing my mother's face—pale, gaunt, with sunken eyes—and the 'chemo cap' she wore even at home over her bald head. She'd stare at the screen, her lips moving along with the words. She knew every line, every gesture, in every movie. I haven't watched any of those movies since she died. I'll probably never watch them again.

Blue is staring at the ceiling as if he could bore a hole in it with his eyes. I wave a hand in front of his face. "Blue? You still with me?"

"I'm sorry." He runs his fingers up and down my spine, then touches his lips to my forehead. "I was just thinking about how I'm going to stop the guy. I *will* stop this sonofabitch. You shouldn't have to deal with this shit. One way or another, I am going to make it stop."

I shiver, maybe from the cold. We stay like that for what seems like a long time. And then my phone buzzes. I come up on both elbows and stare at the dresser.

"Just leave it," Blue says, his voice hoarse. "Can't you just turn it off?"

I sit up and let my head fall forward. "We already went over this." I shift my feet toward the floor, but before I can stand up, Blue springs off the bed and grabs the phone off the dresser. I see his mouth tighten as he stares at the screen. Then he punches a couple of buttons and puts the phone down.

"Was it him?"

He nods briefly and comes back to the bed, folding his body around mine. "Yeah, it was him. The same nasty shit as before. I deleted it."

"Detective Lugner's not going to like that. I'm supposed to show him all the texts when I meet with him tomorrow."

"Fuck Lugner! He's got plenty of evidence already, and he doesn't seem to be doing much with it. You shouldn't have to keep seeing this vile crap."

I collapse on his chest again. Neither one of us speaks for a while. I'm almost asleep when Blue starts talking, slowly, with a raspy edge to the words.

"We were brothers."

That's all he says for a couple of minutes. I'm beginning to wonder if I imagined the words. But then he continues. "Richie Cunningham,

Jonathan Monti, Kyle Hudson." He inhales slowly and then blows it out. His heart, right under my ear, starts beating faster.

I come up on one elbow and let my hair fall onto his chest, covering the tattoo. "The names on the guitar?"

He nods, slipping a strand of my hair between his fingers. He doesn't meet my gaze. "I don't have any brothers or sisters," he says. "I had friends in high school, but nobody I was really close to. Except my mother." Now he smiles, lifting my hair to his nose. "I guess that makes me a mama's boy, huh?"

I kiss him, then settle down again. "I like mama's boys," I say.

He makes this sarcastic hissing sound.

"Well, I like boys who treat their mamas right. I guess that's not quite the same thing." He kisses the top of my head. After a moment of silence that makes me shiver again, he goes on.

"I sure wasn't close to my old man. But when I got over to Afghanistan, especially when I got assigned to route clearance, the guys I served with, man, we got close. Like I said, we were brothers. We'd have done anything for each other. I would have died for those guys. I *should have* died for them."

The last sentence comes out between clenched teeth. I feel Blue's hands curl into fists on my back. He starts shaking. That seam that is sealing our skin together gets slippery. He's sweating.

"Blue…" I try to make that one word comforting, reassuring. But instead, I sound unsteady and scared. Because I am. Something's happening that will change the way things are between us. I can sense it, and, selfishly, I want to stop it. "Blue." I sound stronger this time. "It's okay. You don't have to tell me." I stroke his cheek. Even in the nearly dark room, I can see his contorted expression. "It's okay."

"No, Keegan. It's not okay." His fingers wrap around mine and pull my hand away from his face. He closes his eyes for a second. "I *have* to tell you this. We can't go any further until you know this. I have to tell you."

Just stop talking. Just don't say another word. A tear slips out of the corner of my eye and falls on Blue's chest. He presses my body against his so hard it hurts. "*I* should have died for *them*, Keegan. The whole thing was my fault. They were out there trying to cover *my* ass. Trying to keep my stupid, sorry ass from getting in trouble. It should have been *me* in pieces all over that fucking road. I killed them! I killed my brothers!"

I try to kiss him, try to block the anguished words coming out of his mouth. But he wrenches his face away from mine and goes on, his teeth clenched again, his voice full of self-loathing. "And that's not even the worst part..."

And then the blare of a car stereo, turned up as loud as it can go, tears into my room through the open window. The booming bass pounds against my eardrums. The car is obviously parked right in front of the Embassy.

"What the *fuck*!" Blue whips the covers off and jumps out of bed. He leans out the window just as the music abruptly stops. I hear car doors slamming, then raucous laughter and the sound of footsteps on the front porch. After a few seconds, I hear Hunter whooping on the stairs. "C'mere baby! Come to Daddy!" Then a loud, drunken giggle I instantly recognize. I sit up. "It's Megz."

Blue's standing in the middle of the room, staring at the door. It sounds like Hunter and Megz are running up the stairs. And then we hear someone hit the wall, hard, right outside my door, and the unmistakable sounds of two people in the throes of passion.

"Oh. My. God," I say. Blue seems to be frozen in place, his hands still fisted. I bury my head under the sheets. I don't really want to hear Megz and Hunter going at it. And then, to make things even weirder, we hear Max barking. It sounds like he's right outside the door as well.

"Max! Get out of here!" Hunter's strangled, furious shout does nothing to quell the dog. "Get the fuck away from..."

I hear a solid thump, followed by a pitiful whimpering that fades as Max apparently retreats down the stairs. Blue, still naked, moves so fast across the room that I don't even register it until he yanks the door open so hard it crashes against the wall.

"What did you do?" he screams at Hunter. He sounds enraged, even *unhinged.* "Did you kick him, you sonofabitch, did you kick my dog?"

Then the sounds of a fight: thuds and grunts and snarls, feet slamming on wood. And I just stay there in the bed, Keegan the coward, covering my ears. But I clearly hear Megz. "Hunter didn't kick your fucking dog, Blue, you stupid asshole!" Her voice is harsh. "*I* did! And I'd do it again."

The fighting sounds stop, and there's a moment of heavy silence. Then Blue sputters, "Don't touch my dog again, either one of you." I see him outlined in the door.

When Hunter starts yelling again, it looks like Blue cringes. "You're fucking crazy, soldier boy, you know that? Totally, *fucking* crazy! You're certifi—"

Blue slams the door so hard it makes the walls shake; it cuts off Hunter's last, ugly word. Then Blue leans against the door and puts his hands to his face. I scramble out of the bed and raise my arms to put them around his neck. But he holds me away from him. We stand like that for a moment. Blue's fingers cut into my arms. The streetlight shines on his face just enough for me to see glistening tears.

Hunter's door slams, and it is quiet.

Blue swallows hard, then brings my hands together and leans down to kiss my palms. I can't see anything clearly after that, just the shape of his body through my tears. His voice, when he finally speaks, is measured, controlled, heartbreaking.

"I'm going to sleep in my room tonight, Keegan. Alone." He lets go of my hands and brushes my lips with the barest of kisses. "I'm sorry." And he slips out of the room.

15

MOJO

Blue

We're sitting in cheap, vinyl chairs in a dreary, ice-cold hallway at the Hickory Flat Police Department, and I can barely keep my eyes open. A mostly sleepless night is catching up to me. I spent hours just lying in my bed, replaying in my stupid head the whole Blue-kinda-sorta-comes-clean-to-Keegan catastrophe that unfolded upstairs.

Why did I decide right then, at the end of one hell of a day, to plunge into a confession of the biggest secret of my life? Beats the *fuck* out of me. And *then* I'd only done a half-ass job of it and topped it off with a complete fucking flip-out over the dog. I wanted to fall asleep holding Keegan that night as much as I've ever wanted anything. But I didn't dare. I didn't know how I might wake up. Another appearance from my howling, flashback-flooded self might scare her off for good.

Keegan has to be wishing she'd never met me. Yet here I am, sitting next to her outside the office of Detective Frank Lugner, staring at the name plate on his office door and wondering why the hell he's making us wait so long to see him. I feel Keegan shiver beside me just before she wriggles her hand inside mine; just that small gesture from her almost makes me break down and sob.

"Your hand is so cold." I clasp both my hands around hers. "I don't know why they've got the A/C blasting in here. It's, like, 50 degrees outside, at the most."

She's wearing this soft pink sweater made of that expensive stuff that chicks really like, and her jeans clung to her body so perfectly it makes me ache, and not *just* in a horndog way.

When Keegan texted me that afternoon, asking if I'd come with her to see Lugner, I'd been almost pathetically eager to be with her. I skulked around in my room, pretending to be asleep, until she left the house this morning. I couldn't bring myself to face her. I was scared of what I might see in her eyes: wariness, rejection, fear.

And when I finally crept out of my room not long before noon, I had a cabinet-slamming contest in the kitchen with a grim-faced Hunter. We didn't say a word to each other. No sign, mercifully, of the dog-kicking blonde named Megz.

I put my arm around Keegan, there in the police department, and pull her close. Is it just my imagination that she hesitates for a fraction of a second before leaning against me? I'd basically spent all night moderating a crazy-ass argument between the two sides of myself: Blue the calm, rational realist and Blue the hot-blooded hunka burning love with an unfortunate case of PTSD. No point in denying it any longer.

Cool Blue made the decision about half a dozen times to break it off with Keegan. She needs someone more stable than me, more *everything* than me. But then, over and over, Blue the Hunka Hero talked me (us) out of that decision. Keegan and I have something truly special. I can't give it up. She needs me as much as I need her. I'm sure of it. And I am *so* close to getting my shit together.

Keegan smiles tentatively at me.

"So, how'd the sponsor visit go this morning?" I ask.

She shrugs. "It went okay, I guess. You could tell they were concerned. They kept looking around the newsroom at all those terrible words. It was *so* awkward. But I got through it. We have some great stories coming up this week and next, so it helped to talk about that."

She swiped a hand across her forehead. "I don't know, Blue, I can't help feeling this stalker thing is hurting the paper, hurting the j-school. And it's because of me."

I've just opened my mouth to tell her everything's going to be okay when Lugner's door opens with a swoosh. His belly comes into view first, followed by short, polyestered legs and the slack, pissy face of a middle-aged man who has soured on life. Keegan and I stand up at the same time, and Lugner looks me over, then turns to address Keegan.

"Sorry to keep you waiting so long. Who's your friend? I understood you'd be coming alone. We have a lot to talk about."

"Um, this is Blue Danube. He's my..." She seems to teeter between word choices: s*oul mate, lover, lunatic. All of the above.* I stick my hand out to the detective.

"I'm Keegan's roommate." I stick my hand out, and he takes it, reluctantly, then lets it drop after a couple of limp shakes.

"I thought your roommate was a *girl,*" Lugner frowns. "Megan, wasn't it?"

"Oh, yeah, I didn't tell you. Megan *was* my roommate, but I moved out of the dorm a couple of weeks ago after the guy made some really awful threats and made it clear he knew exactly where I lived."

Lugner shakes his head like he disapproves, and Keegan's tone turns slightly apologetic. "I got freaked out, and so I moved into a house just off campus. Blue is one of my new roommates. I didn't want to drive my car down here today because it's still got all this horrible stuff painted all over it. The police—your guys—just came this morning and took pictures of it. So I asked Blue to bring me."

"Besides," Keegan touches my arm, and I pretty much dissolve into putty inside, "I *want* Blue here with me."

The detective's eyes slide over to me, and he lifts an eyebrow. "*Blue Danube?*" No mistaking the mockery in his voice. "Is that a stage name or something?"

"Or something." I stare him down. Two minutes after meeting the guy, I am surprised at how much I already dislike him.

He ushers us into his office, which has standard-issue, small town police department décor: cheap, L-shaped desk and metal file cabinets, an older desktop computer and printer, and surprisingly few personal items. There's one framed picture on the tallest file cabinet of a much younger and slimmer Lugner with his arm around a teenage boy, both of them wearing the same distant, wishy-washy smile.

We sit in another set of uncomfortable chairs while the detective settles with a sigh into the desk in front of us and grabs a Kleenex to mop his sweating forehead. His shirt is stretched so tight across his stomach I half expect buttons to come flying in my direction at any moment. He pulls a file folder from an overstuffed wire rack on the desk. *Seriously, you're still working from paper files? What is this, 1990?*

"Well, it seems our stalker has moved from text messages to vandalism and trespassing," he mutters, flipping through pages in the file. "Hmm..."

Another Kleenex swipe across his face. Even in the ridiculously chilled air, Lugner seems to be drowning in sweat. He slips on a pair of reading glasses and peers at several printed pages. "Do you know of any reason that he would escalate things now, Keegan?" He looks at her over his glasses.

Maybe because he can, you ass-clown, because no one's doing much of anything to stop him. My jaw has started to hurt lately. I'm clenching it too much. But this is not the time to stop.

"Uh, no, I don't," Keegan begins, "I–"

"So what *exactly* is the Hickory Flat PD doing about this?" Even to my ears, I sound obnoxious, but I don't care. Keegan flinches beside me. I didn't mean to cut her off, but I can't sit there silently another minute. Lugner's eyes, squinting into a ray of dust-dotted sunlight coming through the window blinds, glare at me. "Keegan could be in real danger," I go on. "It doesn't seem like this is being taken as seriously as it should be."

"We're doing everything we can do right now, Mr. Danube, especially given our limited resources." He uses exactly the cold, condescending tone I expected. "I am quite certain this is someone Keegan has stirred up with her *activities.*"

"What *activities*?" Keegan asks, her voice sharp. She's sitting up straight now in the chair. She is, finally, getting mad. "You mean doing my *job* as editor of the paper?"

Lugner pulls his glasses off and takes a deep, exasperated breath. "I am just trying to give you my professional opinion, Keegan. I think this has to do with the things you write in your newspaper, or maybe your, um, *notoriety* from that blog thing you were doing. There are a lot of people who will zero in on someone putting themselves out there as much as you do, especially given your family connections. You've made yourself a target."

Blood is pounding in my ears, and my vision narrows for a moment so that all I can see is the spit built up in one corner of Lugner's mouth. The guy enrages and repulses me, but I'm not completely sure why. "That sounds an awful lot like blaming the victim," I say.

Lugner turns red, and his double chin wiggles back and forth as he places both hands flat on the desk. "That's not at *all* what I am doing, and I think, Mr. Danube, that you should..." Keegan's phone starts dinga-linging in her purse with the old-fashioned ringtone I've teased her about. Lugner's mouth snaps shut. He sits there glaring. Keegan pulls the phone out and turns it over. I glimpse the word *Virginia* on the screen before she pushes the power button and sticks it back in her purse.

"That's the third time she's called today," Keegan mutters, glancing over at me as her voicemail tone pings. "I guess I'd better call her back soon."

Lugner slides pages back into Keegan's file and stuffs the file in among the others on his desk. His mouth is a thin line on his sagging face. He is obviously dismissing us. But I'm not done yet. "I want to know exactly what you're doing to find this guy," I say. Keegan leans forward. I feel her eyes on the side of my face. "It seems like nothing is being done. And how are you going to protect Keegan? Exactly, I mean, how are you going to do that?"

When I was in the service, I relied on what I thought of as the "skin crawl test." It never let me down. If someone made my skin crawl—like a thousand ants all over my scalp—I *knew* that person couldn't be trusted. When Lugner shifts his gaze to me, and I catch the flash of pure venom that lights up his eyes, my head practically erupts with the creepy crawlies, even though it makes no sense.

"Blue…" Keegan shifts uncomfortably in her chair.

"We're doing a lot, actually," Lugner interrupts. "We're waiting on phone records. We're pouring through campus surveillance footage. We've just about pinpointed the IP address that the emails came from. We've questioned Keegan's ex-boyfriend, Tyler Adams. I caught hell for daring to question Pastor Seth Adams' son. We even gave Tyler a lie detector test, which he passed."

"He's not my ex-boy…" Keegan starts, but Lugner cuts her off again. "I *also* questioned Jason Parker, the school paper's managing editor. He comes from one of the founding families of this town, and I caught hell over questioning him too, but I did it." He shoots me a grim look. "And I can tell you, he's *not* the guy. He offered to take a lie detector test before we even asked, and he passed with flying colors."

"Oh." Keegan's surprise is obvious.

"Wait a minute," I say, "why would you question the managing editor?"

"Because he was Keegan's main competitor for the editor job, and he would take over if she resigned, if she left town."

"*What?*" I turn to stare at Keegan. "Why didn't you tell me that? About Jason?"

"I don't know, I didn't think about it." She shrugs. She sounds little irritated. "He was very gracious when I beat him out for the job, and he totally supports me. He's a nice guy." I can't help snorting. Keegan narrows her eyes at me. "His grandma was the first female editor of the paper. Jason told me he was happy if it couldn't be him that it went to another groundbreaking female."

Another snort from me. I shift my glance to Lugner. "So could Jason Parker be pretending to be some nut job who's mad about

Keegan's politics or whatever? He sets my alarm bells off. Has he been investigated? I mean *really* checked into?"

Lugner stands, abruptly. "Maybe you should come back another time, Keegan, when you can come *alone*." He crosses his arms, and I slowly rise to my feet. We stand there glaring at each other. Finally, Keegan stands as well.

"Well, what do we do now?" Keegan asks the detective. "I mean, we *have* to find this guy and make him stop."

"We're working on that right now. Why don't you just let us do our jobs?"

Because you're not doing your job, you fat fuck.

Lugner comes around the desk and puts his hand on Keegan's shoulder, which makes my skin crawl so bad I can barely contain myself. "There are things I can't share with you yet, Keegan," he says, making an obvious effort to soften his voice, "but I can tell you we are making *real* progress, and this should all be over soon. I'll try to arrange for an officer to keep watch at your house. But if you feel like you're in danger, maybe it would be better if you consider leaving town. It might be best so that we can guarantee your safety. How about you just take a semester off? I'm sure your grandmother could put you to work at the Capitol for a few months."

Keegan looks stunned. Lugner pats her back, then steps over to open the door. Keegan walks out ahead of me. As I come even with Lugner, still standing with his hand on the door, I look him right in the eyes, giving him my *You're Not Fooling Me* look. As a teenager, I used to give that look to Bill a lot.

"*Danube...*" Lugner's rubbing his chin. "Any relation to Bill Danube of Bootstrap Enterprises?"

"He was my father."

And then I see the alteration that always happens in people like Lugner when they find out who I am. Or who they *think* I am, anyway. The subtle shift in body language. The change in facial expression. They go from condescending or judgmental or just plain indifferent to envious, fawning, intensely, creepily interested. It's always about the money.

"Well, well. You two make quite a powerful pair, don't you?" No missing the acid in his tone. He's one of the jealous, resentful type. "Didn't your father go down in a plane crash a while back?"

"Yes, five years ago."

"My condolences." He murmurs it in such a perfunctory way that it is clear he doesn't mean it. "I guess that makes you the heir apparent, huh? What're you doing at Ikana, just horsing around while other people work for you?"

We are out in the hallway now, and Keegan and I turn as one to glare at Lugner as he leans against the door frame. I have enough sense not to cold-cock him. Assaulting a police officer would really screw up my life, and it sure won't help Keegan. But my insides tighten and start this lava-slow boil that I know I need to get under control. The sonofabitch is *trying* to piss me off.

"I don't have any involvement with Bootstrap." I say evenly. "I'm completely on my own."

"Uh huh." No mistaking the sarcasm. I curl a fist behind my back.

"I'm really surprised," Lugner goes on, still sarcastic, but looking at Keegan now, "that I haven't heard from the great Virginia Cooke about this whole stalker issue."

"I haven't told my grandmother about it." Keegan sticks her hands in the sleeves of her pink sweatery thing. *Cashmere.* The word has just come to me.

"I don't need her to be involved," Keegan is saying coolly, firmly. "And neither one of our families has *anything* to do with this matter, Detective. So you don't need to bring them up again. I'll expect to hear from you soon." She turns and strides down the hall. She's getting her mojo back or maybe claiming it for the first time. Either way, I'm proud of her. I grin at Lugner. He flushes angrily, then closes his door without another word.

The elevator seems to take forever to make it to the third floor; we decide to take the stairs. As soon as the heavy stairway door slams shut behind us, Keegan leans against the wall, puts her hand on her chest and closes her eyes. "I probably shouldn't have spoken to him like that." She takes a deep breath. "But he made me so mad, Blue. His tone of voice there at the end, when he was talking about our families was so, so..."

"...much like an asshole?" I finish her sentence. "Keegan, you did *great* in there. Don't second-guess yourself. You shouldn't have to put up with being treated like that. And there's something not right about that guy. I can feel it."

I put my hands on the wall on either side of her and kiss her, lightly at first, then more passionately. I'm getting turned on, just pressing against her like this in the empty stairwell. "Hey, you ever wanted to do it on a flight of stairs?" I nudge my knee between her legs. "Now's your chance, baby."

She puts her arms around my neck. "I'm pretty sure doing it in the police department would be a bad idea."

"Aw, come on, walk on the wild side, baby." I push my forehead against hers. She's chewing her lower lip. I know her well enough now to know that means something's bothering her. "What is it?"

"Blue." She drags my name out into two or three syllables. "About Jason." I start to speak, but she puts her fingers on my mouth, shushing me. "I know you have this thing about him. But the thing is..." She kisses me softly. "The thing is that it makes me look bad, you know? Since Jason and I competed against each other, if it gets out that I'm making accusations against him with no proof, it just doesn't look good. So I need you to stop. Lugner said he passed a lie detector test."

I sigh theatrically and grind my crotch into hers. I still think there's something squirrelly about Jason. But I think there's something squirrelly about Lugner too. Maybe I just can't stomach petty, insecure assholes. And maybe my gut isn't infallible when it comes to someone I care about the way I care about Keegan.

"Okay." I press harder, and she catches her breath and moans, tipping her head back against the wall and giving me a look that sets my dick on fire. "Want me to stop this too?"

And then we both almost jump out of our skin as a uniformed police officer pushes the door open and starts down the stairs, pulling up short when he sees us. I've stepped back from Keegan, and neither one of us is undressed, but we probably look guilty as hell anyway.

"Do you two need some help?" The officer stares at me suspiciously.

"No, no, we're just on our way down, thanks." I take Keegan's arm, and we run down the stairs, laughing like crazy when we finally emerge into the cold sunshine.

"Oh my God, that was so embarrassing," Keegan says as we reach the Coupe.

I hit the unlock button on my key and open the door for her. As she settles into the seat, I run my fingers over her cashmere-covered breasts and kiss her. "I can't wait to get you home," I say, then close the door and walk around to my side. I've just clicked my seatbelt into place when Keegan asks me about Bootstrap.

"What was all that heir apparent stuff about? What's Bootstrap Enterprises?"

I twist a strand of her hair, then tuck it behind her ear. "It's the company my old man started years ago. His whole thing was that he pulled himself up by the bootstraps. Bootstrap Bill. He loved to call himself that." I shake my head, then turn the key and sit there a moment as the car purrs to life. I stare out the windshield. "The whole conglomerate is now worth about half a billion dollars."

Then I turn to look at Keegan. Her eyes have widened. "Wow."

"But it's nothing to do with me. I want *nothing* to do with it. Like I told you before, I'm on my own."

Keegan puts her hand on my arm. "Blue." She stares for a moment at her thumb, rubbing my sleeve, then raises her eyes to meet mine. "I know you think you're somehow responsible for … the guys, whatever happened to them. But I don't believe that. It's just survivor's guilt."

I shift my eyes front again because I can't look at her.

"I want to help you work through your feelings about what happened," she goes on. "But I only want you to tell me the whole thing when you're *really* ready to."

We're still sitting in the police department parking lot. I want to shift into drive and race the fuck out of there. But I can't seem to do anything but listen.

"I know all this has happened *unbelievably* fast between us. I know it seems crazy to jump into it so completely. But I think it's real. And I think it's special. I feel *so good* when I'm with you, Blue. I feel so strong and confident and like I can handle anything. I'm not trying to freak you out or come on too strong, but..."

I'm frozen, my hands clenching the steering wheel. "Blue," her voice wavers, "just say something."

I unstrap my seatbelt and take her in my arms, burying my face in her neck, in her hair. We stay like that for a long time, me kissing her over and over and saying things I probably shouldn't. Things that will make it impossible for me to walk this relationship back or end it without a lot of pain. Not that I can ever imagine wanting to walk it back. Keegan has me. She has all of me. I'm at my best with her. I'm the kind of man I want to be when I'm with her.

She needs me. She wants me. And I am *never* going to give her up.

16

KALEIDOSCOPE

Keegan

When I was a kid, I had one of those old-fashioned kaleidoscopes, a gift from my Grandpa. It was made of brass. Grandpa seemed delighted to have a granddaughter who was such an anachronism—a 90s kid fascinated by something invented in the 19th century. For a while, I carried it everywhere, holding it up to my eye and getting a thrill from all the different patterns and colors that tumbled into view.

But then I took it to school one day and tried to show it to my technology-jaded classmates, who laughed me into a humiliated silence. When I got off the school bus at the ranch that afternoon, I ran straight past the main house to the river and threw the kaleidoscope into its muddy waters.

The way I saw myself that day—out-of-date, out-of-sync, weird—is pretty much the way I see myself still. Except when I'm around this sweet, troubled boy burdened with an odd name from a distant time. Maybe that's why Blue and I have such an instant and intense connection. Neither one of us quite fits in.

We've been going around and around, me and Blue—like brightly colored pieces of glass in our own kaleidoscope—starting that afternoon in Detective Lugner's office. Things feel kind of magical, suffused with color and light and red-hot heat, even though winter has set in with a vengeance. You can guess where the heat comes from. We are rarely apart for more than a few hours, and we haven't spent a single night away from each other.

I had no idea how it would change me, being made love to by Blue Danube. Night after fucking night. In his room. In my room. Behind my closed office door in the newsroom. In the Coupe. On the back deck when no one else—except for Max—was home. Almost in the kitchen; we were interrupted by Hunter and Megz walking in the front door.

Yeah, I can say *fuck* more easily now, not that that's any kind of accomplishment. But I still prefer *making love* to *having sex* or *fucking* or any number of other phrases we Millennials use to describe the act. Because that's what me and Blue are doing. We're *making love* in the literal sense, creating something that hasn't been here before. I guess you'd call it my *sexual awakening*. I walk around all day awakened, attuned to some buzz in the air I've never noticed before, this sexual energy that seems to be stuffed into every air molecule and dripping down the walls of every room I enter.

During classes, I have to force myself to stay focused. It's so easy to drift off into daydreams featuring Blue's mouth, Blue's hands, Blue's everything. Sometimes, I drift away anyway, only to be jolted back to reality when someone speaks to me. I'm pretty sure I often have an orgasmic expression that tells everyone what I'm thinking about. I'm a walking, talking, life-sized loin. But I don't care all that much. I am on fire, body and soul, and nothing else seems to matter.

After classes, I race back to the Embassy, even when I only have a spare half hour in the afternoon. I can't wait to see Blue. He makes me feel more alive than I have ever felt before, like any other head-over-heels romance novel heroine. And being with him definitely helps me handle the stress of everything else.

I've stopped hearing from the stalker. It's really weird. Just like that, it all stopped. Maybe the creep finally got whatever he had against me out of his system. But Blue and I are both still on edge every time my phone buzzes or rings. Neither one of us trusts it, this sudden silence. Blue doesn't want me walking to my car at night, when I'm usually the last one left in the newsroom. So he shows up just before 9 PM every night and waits for me to finish. If Jason is still there, they'll usually scowl at each other, but to my relief, it hasn't gone any further than that.

Jason's made some pointed comments about my "controlling" boyfriend, but stopped when I told him to cut it out. Now, he completely ignores Blue, and is cool and businesslike with me. He's apparently jealous. But it's not going to do him any good.

Blue has been making good on his promise to tutor me in music during my rare moments of free time. I am deliberately a dense student. I get a kick out of watching him try to patiently explain something. Sometimes, his voice fades away, and I get lost watching his face, admiring his passion for music, certain of his goodness.

Even when it's freezing outside, we crawl out the window on to the roof, holding blankets, and cuddle up under the stars. The roof is our special place. One night, very late, Blue said he had a surprise for me, and when we were settled in our spot, he pulled the guitar to his chest and began to play a song I instantly recognized: The theme music from *Somewhere in Time.* He played it slowly, tenderly, each note coming off his fingers and chipping pieces out of my heart. It's an unlucky person who doesn't have at least one song that can do that.

My mother used to cry every time she heard the *Somewhere in Time* theme song or watched the movie. When Blue was playing, I closed my eyes and saw her face—on the couch next to me, in the car on the way to yet another doctor's appointment, and finally, in the coffin, looking so unlike herself. I brought the blanket up around my eyes. I didn't want Blue to see me crying. I just stayed like that, shivering a little, until he finished the song. Then I felt his fingers pull the blanket away, and he took my face in his hands. His warm lips kissed my wet cheeks. I could see his breath rising into the cold air.

"I'm sorry. I wasn't thinking. I taught myself to play that song. I thought you'd like it."

"I *do* like it. I *love* it. I love that you went to the trouble to learn it for me." And then, as easily as if I'd said them dozens of times, the words slipped out: "I love *you.*"

And just as easily, the words came back: "I love you too."

And so, the days before Thanksgiving melted into each other. I met Frasier Bryson at an Embassy party where Blue performed so well I swore I saw tears glinting in Bryson's eyes. After the party, we hung out with Bryson and the rest of the band on the back deck, downing tequila shots and "shooting the shit," as Blue put it. He sounded a little starstruck, just being around his hero.

Kendra was there too, with *Henderson* of all people. Turns out she'd been absent from the Embassy a lot because she'd been spending time with my rappelling friend. They'd met at a party a few weeks earlier. Every time she went all moon-eyed staring at him out on the deck, I couldn't help squirming. It was so unlike the Kendra I knew. Not that I knew her all that well. But I didn't trust Henderson. Because Blue didn't trust Henderson.

Kendra and I were in a state of *détente*, to use a term I learned in my American History class. Not friends exactly, but no longer enemies. I'd discovered that I actually liked Kendra. And on the rare occasions when I wasn't attached at the hip to Blue, I think she liked me. Or maybe she just tolerated me. But I was pretty sure she didn't hate my guts any longer. Out on the deck, she'd even drunk whispered in my ear her lewd intentions with Henderson. "It's about time some of the fucking in this house was being done by *me*."

"Oh. Kay, Kendra." I'd put my arm around her for a moment. Seemed like the thing to do.

The morning after the tequila-shot shit shooting, Blue woke up screaming. I'd been lying curled up next to him—my legs tangled in his, the way I loved to sleep—when he bolted upright in bed and looked wildly around like he didn't know where he was. My cotton-mouth and hammerhead hangover made me slow to respond, but I finally was able to sit up and put my arms around him. I pressed the side of my face against his back and closed my eyes against the cruel sunlight coming through Blue's bedroom window.

"It's okay, Blue." Hoarse as a bullfrog, I swallowed a couple of times, wishing I'd stopped after one shot. "It's okay."

I let my face ride up and down along with his rapid breathing. We stayed like that for a few moments, neither one of us saying anything. Then Blue gently pulled my arms away from his body and headed for the bathroom. Just before he closed the door, I saw the pained look on his face. I heard the shower start running. We usually showered together.

I rolled off the bed and stood at the bathroom door, my hand raised to knock. But I didn't. Instead, I went upstairs and got into my own bed, pulling the covers tight around my neck and staring at the ceiling. Just before Blue woke me up, I'd been dreaming about my old kaleidoscope. I was standing by the river getting ready to pitch it into the water. But then I raised it to my eye for one last look inside. And then the dream got really bizarre. I could see Blue and me inside the kaleidoscope, tumbling around and around, grasping each other for support. At first we were smiling and laughing, the kaleidoscope colors whirling around, sealing us in, protecting us. But then, the mirrors inside it began to crack and shattered into pieces around us.

That was the only occasion during that time, though, that Blue's memories or guilt or *whatever* it was still gripping him so tightly broke through, at least when he was around me.

For the most part, things have been really good. I am in love. I am succeeding at the paper and doing well in my classes. We lost one donor to the *Daily* because of the vandalism, but the rest stayed with us. And I've begun to thrive as editor. We broke a big story about some shady financial dealings involving Ikana's president that was picked up by the national media. I was even interviewed on CNN. For the first time, I've allowed myself to believe I'm doing a kick-ass job. That I'm helping the newspaper.

I've even started to thaw toward Virginia, if only a bit. She found out about the stalker when Pastor Seth called her to complain that

I falsely accused his son. Virginia and Seth go way back, but not in a good way. She hates his guts, and the feeling is apparently mutual. They ended up in a screaming match, which naturally made my grandmother determined to prove it *was* Tyler. "It's not Tyler," I've told her over and over. She finally seems to have accepted that. But she does appear to be genuinely concerned that someone is stalking me. She chewed me out for not telling her about it. She also told my dad about it, and he called me up and chewed me out, too. For some reason, all that ass chewing makes me feel pretty good.

Virginia also has surprised me with an invitation to the ranch for Thanksgiving. She's even invited my dad. It will be the first time she's seen him since my mom's funeral. "Buick will be there too. I was able to get his sentence commuted." She left me stunned by that. Virginia once said Buick could rot in prison for all she cared. Not quite believing it, I'd texted the last number I had for my brother: *Are you really out?* And he'd replied: *Yep. Just moved back to ranch. Old lady had a change a heart I guess.*

So here we are, in Blue's car on Thanksgiving Day, speeding toward the Cooke Ranch. I only agreed to come if I could bring Blue with me. We're going to spend one night at the ranch, then go to Tulsa to have a delayed Thanksgiving with Blue's mom on Friday. I am nervous about meeting his mom. Blue says she's almost as sweet as me.

He is driving, with me in the passenger seat and Kendra in the back. I persuaded Kendra to come with us at the last minute, after she'd drowned her sorrows in a bottle of Jack the night before, then walked in on me and Blue, pushing my bedroom door hard against the wall, too wasted to even notice that we were scrambling to cover up. Henderson had dumped her. I didn't think Kendra should be alone in the house over Thanksgiving break.

Hunter and Megz left Wednesday for Oklahoma City, his hometown. Megz is the one sore spot in my life at the moment. She's acting like a stranger. Worse, she's acting almost like we're enemies. She and Hunter are still hot and heavy, but they spend most of their time in her dorm room. When we do encounter each other at the Embassy, Megz looks right through me or else she shoots daggers with her eyes as if I've done something terrible to her. I tried talking to her. I tried texting her. But she ignores me. I just can't understand it.

I look in the backseat at Kendra. She's curled up into a ball, her head leaning against the window. She is hung over and miserable, her green eyes bloodshot. "You getting enough heat back there?" I ask, holding my hand in front of the car's vents. The temperature dropped overnight, and a light snow has been falling all morning.

"Yeah, it's fine." She's still looking out the window, but she feels my eyes on her. She sits up and stretches her arms over her head. "Don't worry about me—what is it Blue calls you? Bar girl? I'm tough as nails, *bar girl*. If I can take some asshole's fist smashing into my face for five years, I sure as hell can handle being dumped by some douchebag."

Flinty words, cocky attitude. But not fooling me. Blue says she escaped an abusive marriage, but he doesn't know why she seems to have no family to go home to for the holidays. "It never came up," he said when I asked him.

"And you never thought to ask her? The whole time you guys were together, you never asked about her family?"

He'd shrugged, a little defensive. "We weren't together very long. Actually, we never were *together*. We just had sex sometimes."

Men.

I study Blue's profile as he drives. Strong jaw, straight nose, thick eyelashes. And dear God, that mouth. Virginia will probably pitch a fit if we try to stay in the same room at the ranch. And I'll be too embarrassed to even suggest it in front of my dad. But after everyone goes to bed, Blue Danube will be sneaking up the stairs.

I must have smiled. Maybe I made some kind of sex-fiend sound. But something makes Blue look over at me, and his eyes light up as he runs a finger down my cheek.

"Do you two have *any* fucking idea what it's like for me to sit back here and watch you?" Kendra punches the back of my seat. "Well I'll tell you, it's nauseating. Absolutely vomit-inducing."

"Sorry, Kendra." Blue puts his hand back on the steering wheel, but throws a quick *told you so* look at me. He hadn't wanted me to invite Kendra along.

"And another thing..." Her words trail off as she stares at the massive gate looming before us. I've seen it so many times, it doesn't even register. But I have to admit it's pretty impressive. Huge logs make up all three sides, and they are set in stone bases. A large, wrought-iron sign—*Cooke Ranch*—hangs from the top. The Cooke brand is carved into each log, along with *1893*, the date the ranch was established.

Blue pulls through the gates and follows the road as it climbs a ridge and then curves around a hill. The tires slide on the slick, icy surface. Blue brakes carefully as we come around the curve. It has stopped snowing. The sun's just broken through the clouds, and the river that winds through Rosewood Valley sparkles in the sunlight. Even in the winter, with the grass a dull brown and the trees stripped of leaves, it's a beautiful sight.

On the banks of the river, the main house twinkles with the Christmas decorations Virginia always has the ranch hands put up in early November. In this weather, all the fireplaces will be blazing, and the inside will be as beautifully decorated as the outside.

I almost refused Virginia's invitation. I don't believe it comes with no strings attached. But when she dangled my dad and Buick's presence in my face, I couldn't resist. And the truth is, I miss the ranch. It's the only place I've ever really thought of as home.

"Wow." Kendra unbuckles her seat belt and leans her forearms on the front seats. "I can't believe I'm actually at *the* Cooke ranch," she says sarcastically. "You sure your snooty grandma will let me in the door?"

I'm a little irritated. It's okay for *me* to say that about Virginia, but not for somebody else to do it. "Yeah, Kendra," I say pointedly, "I'm sure."

"Hey, what about your grandfather, Virginia's husband?" Blue asks as we get closer to the house. "I don't think I've ever heard you mention him."

"Cause I've never met him. He left Virginia before I was ever born. Went back to New York. Told Virginia he'd only married her for her money, and it wasn't worth it to him anymore. According to what my mom told me, anyway."

Then I point toward one of the barns, which has an open garage door. "Pull into that barn," I tell Blue. "The heat'll be on and you can leave the car in there."

"Yes ma'am," he drawls. He's been talking like Cowboy Blue ever since we left the highway. He shuts off the car inside the barn, and I'm slipping my socked feet back into my boots when Kendra makes this odd noise and grips my shoulder.

"Holy Mother of Pearl! Who is *that*?" I look at her, surprised, then turn my gaze out the front windshield, trying to figure out what she's talking about. Buick is standing in the back of a pickup on the other side of the barn, pulling down bales of hay from a stack that rises to the ceiling. He's shirtless. He pauses to wipe sweat off his face. Virginia always wants the heat up too high, even in the barn.

It's obvious Buick spent his time in prison working out. He's seriously bulked up since the last time I saw him. And he's grown his hair out too. I can see it under his cowboy hat, falling in waves to his shoulders.

Kendra's claws are *still* digging into me. "What is your problem?" I pull away from her and start to open the door. "That's just my little brother, Buick."

"Wait! Is my makeup smeared?" She runs a finger under her eyes, then tries to fluff her black hair with her hand. "How bad does my hair look?" She doesn't even pause long enough for me to answer. "Why the *fuck* didn't you tell me you have a brother who looks like that?"

Blue snorts. "So much for Henderson."

I've heard girls go on about Buick being gorgeous for years, but I never paid any attention. He's my kid brother, for Pete's sake. And he's only 18. "Kendra, he's, like, 10 years younger than you!"

"So?"

"And he just go out of prison." I feel bad telling her that. She has her hand on the car door, but my words stop her cold.

"What did he do?" she asks.

I sigh. "He got involved with the wrong crowd and went along when he shouldn't have. Look, Buick's basically a good person once you get beyond this big layer of *stupid* that he carries around, I mean. But he's off…"

She already has the damn door open.

Blue and I get out at the same time. Buick sees us and jumps from the truck bed to the ground. He's grinning. I suddenly can't see very well because of the tears in my eyes. I could have been a much better sister to him than I have been. We'd had a huge fight just before he went to prison. We didn't even say goodbye to each other. I hadn't realized 'til right then how much I missed him.

I wipe my eyes, clearing them in time to see Kendra doing this strange little sashay across the barn floor toward Buick. He puts his hand out to shake hers, and it's pretty obvious she is having to control herself to keep from jumping his bones right then and there.

"Unbelievable," I say as Blue slides an arm around me.

"I can't wait til bedtime," he whispers, his lips against my ear.

I smile at him. "Me either."

I hear footsteps and look up to see Virginia standing at the barn door, wrapped in a Pendleton blanket, tapping one of her booted feet.

"Oh shit, here we go," I mutter.

Blue squeezes my arm. "Steady, bar girl."

17

THE TRUTH

Blue

It's usually the little things that trigger the memories. Like a pair of damn cat eyes glowing in the dark. I'm sneaking up the stairs at the ranch, trying not to make any noise, when I almost step on Boots, Virginia's standoffish Siamese. His eyes—an eerie blue—flash at me before he rushes through my legs with a cranky meow.

And just like that, I'm back in Aziza's village, sneaking around behind the mud-walled house she had shared with her father and four brothers. I'd heard a noise then and froze, my heart thumping, until a black cat crossed the alley in front of me, its yellow gaze sending a shiver of fear down my spine. I should have listened to my gut, which was screaming at me to get out of there. But I'd been determined to find Aziza and bring her back to the base before she ended up trapped in a forced marriage, like so many other girls. Blue to the fucking rescue, as usual. But it didn't turn out that way.

I shake my head, trying to force out the flashback, and have to grab the stair railing to keep from tumbling over.

Jesus, Blue. Get it together.

I take a couple of steps up. The stairs squeak loud enough to wake the dead. Virginia's room is the closest to the top of the stairs. It would be my luck to wake her up while I'm trying to slip into her granddaughter's bed.

Virginia Cooke. Her eyes, so like Keegan's and yet so *unlike* them at the same time, gave me chills as she glared at me across the table this afternoon. She examined me like an unwelcome insect scurrying around on the ceiling. I couldn't decide whether to return the stare or ignore it and focus on the lavish spread before me. It'd been a long time since I sat down to a Thanksgiving meal like that. Mama always puts out a spread. But I haven't been home for the holidays in a while.

So I stuffed my face and gave Keegan's grandmother a big, shucks-I'm-just-glad-to-be-here smile. It was the same kind of dumbass grin I used to give Bill. I'd figured out it was far more effective than a head-on challenge.

I stop outside Virginia's room and listen for signs of movement, then scuttle like the rodent she apparently thinks I am toward Keegan's door at the end of the hall. I have to pass her dad's door and Buick's as well. Hard to tell how they'd react to my presence in Keegan's bed, although they've both been much friendlier than Madam Matriarch. Mark Crenshaw's deeply lined, lived-in face and guileless, light blue eyes give off such an impression of kindness that it gave me a lump in the throat. I liked him instantly, and for me, that's rare.

Buick is harder to figure out: wary, wanting you to think he's prison-hardened, but his bravado feels only skin-deep. And he completely failed to play it cool with Kendra; not two hours after they met, they seemed unable to keep from touching each other as they sat side-by-side at the table. Buick was actually blushing all the way from his neck to the roots of his hair. And Kendra sure as hell wasn't thinking about Henderson anymore.

No wonder Virginia looked pissed during the meal. She thought she was gathering only her fractious family members back at the ranch. Keegan is convinced she has some nefarious purpose for it. Whatever her reason, Virginia wasn't expecting a couple of interlopers to tag along. Oklahoma's most powerful politician would really shit bricks if she knew my complicated sexual history with both Keegan *and* Kendra. Buick might not be too pleased either.

I turn the knob, cringing as Keegan's door squeaks as loudly as the stairs. Then I forget all about the noise or anything else for that matter. All my mind—and my suddenly raging dick—can focus on is the gloriously naked girl sitting on the canopy bed in front of me, the flames from the fireplace throwing flickering shadows on her skin. She's smiling. She shakes her hair, and it cascades over her shoulder, over one breast. She's the most beautiful thing I've ever seen.

Every once in a while, I seem to step out of myself, kind of like those near-death experiences you hear about where somebody's spirit rises up out of the body and lingers around on the ceiling, watching what's going on below. Not to get too mystical about it, but that's how it feels: as if some other, shimmery Blue steps out of my body and stands there looking at the other me, who is standing there gawking at Keegan. And other Blue—the one without a hard-on, the one with a coolly functioning brain—says "You will remember this moment for the rest of your life."

The same thing happened to me back in the village right after I saw the cat's eyes and made the mistake of thinking I was safe. *Only a cat.* That's the thought that slipped into my mind the second before I felt the muzzle of an AK-47 pressing into my side and heard the voice—hate-soaked, in broken English—spitting in my ear. I had no doubt I would never forget *that* moment or what happened in the hours that followed.

My back is burning. Not that I notice it much at first. I've turned into one walking, throbbing penis at that point. But when I reach the bed and lift Keegan into my arms, she puts her hands on my back, and I cry out.

"Oh I'm sorry! I didn't mean to…"

"It's okay. You didn't." I kiss her, then carry her swiftly over to the fireplace, dropping down on my knees and laying her gently on the plush white carpet. I ignore my sizzling scars as I whip off my shirt and pull off my jeans and underwear, kicking them aside. It's ridiculous, the way my brain sometimes tricks me into believing the skin on my back is once again flayed open, shredded by the whip wielded by Aziza's oldest brother. I am determined to ignore it.

My mouth finds Keegan's breast, sliding to the nipple, where I let my tongue linger as she arches her back and moans. I move to the other breast, nuzzling the side nearest the fire. The skin's warmer there, kind of smoky tasting. She moans again and says my name. I close my eyes and bite my lip so hard I taste blood. Better blood than the tears threatening to spill all over her body. Just the sound of my name coming from her lips is enough to make me want to cry.

"Keegan." I fall on top of her, kissing her mouth, chin, neck, stomach, running my hands and my face through her hair, dragging my lips down, all the way down until my breath exhales against her thighs. Then my tongue searches for, and finds, the spot that I've learned sends shudders throughout her body. Finally, a bolt of electricity seems to lift her off the floor.

After a few delicious moments, I stretch out above her. We're both panting. I stare into her eyes. They glow, reflecting the fire next to us; they're soft, happy, full of life. So different from Virginia's cold, dead gaze. "Keegan." I'm not even aware of forming words; they just seemed to suddenly be there between us. "I love you." She melts her lips against mine. Liquid heat, running into my mouth and down my throat. "I never want this to end."

I clench her hands in mine, then roll onto my back, pulling her on top of me. I close my eyes as her hair tickle my cheeks. "I never..." I hear the tremor in my voice. *Fuck, Blue, act like a man.* She kisses me. "...want this..." She kisses me again, and I open my eyes, trying to finish the sentence. "...this feeling between us to..."

One side of her face curls up in a mischievous half-smile as she slides her body against mine. She pushes down until, suddenly, I'm inside her. "...end." The last word comes out as something between a sigh and a shout. She's so unbelievably warm and tight and all-encompassing. I want to be far inside Keegan, so far that I stop being me, at least the me that ever has to be apart from her. I don't want to be the phony with a burning back. I don't want to be Blue the failed hero. I want to start over.

"Keegan…" I can't seem to stop talking. She shushes me by lifting her head and, at the same time, grinding into me. I make some kind of cartoon wolf howling sound. We move together then, a slow sensual rhythm that Keegan is completely in charge of. I watch her—eyes closed, lips parted, hair falling across her face, almost oblivious to my presence—this girl who only a few weeks ago had been so uncertain and inexperienced. Now she is using me as a very willing sex toy.

I am so turned on that things are in danger of, um, *coming* very rapidly to, yeah, a *head. Don't blow this, Blue. Fuck.* I can't seem to stop with the double entendres, even in my own head … *brain. Focus, you jackass. Think of something else.* I don't want to spoil this spectacular moment with poor timing.

But then Keegan's eyelids flutter, and she's gasping, running her hands through her hair, down her neck, over her own breasts as flame shadows dance across them. She calls my name, over and over. I can't hold it off any longer. I'm pretty sure I do a full-on howl at the moon. I know I call out Keegan's name more than once. It's blinding, white-hot bliss. And it's loud.

We collapse on the carpet side-by-side, rolling on our backs, our hands automatically clasping. After a few minutes filled only with our that-was-incredible heavy breathing, Keegan detaches her hand from mine and covers her face. "Oh God, what if everyone heard us? What if Virginia heard us?"

"I was just thinking the same thing. I'm actually surprised your grandmother hasn't already busted into the room and had her ranch hands drag me away for some country justice." I turn on my side, prop up on an elbow and run a finger down her arm. "But it would absolutely be worth it."

She chuckles, but casts a wary glance at the door. I get up and pull a blanket from the foot of her bed, then lay down right next to her, and she curls into my chest. We lay there in silence for a few minutes, under the blanket, listening to the crackling fire.

"Blue," Keegan finally says, drowsily, "you know you're my hero. That probably makes me sound like a little girl, but it's true. You're so different than anyone else I know. You've served your country. You've made a *difference.* That's heroic. That's how I think of you."

I can't help wincing at the words. She raises her head to look at me. "What's wrong?"

"Nothing." I kiss her nose and pull her into my chest again, holding her a little too tightly. "Go to sleep, baby."

Then, just before we both drift off, she says softly, "Hey Blue?"

"Yeah?"

"What time do we have to leave tomorrow to get to your mom's on time?"

"I guess about 10. Why?" I bend my head down to look at her. She's chewing her lip.

"Can you ride?" she asks.

"You mean a horse? Yeah. I actually took riding lessons in middle school." I snort. "Bill seemed to think it was necessary." I squeeze her again, inhaling the scent of her hair.

"Will you come riding with me in the morning? It's supposed to be sunny and a little warmer. We can go early and be back in time." She reaches up and runs her fingers over my face, circling my mouth. "There's something I really want to show you."

You don't think about things in order, like you should. Your brain, after war, doesn't work like that anymore. Shit's just jumbled around all over the place.

So that crisp, clear morning—the day after Thanksgiving—I am following Keegan, watching her hair streaming behind her, admiring the way she handles her bay gelding, staring at her ass bouncing around in the saddle. And then, just when my thoughts should move on to pleasantries like the way her ass bounced around on top of *me* the night before, my head's instead suddenly filled up with a vision of Cunny's bloody face.

He was the only one still alive when I got to the Buffalo. His hand still gripped the goddamn radio so tightly I had to pry it loose. He'd been sitting in the back when the Stinger hit; it was the only part of the vehicle that hadn't been completely incinerated. I tried to keep my eyes off what was left of Monti and Hud and focus on dragging Cunny away from the Buffalo.

It's all kind of hazy now. I remember hearing the explosion. I was sitting slumped against the wall in a small room in Aziza's house, my bare back on fire from the beating I'd gotten. I'd been sitting like that all night, since they cut me down. When one of the brothers—who'd been ordered to guard me—was distracted by the noise, my instincts took over. I was on my feet and across the room in an instant, grabbing the AK out of his hands and smashing it across his face to knock him out. I'd have shot him if I had to, but I didn't want the sound of gunfire to bring all the others running before I had time to escape. And, in spite of what they'd done to me, I didn't especially want to kill one of Aziza's brothers. As horrible as they'd been to her, she still loved them. She was that kind of person.

I slipped through the house, praying I wouldn't stumble into any of the others, and out into the back alley. I realized later they'd all been drawn outside by the sound of the Buffalo being blown apart. But I didn't know at the time that it *was* the Buffalo. I didn't know Cunny, Monti and Hud were inside. My brothers, who'd come to rescue me.

I made it to the edge of the village, to the bike I'd thrown into a ditch after riding it the night before the short distance from the base. I figured a bike ride at dusk was a lot safer than trying to barrel into the village in any kind of vehicle. Not to mention a better way to not draw attention to myself since I was off base without permission. I had just jumped on the bike, meaning to race back to the base, when I saw the Buffalo, black bilious plumes of smoke boiling above it.

I don't remember getting to it. I don't know how Aziza's brothers didn't see me running and grab me again. Maybe they did see me, but they also heard the choppers already on the way. Cunny had managed to call for help, I found out later. First thing he thought to do, even before trying to save himself. I don't remember scrambling through the flames toward him, burning the torn skin on my back to a crisp, or pulling Cunny out. I do remember begging him, as the choppers closed in, to stay alive; I remember begging him—begging *them*—over and over and over to forgive me.

I remember my heart pounding in my ears so loudly I could barely hear anything else. So maybe it's my horse's pounding hooves that brings it all back in a rush as I spur him into a gallop to keep up with Keegan. I am riding Buick's gelding, Okie. Keegan assured me Buick wouldn't mind. I sure hope that's true. There'd been no sign of Buick or anyone but the housekeeper when we snuck out of the house at dawn and quickly saddled up in the barn. I'd forgotten how good it feels to be out on a horse, barreling across the prairie, enveloped by a clean, grassy cow shit-laced scent that smells like freedom. I could stay out in that forever.

After about 15 minutes, Keegan slows to a trot and turns east toward the river, following it for a couple of miles until she comes to a spot where the water's shallow. She urges her horse across, and I follow, squinting into the rising sun. On the other side, Keegan breaks into a gallop again, racing up a heavily wooded hill. And again, I follow.

When we reach the ridge, she slows, turning back to smile at me. "We're going down there." She points about 100 yards down, where I see a rocky bluff jutting out beyond the trees. Way below the bluff, I can see sun-speckled water.

"Is that the same river we just crossed?" My voice sounds heavy, froggy. I've barely spoken since I got up with what felt like a lump of concrete pressing on my chest and bile in my throat. All fucking night, I kept hearing Keegan's voice: *Blue, you're my hero.* She has no idea how horribly wrong she is.

"Yep, it sure is. The Illinois. It curves back around and runs under the bluff. See that old cabin down there?" She points at a weathered A-frame that faces the bluff and is just visible through the trees. "That's where we're going." She kicks her gelding's sides, and he starts down a steep, rocky path toward the cabin.

There's a hitching post next to the cabin. We tie up our horses, then use the two log steps to reach the front porch. Keegan lifts her face into the sun with a happy smile. "My great grandfather built this cabin. Virginia's father. He told everyone he needed it to get away from his wife." She snorts. "If Virginia's mother was anything like *her*, I understand why."

I've got my face raised to the early-morning sun too. "Yeah, Virginia *is* pretty intense."

Keegan puts her arms around me and tucks her face into my neck. My arms tighten around her body. If I could only shake the sensation that I can't breathe. I know it's psychosomatic, but I feel like a fucking elephant is sitting on my chest.

"I saw the way Virginia was looking at you yesterday." Keegan's voice is muffled by my shirt. She raises her head and looks into my face. "The disgusting thing is that if I'd told her who you are—and who your father was—she'd have treated you completely different. Which is why I didn't tell her. She's the world's biggest snob." She is studying me. "You okay? You look a little … *off*."

Don't fucking cry. I twist my face to the side so she can't see it. "I'm fine, bar girl. Any time I'm with you, I'm always going to be fine." We stand there for a moment, my chin pressed against her forehead, our eyes closed. When I open my eyes, I see a pair of bald eagles circling lazily above the bluff. "Hey look, two bald eagles." I point them out.

Keegan shades her eyes and watches the pair plunge toward the river, then soar back up and sweep over us again. "Yeah, we see them every winter here. Aren't they beautiful?" She gives me the soft sweet smile that's now imprinted on my soul. "Did you know bald eagles mate for life?"

It should be a precious moment. I should say something romantic. She's practically begging me to say something worthy of a hero, of the knight in shining armor she thinks I am. But I can't speak because of the acid guilt choking my throat. So I just stand there.

After a moment, Keegan grabs my hand. "Come on, I want to show you the inside of the cabin. And then I'm going to *really* make your day."

The door opens with a creak, and she pulls me inside. It's chilly but quaint, full of hand-carved furniture and quilts. In one corner is an old-fashioned, wood-burning stove. In the middle of the combination living room/kitchen, a staircase made out of logs rises to a loft. I can see a quilt-covered bed up there and a wooden dresser.

"Wow," I say, "This is really cool."

"Yeah. I used to come here all the time when we were living at the ranch. It's my favorite place to be. I used to sit up in the loft or out on the front porch and write everything down in my journal. Typical girl stuff." She blushes. "Only drawback is there's no bathroom, just an outhouse in the back. I always worried about snakes in there. Don't know why they never added on a bathroom."

Keegan sighs and walks around the room, running her fingers over old photographs hung on the log walls. "That's Virginia as a little girl, with her parents." She taps on a black and white picture of a somber-looking girl with a long brown braid. I step closer to the picture and stare at it in amazement.

"She looks exactly like you. Or you look exactly like her, I guess would be more accurate."

Keegan groans. "Everybody says that. I hate hearing it." She touches the picture again. "Apparently, Virginia had a pretty awful childhood even though she was rich and privileged. Still, it's not an excuse for the way she's acted." She shakes her head and moves away from the picture.

I spot another one, a close-up of a blond teenager with a Farrah Fawcett hairstyle and haunting blue eyes. She's on a horse. Next to her is what looks like a much younger Mark Crenshaw, also on a horse. "Is that your mother?" I touch the photo. It's hard not to react to the blonde's pretty face and tender expression.

Keegan nods and swallows hard, then puts her hand over mine so that our intermingled fingers rest on the picture. "Yeah. Wasn't she beautiful? My dad says he fell in love with her the first moment he saw her. At Keegan's bar, remember?" She smiles at me. "It was after a rodeo, when my mom was still in high school, and a group of her friends used fake IDs to get in. My dad was there with some of the other bull riders. He used to be really good, 'til he broke his back. And his leg in two places. And a bunch of other bones."

I'd noticed when Mark Crenshaw got up from the table that he walked slowly, with a limp. I let my arm drop from the photograph, but Keegan's fingers continue to trace her mother's face. Her brows knit in a pained frown, and her eyes fill with tears. "God, I miss her so much."

I run my hand down her back, but I don't say anything. After a moment, Keegan wipes her eyes. "Virginia never forgave my dad for talking my mom into getting married right out of high school. She never went to college, never got a chance to meet the 'right' kind of husband, at least in Virginia's mind." She piles her hair on top of her head before letting it cascade around her shoulders again. That's all it takes to make the crotch area of my pants tighter than a duck's ass in a windstorm, as Monti used to say.

"Virginia cut her off, and neither one of my parents was very good at keeping a job, so we kept having to move." Keegan takes a deep breath in and blows it out slowly. "They'd make up with Virginia, and she'd let us all move back here to the ranch. Then they'd get in another huge fight, and we'd move out again. It was ridiculous."

Keegan shifts her gaze again to the picture of her grandmother as a little girl. "Then my mom got sick, and they had no health insurance. You know what it costs to get cancer treatment in this country if you have no health insurance?" Her mouth twists bitterly. "Too *fucking* much." She puts her hands over her face.

"Keegan." I try to load her name with compassion, love, understanding. My voice still sounds weird.

She takes my arm. "Anyway, they waited way too long to tell Virginia about it. 'Til we were about to be evicted from the trailer park we were living in. 'Til my mom was beyond saving. Virginia paid all the medical bills and let me and Buick move back to the ranch. But not my dad. She was so angry at him. That's why I'm still shocked she invited him here for Thanksgiving."

"Maybe she's not as bad as you think she is."

She gave me a look. "*Maybe.* Anyway, I don't want to think about that right now. Look at *this* picture." She pulls me toward the back wall, where a faded black and white, clearly much older than the others, hangs in an elaborate frame. "These are my great-great-great grandparents, who founded the ranch back in 1893. Funny how no one smiled in pictures back then, huh?"

I peer at the woman in the photo, clothed head to toe in some godawful black dress. Even in the blurry picture, I can still see the family resemblance. "She looks like you, too." I twirl a strand of Keegan's hair around my finger. "A long line of strong, beautiful women. Too bad about the clothes they had to wear back then."

That makes her smile, and then she shivers. "I wish we had time to light the stove. It really makes it cozy in here." She tugs on my arm, guiding me toward the log stairs that lead to the loft, and throws a seductive smile over her shoulder. "We'll have to think of another way to stay warm."

More quilts hang on the loft railing. You can look out a circular window cut high up in the front wall and see over the bluff to the gleaming river below. Beyond that are winter-brown pastures, dotted with hundreds of cattle. "This place really is something," I mutter.

Keegan wraps her arms around me from behind and pulls me to the four-poster log bed, sliding off my jacket, then feverishly unbuttoning my flannel shirt and yanking off my undershirt. And naturally, I reciprocate, lifting the three layers she's wrapped herself in with one swift gesture. Then she climbs into my lap and closes her eyes as I take my time removing her bra, easing each strap down her shoulders slowly with my teeth and sliding my hand around her to release the clasp.

"Blue." I will never get tired of hearing her say my name like that. I toss the bra on the floor and roll my entire face over her breasts. I'll never get tired of doing that either. I've just taken one nipple in my mouth when she says it.

"Blue, you're my hero." She means to be kind and loving. She means to build me up, make me feel good. But the word is like a lit match thrown into a bucket of gasoline. It sends me jolting to my feet.

I've been able to tamp down my fury, my self-hatred, in the last few weeks. Things have been good. The asshole stalking Keegan has apparently moved on. I'm doing great with my music and at least not failing any of my other classes. And Keegan has been on fire, at the newspaper and in her classes. I've loved just watching the joy she gets out of succeeding. She's so unbelievably fucking smart and passionate. I am in awe of her.

I think about this girl all day long. I can't wait to curl up with her at night. I am crazy about her. But I've also been worrying that I'm dragging Keegan down. I have certainly been lying to her. It's clear she's falling for me too. At least, for the person she thinks I am. I need to tell her the truth. But what happens when I do?

In that one split second, with that one word, all my raging emotions detonate inside me.

At least I don't dump Keegan on the floor. I bring her up with me and stand there holding her, staring at the red mark around her nipple where I ripped my mouth away. Then, without even thinking, my body rushes toward the wall and slams us both into it. Not hard enough to hurt, really, but hard enough to scare the shit out of me, anyway.

Keegan seems to think I am being all alpha male and passionate. And she seems to like it. She grabs my face and kisses the hell out of me, wrapping her legs tight around my waist and using her thighs to pull me against her. She still has her jeans and boots on.

I can still do this. I can still act the way she wants me to act. I kiss her back, hard, pressing my lips into hers 'til I can feel the ridges of her teeth through her lips. I let her slide down the wall until her feet touch the floor. Then I grind into her, my whole body pushing into hers as if it can disappear inside her. I pull her hands above her head and run my tongue from her collarbone up her throat, tasting the cold air and the wind-swept plains on her skin. Then I kiss her again, a little softer this time.

But then she says it again. "Blue. You *are* my hero." She makes this sweet little moan right in my mouth and then turns her face to the side, her eyes closed.

Shit. Shut the fuck up. And suddenly, I am furious. Not at her, not really. But that word, it just fucks with me every time I hear it. That word sets off a fucking flash bang in my head, filling it with memories, one after another: Cunny's tore-up body, his chest heaving with a final breath; Monti and Hud, burned and lifeless; Acrid, black smoke stinging my eyes and throat as I screamed and cried. That word makes me nuts.

I hold Keegan's face between my hands, squeezing it, squeezing her mouth closed. "Don't call me that. Just *don't* call me that!" I don't mean to sound so harsh. Her eyes widen with shock. I release her face, run my knuckle down her cheek. "I'm sorry, Keegan. I'm sorry. It's just that … I just…"

The images are still crashing into my brain: The CASEVAC chopper ride where my seared back had me in agony; the debriefing on base where I realized everyone thought I was the lone survivor of yet another insurgent attack. Where I realized they didn't know I'd been AWOL, didn't know what the Buffalo was *really* doing near the village when it was hit. Where I kept my mouth shut so they'd go on thinking I was a fucking hero. I keep seeing my face that first night after the guys died, when I stood hunched over a sink, staring into the mirror at a bruised, haggard bastard I didn't even recognize. A lying bastard.

Tell her, you lying bastard. Tell her the truth.

Keegan is staring at me with the same frightened expression she had the first morning we woke up together. I slump down on the bed and bury my face in my hands. I can't stop shaking. The bile is back, inching up my throat, dripping acid into my stomach. I'm about to be sick in Keegan's favorite place. I bend over, gripping my stomach, willing myself not to lose control. Keegan puts her soft hands on my face, and I close my eyes.

"Blue." Her voice trembles. "Blue, what is it? What's wrong?"

"I can't do this anymore, Keegan." I open my eyes, not even trying to keep the tears away now. "Not unless you know the truth about me."

There's a long moment where neither of us says a word. We just stare into each other's eyes. I open my mouth over and over, but nothing comes out. Finally, I get off the bed and turn away from Keegan, looking out the window toward the river.

"I've never told anyone this." I speak quickly, keeping my eyes on the distant, glimmering water. "Not even my mother. *Especially* not my mother. But I need to tell you. We can't go any further until I tell you the truth, Keegan."

18

SHOW ME A HERO

Keegan

Show me a hero, and I'll write you a tragedy.

That F. Scott Fitzgerald quote slithers across my memory as Blue grips the steering wheel so tightly his knuckles show white. I read the quote somewhere a few years ago and wrote it down in my journal, liking the irony and poignancy of it, but not really understanding its meaning. But now, staring at Blue's tense face as he drives away from his mother's house, the words swirl around my brain with new meaning. I've had a sick feeling in my stomach ever since Blue told me what happened while he was a soldier.

Over there. Afghanistan. I'm not even sure I can find it on a map. I've never given the place, the war that's kind of sat on the back burner most of the time I was growing up, much thought. I'm a privileged little shit, self-righteously skewering politicians in my blog, keeping the campus powers that be honest—or so I like to think—from the safety of my newspaper office. And all the while, people like Blue are being shipped halfway around the world to fight and die in a strange, hostile landscape, doing things I can't even imagine having to do, making decisions I will never have to make.

There are girls over in Afghanistan too, girls with the same hopes and dreams I have, girls—like the 14-year-old Blue tried to help—who will never get to make the choices I take for granted. Like who to love, who to marry. Or *whether* to get married at all. Blue tried to be a hero, tried to come to the rescue of one of those girls, just like he did for me. And it's cost him everything.

Things have changed between us, been weird ever since Blue choked out the story of how the guys in his patrol died. *Why* they died. And how he lied about it. He'd twisted the old quilt on the bed in the cabin with his fists until I thought it might rip apart, and he sobbed the words with a self-loathing tone that broke my heart. I'd reached out to comfort him, running my hands down his heaving shoulders and then up to his lips, trying to stifle what was coming out.

But he'd yanked away from me, stumbling off the bed and leaning against the loft railing again. For a moment, I thought he was going to hurl himself over it. Instead, he spoke quietly, not looking at me. "So now you know, Keegan. You know what I did. What I am."

I wanted to rush to him, throw my arms around him and hold on for dear life. But I wasn't sure how he'd react. So I sat there and searched for the perfect words, the just-right sentences that would take away his pain, but I couldn't find those words. I wasn't judging Blue. I knew I might have done the same. I wasn't horrified by what he'd done. I was horrified by what he'd been forced to do.

And ever since he told me the whole story, I've been trying to imagine the agony and guilt and fear that must have saturated Blue's every second since it happened. He'd tried to help a girl over there. He'd said her name was *Aziza.* He meant to get her back to the base, back to the aid worker who'd promised to smuggle her to a sympathetic uncle in the capital city. He meant to be a hero.

No good deed goes unpunished. My dad says that a lot.

Hot, stinging tears fill my eyes. I shudder, afraid of what might happen to Blue if anyone else finds out. He could get into serious trouble, that much I know. I could lose him, just when I am realizing how important he is to me. Just when I am certain I *cannot* lose him.

I should have said something deep, something comforting there in the cabin. But I had nothing to say. So we rode the horses back in silence and said a solemn goodbye to Virginia, my dad, Buick and Kendra. They must have wondered what was wrong, but no one asked any questions.

Kendra and Buick were probably too starry-eyed over each other to even notice anything amiss. Buick had offered to bring Kendra back to The Embassy on Sunday, so she was staying on at the ranch. She'd squeezed my arm and smiled as we left, her eyes bright and happy. "Now *that's* something I would *never* have seen coming," I muttered in the car as we pulled away from the ranch, watching Kendra and Buick wave giddily from the front porch.

"Huh?" Blue didn't seem to notice.

"Nothing."

He barely spoke on the drive to his sprawling, Tudor-style house in Tulsa. We'd just parked in the circular drive when Blue's mother, Maria, rushed out the ornate front doors and pulled me into her arms. She was plump and warm and pillowy, her eyes the same heart-stopping color as her son's.

"Mama, give her a chance to get in the door!" Blue sounded impatient, on edge. His mother placed her soft hands on my face.

"Blue told me about your mama, you poor little thing." Her accent was pure Okie, just like my Grandpa's. And my dad's. I closed my eyes for a moment, wanting to melt against her comforting body like a little kid would, my breath snagged by the sharp pang that sliced through me as she spoke.

"You sound just like my Grandpa," I murmured, the words mangled by Maria's palms squeezing my cheeks.

"Mama doesn't really *do* boundaries," Blue said apologetically.

Maria planted a kiss on my forehead, then turned away from me to throw her arms around Blue, burying her face in his chest just like I'd done a zillion times. "It's about time you came home." She pulled back and put her hands on his shoulders, staring into his eyes. "I've missed you." She said it gently, without a trace of bitterness, but Blue still flinched as if she'd slapped him.

"I'm sorry, Mama, I didn't really mean to stay away so long." A look of shame had settled over his face.

Maria tilted her head and narrowed her eyes, obviously puzzled. Then she touched Blue's cheek and smiled. "I know you're busy, son, setting the world on fire with your music and all. It's *okay*. Just try to occasionally remember your old mother."

Her cheerful words only seemed to make Blue more miserable. He'd given her a wan smile, then pulled me up the grand staircase on the pretext of giving me a tour of the house. He could barely look his mother in the eye the whole time we were there.

We'd spent one night in Tulsa, and this time it was me sneaking into Blue's room, although I doubted Maria would have cared if we'd just openly shared the same bed.

I could sense that Blue's mom, underneath her warm exterior, was sad and lonely. Blue felt it too. "You should sell this place, Mama, move into a condo or something so you can be around other people," he said as we were leaving the next day.

She'd made a little shushing sound to dismiss his words, then hugged him so long I thought she wasn't going to let go. When she finally did, she turned to me and wrapped her arms around my shoulders. "Take care of him," she whispered in my ear. "I know something's wrong, but he won't tell me what it is. Just take care of him." Her voice wavered, and I nodded, squeezing her hand.

"I really like your mother," I say as we're driving back to campus, desperate for something to fill the gloomy silence between us.

Blue nods, but doesn't take his eyes off the road. "Yeah, everybody does."

After several more silent moments, he adds, "She liked you too, bar girl. A lot." His voice has warmed up, and he gives me the ghost of a smile. He takes one hand off the wheel and raises my hand, kissing it. Then he picks up his phone and taps the screen with his thumb. "We need to get back to your tune teachin' young pupil. You've still got a *lot* to learn." He says it with an exaggerated twang.

I let out an exaggerated groan, happy that his mood seems to be brightening. "*Not* more Bryson, I beg you. I can't take any more." I want to keep this playful mood going.

Blue gives me one of his grins. "Nope, we're getting back to the Man in Black."

I swallow the lump in my throat. I haven't seen one of those naughty grins in a while, and I've missed them. I know enough now to be aware that Johnny Cash was the Man in Black, so I smile at Blue and sing along to *Ring of Fire* as it blasts out of the car speakers.

"Very good, bar girl. You know all the words." Blue runs his fingers down my cheek. Then we sing along to *Jackson, Sunday Morning Coming Down, I Walk the Line,* and, of course, *A Boy Named Sue.* Except that I say *Blue* each time instead of *Sue.*

We're almost back to Hickory Flat when my phone dings. A text. I haven't heard from the stalker in a few weeks. But now, I hesitate to pick up the phone. "Want me to look?" Blue's eyes search mine. He can read me so easily. I shake my head.

"No. I'm tired of being afraid of my own damn phone. And it's probably just somebody from the *Daily.*" I turn the screen up and squint to see it in the sunlight. "It's from Kendra." I can hear the relief in my voice. "She says she just walked out on the back porch and caught Virginia crying her eyes out." I shake my head again. "I can't figure that woman out. She acts all pissy Thanksgiving Day, treats *you* like crap, then is all nicey nice before we leave. She even asked me about the stalker thing, said she wanted to be sure I was safe. And I've *never* seen Virginia shed a tear, much less be 'crying her eyes out' where people can see her. It's weird. I don't know what's going on with her."

Blue is tapping the steering wheel in time to the music. "I just get the feeling there's a lot more to your grandmother than power-tripping bitch, you know?"

I've just started to argue when I hear Blue's ringtone. He takes his phone out of the center console and glances at the screen, then puts the phone to his ear. "Hi Mama." His face quickly turns red. He keeps nodding. "I know, Mama. I know. Mama…" He says it several more times. "It's not your fault." His voice shakes. "Mama, I know you're worried about me. I'm sorry I was so…" I can hear Maria on the phone. She is crying. "Mama…" Blue grips the wheel. "I'll call you later. We'll talk later. Okay?"

He throws the phone into the console and stares at the road. I look straight ahead as well, for a few minutes, not sure what to say. Then I hear Blue gulp. He is swiping at his eyes. "She's blaming herself," he says furiously. "She always blames herself. She did it with Bill, took responsibility for every asshole thing he did, like *she* made him do it. Now she's doing the same thing with me."

"Blue." I blink back my tears and try yet again to find the right words.

"I couldn't even look at her while we were there, Keegan. I couldn't *wait* to get out of there. It's why I haven't been home in so long. I can't *stand* the way she stares at me, adoringly, like I'm the greatest thing since sliced bread, like I'm some kind of fucking hero. And she thinks *she's* done something wrong. She thinks it's her fault!"

"Blue." I am feeling *so* worthless right now. All I can do is reach out and loop my fingers around his arm. Then I unbuckle my seatbelt and move over next to him, leaning my head on his shoulder. After a few minutes, I say the only thing I can think of. "Blue, why don't you just tell her what happened? She'll understand. It wasn't your fault. It was an accident. It's not your fault that they died."

I can hear the false note in my voice, the knowledge that what I'm saying isn't completely true. And Blue can hear it too. My head bounces off his arm as he slams his fists into the steering wheel.

"Yes it was my goddamn fault, Keegan!" he screams. "Yes it was my fault. It was no *accident!* It was *all* my fucking fault! And you know that!"

The car swerves all the way off the road, and I can't help crying out as my body is thrown against the passenger side door. Blue applies the brakes slowly and gets the car back on the road as an 18-wheeler passes us on the left, the driver laying on the horn and gesturing wildly at us.

"Keegan." Blue's voice is shaking. "You need to put your seatbelt back on right now." He's panting. "*Right now.*"

I sit up and click the belt into place. Gradually, we pick up speed again. Blue's still breathing heavily, his cheeks still wet, the jaw muscle working overtime. I stare at his stretched-white hands on the wheel. "I'm so sorry, Keegan," he says after a few minutes. "I'm sorry. But I just can't *do* this. I can't control myself sometimes." His voice splinters. "I have to…" He inhales and exhales a couple of times, then goes on more calmly. "…this is not fair to you, Keegan. You know that. I *know* you know it!"

I shake my head vehemently like I can prevent his words from entering my ears. "Don't, Blue." Tears roll down my cheeks. I don't wipe them away. "Don't say it. I don't want to hear what you're going to say!"

And so we're silent until we pull into the Embassy's driveway. My newly painted Nissan is still parked by the tree. Blue paid for the paint job, saying it was my birthday present. I release my seatbelt and squeeze Blue's arm, then kiss it. He opens his door and steps out without saying a word, without even looking at me.

The living room's cold and seems even emptier than usual. We'd gotten rid of the leftover kegs and trash bags holding hundreds of red cups before we all left for the Thanksgiving break. Blue and I just stand there awkwardly for a few minutes, not looking at each other. Hunter and Megz are obviously still gone. Blue and I are alone in the house.

Finally, he speaks, without looking up from the floor. "I need to be by myself for a little while, Keegan. I just need some time to think." I nod, also staring at the floor. His voice pleads with me, but his words are already putting distance between us, already building a wall. I blink back tears. *Dammit, do not cry.* Whether he realizes it or not, Blue sounds like a guy trying to walk away. I keep my eyes on the dusty boards until I hear the quiet click of his bedroom door.

❦

I spend the next couple of days in a fog, that pea-soupy mental state your brain sometimes steers you into so it can avoid thinking about painful stuff. Or maybe it's your heart that does it. Either way, I am going through the motions, cleaning my room and the bathroom, organizing my portion of the kitchen, even picking up dog crap in the backyard, just for something mindless to do.

Max, the source of all the crap, keeps showing up at my door, scratching until I let him in, then curling up next to me as if he knows that's exactly what I need. And after he's been with me a while, Max will head downstairs, and I'll hear him scratch on Blue's door. When Blue opens it, I'll hear a blast of music—usually Bryson—before he closes the door again. Max goes back and forth like that, a self-appointed canine counselor. Good old Max. He really tries. But I need more than he can give.

By Sunday afternoon's editorial meeting—the last one of the semester—my stomach's churning, and my head seems to be on a fault line that an earthquake's just ruptured. I can't focus, can't stop scowling and snapping at the newspaper staff. I know I'm screwing up, making a fool of myself. But I can't stop. I can barely manage to put a coherent sentence together. I am furious at myself. *Focus, Keegan. Dammit, focus on what you're doing.* But I cannot focus, can't seem to think straight; I can only grab hold, metaphorically, of the thoughts swirling wildly around my head and try to hang on. I don't know how to feel about what Blue told me. I don't know what to do, what to say. I wish I could simply remove his secret from my brain. I wished he'd never told me.

By the time I get back to the Embassy Sunday night with a pizza I picked up on campus, I am aching to do what I've done for years when I'm boiling over with emotion. I put my earphones in and pull up some good crying music on my phone. At first, I go with my go-to sad songs, heartbreak tunes by Adele, Bonnie Raitt, Amos Lee, The Fray. Then I switch over to the stuff my mom and I used to listen to together, the songs she'd play over and over again. Especially Karen Carpenter. Especially *Rainy Days and Mondays.* It's not raining, and it's not Monday, and it's sure not the 1970s. But still, it fits my mood.

I sit on my bed, stuffing one slice of pizza after another in my mouth. I pull my journal out from under my pillow. And I write it all down—starting with the Fitzgerald quote about a hero—while the music whips my every emotion to a fever pitch. Somehow, in a weird way, it's comforting. I write about the trip to the ranch. About Virginia and my dad, Buick and Kendra. Every mind-blowing, heart-wrenching detail. The passionate night in my old bedroom, in front of the fire with Blue. The early-morning ride in the crisp air and sunshine. The beauty of the ranch. The cabin and all its memories. And then, Blue's deep, dark secret. Blue's agony. And my fear.

I can see something like film footage in my mind as I scrawl the words with my Mont Blanc pen: Blue slipping into Aziza's village; Blue being beaten by her brothers; Blue screaming and sobbing over the bodies of his comrades; Blue staying silent over what really happened; Blue accepting a Purple Heart, hating himself for it, pretending everything was all right while his own heart shriveled up and broke into little pieces.

I cry as I write. Like I want to. Like I need to.

I'd just written the last line when headlights hit my windows as they do whenever a car pulls up in the Embassy's bricked-over front yard. I can tell by the bass assaulting my eardrums that it's Hunter's BMW. The rude SOB always plays his stereo at obscene levels. And if it's Hunter, Megz is probably with him. I've been thinking a lot about her lately, and I'm determined to find out why she suddenly shut me out. If it's because of the tension between Hunter and Blue, I want to talk it out with her. I'm not going to let Hunter come between us. Or any guy, for that matter. I am not going to give up on our friendship that easily.

Heavy steps on the stairs reach my ears a few minutes later, followed by laughter and then whispering I can't quite make out. I hear Hunter's door squeak as it opens, and a second later, there's a sharp knock at my door.

Megz sticks her head inside and gives me a hesitant smile before I have a chance to answer. "Hey, Kee Kee."

"Hey yourself."

Megz is one of those girls who look just as good all disheveled the way she is now—hair a wild mess, makeup smudged—as when everything's in place and perfect. She slips inside and closes the door with her back, her hands clutching the doorknob behind her. Her cheeks are red from the cold wind. She is wearing skinny jeans tucked into an expensive-looking pair of black, high-heeled boots I've never seen before and a red cashmere sweater. The small red Coach purse she bought right before I moved out of the dorm dangles from her shoulder.

Megz has always been a little mysterious about where her money comes from. I know that, as a former foster child, she gets her tuition paid by the state. She says her waitressing money covers the rest of her expenses. I sometimes wonder about that. I once accused her of having a sugar daddy.

But Megz doesn't have parents—or in my case, a wealthy grandmother—to pay her bills, so I don't question her too closely. Maybe I am ashamed to. I'm not proud of the fact that Virginia's funding *my* college education. But my dad has no money, and my editor job pays peanuts, even though it takes up most of my time. So when Madame President Pro Tempore shocked me after the whole blog story exploded by not rescinding her offer to pay my way at Ikana, I was happy to take her money. It's not the only part of my life that's blatantly hypocritical. Maybe Blue's right that Virginia isn't as bad as I make her out to be. Maybe the *real* bad actor in all this is me.

"Can we talk?" Megz is staring intently at me. "Um ... is something wrong?"

"Nah." I wipe my eyes, realizing it's probably obvious I've been crying. "I was just thinking about coming to talk to *you*."

There's this pregnant pause, the kind of space that naturally arises between strangers. Megz and I had that space around us for a short time when we first started sharing a dorm room; it dissolved quickly as we got to know each other. But sitting there watching her lick her lips nervously and smooth down her hair, it suddenly hits me that the space has been growing back between me and Meg for a while, even before she met Hunter, even before I moved out of the dorm. Things have been different between us ever since we returned for sophomore year. I can't put my finger on exactly why. But *something* has changed.

"So, what'd you want to talk about, Kee?"

"Hopefully the same thing *you* want to talk about. What's going on between us? Why the cold shoulder lately, Megz?"

She looks out the window toward the tree for a long moment, appearing to weigh what to say next. "Oh, Kee Kee, sometimes I forget how naïve, how *sheltered,* you really are." She says it with a bitter smile, still staring out into the darkness.

"What do you mean?"

Megz shakes her head and walks over to the bed, sitting next to me. "Nothing. Forget it." She taps my open journal with her finger. "Got your *diary* out, huh? Must be important." Just a hint of mockery in her voice. Megz has always seemed amused by my journal writing. And kind of contemptuous of it.

I try to subtly move my hand over the last few paragraphs on the page. I don't want Megz to see what I wrote about Blue. "Yeah, you know how I like to write every silly little thing down."

She gives me that laser look again, and I stare at the mascara smudges under her eyes, wondering if she'd been crying. But then, judging by the just-fucked state of her hair, probably not. Megz puts her hand over mine. Her skin is cold. "Sorry about being kind of standoffish lately, Kee. We can't let *any* guy get between us. Sisters before misters, right?" She punches me lightly, playfully, on the arm. "I just forgot that for a little while. You forgive me?"

I smile and close the journal, sliding it off my lap and on to the bed. "Sure I do, Megz. Sisters before misters. Always." I pull her into a hug, and for a second, she stiffens. Then she hugs me back. "So," I say when she lets go and moves back away from me slightly. "How was your Thanksgiving? What was it like at Hunter's? What is his family like?"

"Oh. My. God. You will *not* believe it!"

She sounds like the old Megz then, and we sit there for a while, talking and laughing, just like we used to. But the pizza I wolfed down is not interacting well with my tied-in-knots stomach, and I start to feel sick. I'm pressing an arm into my body as if that'll help when Megz notices and pauses mid-sentence. "You okay, Kee Kee?"

I start to say I am fine, but a wave of nausea sends me to my feet. "Sorry, Megz," I say on my way to the bathroom, "I think I ate too much too fast."

I've been in the bathroom for a while when Megz knocks softly on the door. "You still alive in there, Kee?"

"Yeah, I'll be out in a minute. Sorry about this."

"No worries." I can hear her fingers tapping on the bathroom door. "Look, I'm exhausted. I'm going to go back to my boy now, okay? We'll talk more tomorrow, huh?"

"Sounds good. Thanks, Megz. Thanks for coming to talk to me."

I think for a moment she's already gone back to Hunter's room. But then I hear her voice outside the door. "No, Kee. Thank *you.*"

19

SNAKES

Keegan

My Monday morning class was canceled, and I was happy to be able to sleep in the next day. Maybe that's why I'm so hard to wake up. Maybe that's why I hover on the edge of consciousness, close enough to reality to know someone is calling my name, but unable to pull myself completely out of the dream I'm having.

It's the snake dream again. Just like before, I am on the river, on an air mattress, surrounded by my family. And just like before, we're being pursued by water moccasins with familiar faces: Megz, Jason, Blue, Hunter. Only this time, the largest snake, the one leading the slithering nest with its mouth wide open and poison dripping from its fangs, has Detective Lugner's face. And instead of being buoyed along by the prickly heat of summer, we are shivering as winter's chilly gray mist settles into our bones, making us heavy and slow. Cold, muddy water sloshes in waves over our bodies.

Just like in my earlier dream, my mother's laughter suddenly turns into long, horrible screams. But I can't go to her, can't do anything for her, because Buick is trying to get my attention. "Keegan." His outstretched hand shakes me. "Keegan."

My dream brother's voice is urgent, demanding. I try to pull away from him. I am angry at Buick. I've been angry at him for a long time.

He is slowing me down, trying to tip over my air mattress and toss me into the dark, deadly water. And I can feel Lugner's reptilian breath on my heels; Lugner's hissing, getting ready to strike.

"Keegan. Wake up." Buick's hair tickles my cheek.

"Get a haircut," I mutter, climbing through the remaining wisps of the dream world and opening my eyes to a painful blast of sunlight.

Buick, wearing the same flannel shirt and jeans he had on Thanksgiving Day, is sitting next to me on the bed; his hand squeezes my shoulder. "Huh?" He stares at me like I'm crazy. No idea why I mentioned his hair. I might have heard Virginia complain about his long locks at the ranch.

I sit up quickly, grabbing my head with both hands, trying to suppress the beginnings of a migraine. "Never mind. What are you doing in here, Buick? I thought you were dropping Kendra off yesterday. Why are you here now, waking me up?"

"Do you know where Kendra's car is?"

"What?"

"Kendra's car! She says she left it parked in front of the garage. But it's not there. We just got here, and her car is gone. Do you know where it is? Keegan! Get it together!"

I give him a sour look, tempted to launch into a lecture about the rich irony saturating the concept of *Buick* telling *me* to get it together. But I just shake my head, trying to clear away the last drowsy effects of my dream. "No, I have no idea where Kendra's car is." I'm only vaguely aware that Kendra drives a battered-looking car of some kind and usually parks it in front of the house's detached garage.

"You didn't notice when you got back that it was gone?"

I start to get out of bed, then remember I have nothing on but a T-shirt and thong. "No, I didn't notice. I had other things on my mind." *Like the guy I'm in love with walking away from me.* "Would you get out of here so I can put on some clothes?"

I come out into the hall a few minutes later in a pair of sweatpants and the ratty house slippers I've had since I was 15. Kendra is leaning against the wall next to her bedroom door, holding some kind of document in one hand and taking a long drag on a cigarette with the other. Blue and Buick are standing on either side of her. Blue's wearing only a pair of gym shorts and a bleary-eyed look that tells me he's been roused out of bed too.

Not my bed, though. For two nights now, we've slept apart. And it's seemed like forever.

I try to avoid looking at Blue. But just like on the day we met, my body ignores my brain's instructions. My eyes roll all over him, touching his chest and arms and abs, his hands and lips. *Oh God, his lips.* Then my tongue practically breaks through my teeth trying to follow suit. And my lately-happy loins start some kind of crazy war dance. They are in revolt. They miss Blue. Every part of me aches for Blue.

He raises his eyes to mine just as I'm trying to tear my gaze away, and I can't help taking a sharp breath at the blazing mix of longing and pain that shoots through me. We stand there staring at each other until Buick clears his throat and waves a hand between us.

"Uh, sorry to interrupt *whatever* this is, but we need to help Kendra."

I am still getting used to being around Buick again, and I'm sure not ready to wrap my head around this lightning-fast thing he has going with my prickly roommate. His man-in-charge tone really rubs me the wrong way too. It doesn't sound like Buick; not the Buick I thought I knew anyway. I put my hand up as if to block out his face. "What are we talking about?" I sound irritable, but I don't care. "The car? Was it stolen?" I look at Kendra. "Shouldn't you call the police?"

She lets out a long, smoky sigh in my direction. "It's worse than that."

I wave my hand in front of my face in disgust. "I didn't know you smoked."

Kendra twists her mouth away from me and blows out again. "I quit last year," she says, grimacing. "But I just started again. Like, *just* this fucking minute." She shoves the papers in her hand at me. "Because of *this* unbelievable shit."

I take the document from her and try to focus on it. A Notice of Repossession.

"My fucking ex stopped making the payments." Kendra's voice wavers. "It was part of the divorce agreement. He was supposed to keep on paying for my car. And he just quit doing it." She shrugs helplessly. "My credit was already crappy because of him. Now it'll be completely ruined. I can't afford to buy another car. I don't know what the fuck I'm going to do!"

A tear rolls down her cheek. And Buick tenderly scoops it off with his finger, then caresses Kendra's short, dyed-black hair. *Who are you and what have you done with my idiot brother?*

Kendra curls her free hand around his finger and smiles at him gratefully. It's sweet. And kind of nauseating. And it sends a tremor of worry through me. Buick is just starting to get his life together. He's not ready for some big, heavy relationship. At least, I don't think he is.

He certainly isn't naive when it comes to sex. Not that it's something I even want to think about. But I'm pretty sure he's had lots of experience. Buick has been turning female heads for years. Girls can't seem to keep their hands off him. But he's always been a Wham Bam Thank You Ma'am kind of guy. As far as I know, he's never been in love. I've never seen him act the way he is acting with Kendra. And they've only known each other a few days. It's ridiculous.

Compared to Buick, Kendra is practically ancient. Plus she's carrying around a *lot* of baggage. I'd pretended to write off Buick when he was arrested, just like Virginia. But he is my kid brother. I don't want to see him get hurt.

"You can use my truck," he is saying to Kendra. "I'll catch a bus back. You use the truck until we figure something out."

Kendra shakes her head. "No, I can't do that, Buick. But thank you. You have no idea. Thank you." I watch her eyes rake his body in exactly the lusty way mine had raked over Blue a few moments earlier. *Eww.*

"It's not your truck to loan, Buick." I know I sound snippy. But grandson or not, Buick will find his ass fired if he lets someone borrow a Cooke vehicle without Virginia's permission. He needs his job at the ranch. "I can let Kendra borrow my car when I don't need it, and I'm sure Blue can, too. Shouldn't you be getting back to the ranch? Virginia's not paying you to be off..."

I've just registered the annoyed expression crossing Buick's face when a whoosh of air from Hunter's thrown-open door makes me stop talking. Hunter is standing there with his hands on each side of the door frame. He's naked and looks royally pissed off. And yeah. There is a piercing *there.*

"Do you people *have* to hold this stupid conversation right outside my fucking door at this ridiculous time of day? Huh?" I can see there's someone in Hunter's bed, presumably Megz, but I can't tell if she's awake. "What time is it, anyway? Why the *fuck* are you waking us up this early?"

Blue crosses the hall in two long strides and gets right in Hunter's face, his fists clenched at his sides. "Jesus, Hunter, put some fucking clothes on. How many times do we have to be forced to see your dick? Do you think it's something special, that *everybody* wants to take a look? Put your fucking pants on, you arrogant piece of shit, and *then* maybe we'll listen to you bitch about being woke up!"

Something about Hunter sends Blue into a white-hot rage every time they are together. I think for a moment Blue's going to slug him. "Blue..." I say. He ignores me.

Hunter leans closers so they're only a couple of inches apart. He's acting like he's going to spit in Blue's face. But then he smirks and steps back, holding his hands up. "So sorry, Soldier Boy. *No* disrespect intended. I wouldn't dream of comparing myself to you in the dick department." His eyes flicker over to me, then back to Blue. "I'll do just what you said, *Private* Danube. I'll go put my pants on like a good little boy."

He slams the door in Blue's face.

"*So,*" Buick drawls after a moment's silence, "*that's* Hunter." Buick has this dry sense of humor that used to crack me up a lot when we were kids. This time, it's Kendra who laughs.

"Yep. That's him," she says, taking another drag on the cigarette, then stepping into the bathroom to throw the butt in the toilet. "And in a weird way," she adds cheerfully on her way back, "*that* little bit of drama with Hunter makes me feel better. A little better, anyway."

She yanks the paperwork out of my hand and grabs Buick by the arm, leading him into her bedroom. "I'll deal with the car problem later," she says to me and Blue as she's closing the door. "Right now, I want to say goodbye to this cowboy in a way he won't forget." Just before the door shuts with a click, I catch a glimpse of my brother's big-ass grin. *Eww.*

Blue hasn't moved. He just stands there staring at Hunter's door. I step toward him and wrap my arms around his waist, pressing my forehead into his back. He flinches, then gets very still. "Come to my room, Blue," I whisper into his skin. "Come talk to me. Come … just … hold me. *Please.* I need you. Don't shut me out. *Please.*" I sound desperate. I sound needy. I don't care.

Blue grips my hands, still wrapped around his waist. I think he's about to shrug me off and walk away. Tears prickle my eyes, getting ready for what's coming. But then he whips around and pulls me into his arms, holds me against his chest like he will never let me go.

"Keegan." That's all he says. That's all he needs to say.

After a few moments, we turn as one and walk into my room, me clinging to Blue as he kicks the door closed.

I sleep through my one o'clock class and wake with a start just before three. The afternoon sun is piercing Just Brenna's curtains and lighting up my room. Deep, regular breaths touch my shoulder. A leg's thrown over mine, and a pair of arms clutch me in a warm embrace. I am tangled up in Blue.

I want to stay right where I am. All day. All night. I take a deep breath and close my eyes, trying to imprint on my memory the wonderfully heavy feel of Blue's body on mine.

But I'm late getting to the newsroom, and I can't stop thinking about *The Daily*. I've got a lot of work to do.

Finally, I lift Blue's arm with one of my hands and slowly ease out of the bed, then stand for a moment watching him sleep. He looks so peaceful, so untroubled. I kiss his forehead and grab some clothes, heading for the bathroom.

The newsroom has a different vibe for the semester's last issue of the paper. Everyone is in a hurry to put it to bed and start studying for finals, start preparing to head home for the holidays. Editors and reporters snap at each other, argue over insignificant details, explode over issues that normally would have had them joking and laughing. And Jason's the most cranky of all today. He snarls and rants, chews people out for the slightest thing. You can practically see the black thunderclouds forming over his head as he stalks from one desk to another before he finally retreats into his office and slams the door.

But none of it bothers me much. I'm blissfully happy. I am enmeshed, immersed, bound up— body, mind and soul—in Blue Danube. He's come back to me. He loves me. Nothing else matters.

By 8:30 PM, only Jason and I remain in the newsroom. I've just shut off my computer when he steps into my office and stands there looking at the bound, old copies of *The Daily*.

"So are you feeling less pissy now that we're all done for the semester?" I ask jovially. He doesn't respond, does not look at me. I try again. "Man, I've *never* seen you so crazed before. You scared everybody." I laugh to show him I understand. "But it's all done now. We can relax 'til next semester."

Jason smirks and very slowly shakes his head. "*Absolutely unbelievable.*" The words are loaded with sarcasm; they almost feel like a slap across the face. He finally looks at me, his eyes so full of hatred and resentment it makes my jaw drop. "You can't really be this stupid, Keegan. *Nobody* is that stupid!"

"What ... what do you mean?"

Jason doesn't answer, just turns as the door to the newsroom opens. And all my elation vanishes, dissolved in an instant by the venomous sneer on Detective Lugner's face.

"Hey Uncle Frank."

It takes me a few moments to register Jason's words, as well as his smug tone. I seem to be frozen, iced over from the inside out, my thoughts traveling in slow motion, trying to catch up with the wave of cold horror that's washing through me. Something is wrong; that much I know. But as I sit there watching Jason and Lugner exchange knowing smiles, I can't speak, can't move, can't think straight. I try to swallow, but I can't even do that.

Lugner walks into my office and slips an arm around Jason's shoulders. "Did I happen to mention, Keegan, that Jason is my nephew?" It sounds like the mildest of questions, but it's laced with poison. "He's my sister's son. My sister, who was editor of this paper in the 80s. Our mother, Jason's grandmother, was editor of this paper in the 60s. And my nephew *should* have been editor this year. Until *you* came along."

His voice gets a little higher and more caustic. "Until *Virginia Cooke's* granddaughter comes sailing in here with her stupid blog and her powerful family. A *sophomore* who somehow manages to get herself chosen as editor." Flecks of spit fly out of his mouth and land on my arm. I find myself staring at the overburdened shirt button at the apex of his belly. I'm having a hard time raising my eyes to meet his.

"Well, we know how she did *that,*" Jason scoffs. That makes me look up. I glare at Jason. There's something in his voice, some slight note of hesitation, that tells me he is not completely comfortable with what's happening, that he's following his uncle's lead.

"You couldn't just wait your turn, put in your time like Jason has done, could you?" Lugner's arm drops away from Jason, and he puts his hands on my desk, leaning closer to me, again spewing spit. "You had to get that bitch of a grandmother of yours to pay off the journalism board, buy the job for you, like you thought you were *entitled* to it."

That's when I go from ice-cold to boiling hot in one surge of rage. I'm on my feet before I even know it. "That's a lie!" I shout in Lugner's face. "She didn't buy anything. I *earned* this job. They wanted me because I was better at it than your nephew. He had his chance. He had a better chance than I did because he's a senior. And he blew it!"

Jason sputters, and whatever ambivalence I may have sensed in him vanishes. "There's no way you earned it!" His face is contorted into a grotesque sneer. "It was *my* job, and you stole it. You fucking stole it, Keegan. *My* senior year, my only chance to be editor. And you took it away from me!"

I close my eyes and take a deep breath. I'm still playing catch-up, mentally, still connecting the dots. Then I open my eyes and glare at them. "You're the ones who've been stalking me? So, what, you thought you could drive me away from here by sending me all that nasty crap? By writing all that horrible stuff all over campus? You thought you could scare me into giving up this job? Are you *crazy*? Did you really think you could get away with this?"

"It was working," Jason says. "You were scared shitless and doing a crappy job as editor. You were doubting yourself, and you were screwing things up. It was obvious to everybody. It was working until..."

"...until you started fucking some fake war hero who thinks he's tough shit," Lugner cuts in. "And he had my nephew thinking it too." He casts a snide look at Jason. "*Somebody* got cold feet and called it off when he thought *Blue Danube* was going to figure things out."

Jason flushes angrily. "He would have figured it out, Uncle Frank, and then we'd have been in trouble, both of us." There's a whine in his voice.

"Oh, horseshit." Lugner waves a hand in front of his face. He sounds disgusted. "You think I couldn't have handled him? Anyway, none of that matters now, because we ended up with something much better." Lugner gives me a sinister smile as he pulls his phone out of his pants pocket, and my stomach twists. The smile stays on his lips as he punches at his phone. When he looks up at me, his eyes gleam with triumph.

"You really should be more careful about who you choose as friends, Keegan." He thrusts the phone at me.

And even before I see the image on the screen, I know. All kinds of little clues are coming together in my head, and I know. Still, I gasp when I see the picture on Lugner's phone of my journal, flipped open to the last page I'd been writing on when I closed it and left it on the bed last night.

"And you *sure* as hell ought to do a better job choosing your *heroes,"* Lugner sneers.

And when Jason chimes in, mocking the quote I'd written about Blue—*Show me a hero and I'll write you a tragedy*—I feel my legs give way. I sit down, hard, with one word on my lips. "Megz." A hot ache swells at the base of my throat. It makes me look weak, but I can't stop the tears that fill my eyes. "But why would she…?"

"She's been helping us since the beginning of the semester," Jason says, scornfully. "She was stupid enough to get caught shoplifting. It didn't take much to convince her to help us out, let us know where you were, what you were doing, how you were reacting. Some friend she is."

I try to say something, but all that comes out is some kind of croak. I swallow and try again. "You blackmailed her?" All the expensive items Megz has shown up with over the last year flash into my mind. She's been stealing them.

Lugner picks up his phone. "Like Jason said, it didn't take much convincing. She put you down as the contact on her arrest record. And there she was, sitting in my office, crying her eyes out, giving me this sob story about being a foster kid and losing her scholarship from the state and *boo hoo hoo.* And I'm sitting there looking at *your* name, the bitch who stole the editor job away from *my* family. And then I realize, there just might be a way to fix it."

"But..."

"But then you decide to move out of the dorm and take up with this ... *war hero,*" he laughs again, "with this *dumbass* name. *Blue Danube?* Are you fucking kidding me?"

Jason laughs too. I stare at him with what I hope are murderous eyes. Lugner's smirk returns. "We don't need to stalk you now, *bar girl,* since you've handed us your chicken-shit boyfriend, your *knight in shining armor.*" He lets out this evil-sounding guffaw that makes me want to claw his eyes out.

Or maybe I should claw my own eyes out. My journal. I'd written all about how Blue called me *bar girl* in my journal. About how Blue was my knight in shining armor. And I'd written all about what happened in Afghanistan. All about Blue's secret. And then, like a complete fool, I left my journal alone with Megz.

Oh, God. Oh God, no.

"We backed off for a little while since my nephew insisted," Lugner continues, rolling his eyes and casting another disparaging look at Jason. "But I told your little shoplifter friend she better come up with something else we could use to run you off if she didn't want to end up in jail." That nasty note of triumph is back in his voice. "And then, lo and behold, she came through."

He gets right in my face, and this time, I can barely make my eyes meet his. Because I know what he's going to say. "Do you know what they'll do to your boyfriend when they find out what really happened over there? That he's responsible for the deaths of American servicemen? That he was off base without permission? That he *lied* about the whole thing to his superiors?"

Lugner's garlicky breath strikes my cheek like a hammer. I twist my hands together, trying to keep them from trembling.

"You really think he's a hero, Keegan? He's nothing but a *coward.* A liar. A *criminal.* Does his mother know the truth about him? Huh? What if the media found out that the heir to Bootstrap Enterprises let his patrol get wiped out?"

I'm shaking my head. The rest of my body is shaking all on its own. I can't do anything else. "No! It's not like that. Blue is not like that!"

"Oh, yes he is like that. And what happens if the press finds out Virginia Cooke's granddaughter, the famous *Screaming Bad Girl,* was helping cover it up?"

Lugner stands up straight. Jason watches him, obviously waiting to be told what to do. "How could you do this?" I spit at Jason. "I thought we were ... I thought *you* were a decent human being. Is *this* really how you want to get ahead? You can't do it the right way? The honorable way?"

And again, for just a second, I see something like regret flash across his face. But then it's gone, and his features harden. "Don't you dare talk to me about honor, Keegan," Jason snarls.

I shift my gaze to Lugner and take a ragged breath. "What do you want me to do? Resign? Fine, I'll resign. Jason can have this *stupid* job." I again can't stop the tears from filling my eyes and weakening my voice. "And if I do resign, you will keep quiet about Blue?"

Lugner doesn't say anything for a moment; he is studying me. "Resign *and* drop out. Leave Ikana. Leave town. Go back to grandma. And keep your mouth shut." I can't stop myself from gasping.

"It's not enough for you to resign as editor," Jason chimes in. "I don't want you around here, in the journalism building, on campus, undermining *me* as the new editor."

I can't catch my breath. There's a loud, whirring noise in my ears: the sound of my world, my future, collapsing. Maybe Lugner sees a hint of struggle on my face. He leans toward me again. "If the army finds out, Blue will spend the rest of his life in a military prison, Keegan."

My heart pounds in my throat, strangling what I'm trying to say.

"But you really haven't known him very long, have you?" Lugner's voice is pure acid. "You can always find some other guy, some other *hero,* to fuck you. So what if Blue Danube rots in prison, huh?"

"You son of a bitch!"

Lugner shrugs. And smiles. I sit there for moment. Nobody says anything. I can hear police sirens outside, the sound fading as they get further away from campus. I nod and turn on my computer. I don't have any other choice. I open a new email message and select the group contact I've stored with the addresses of the entire journalism board.

Lugner walks around and stands behind my chair, and after a moment, so does Jason. *Fucking lap dog.*

"Tell them you're resigning effective immediately due to personal reasons," Lugner commands. "Tell them you have full confidence in Jason as the new editor of the paper." He watches as I type out the message and hit *Send,* then puts his hand on my chin and lifts it up. "And be out of town by tomorrow night." He lets go of my chin and blows out a heavy breath as if he's just been running. "It's late, and I'm tired," he says to Jason, looking at his watch.

And that's when I remember that Blue will be showing up at any time, like he always does, to walk me to my car. "Oh God." I grab my phone and start texting. I don't trust myself to call him. *Hey there, I'm running late tonight. Don't come pick me up until 10, OK baby?*

Lugner cranes his neck to see what I'm typing. I shoot him the most hateful look I can muster. I've never despised anyone so much in my life. "How do I know you won't say anything about Blue after I leave?" I ask, standing up. "There's no way I trust either one of you!"

Lugner shrugs again. "Once you're out of here, I don't give a fuck about Blue Danube. So as long as you leave and keep your mouth shut, we'll keep ours shut. You'll just have to live with that."

My phone buzzes. *Okey, dokey, smokey. See you at 10.* My knees almost buckle with relief. I'd been so afraid Blue would walk through the door. If he finds out what Lugner and Jason are doing, he might kill them. Or try to.

I push past Lugner and Jason, leaving everything but my purse behind. I turn to look around the office, then glare again at Jason. "I hope you're happy with yourself," I hiss. Then I shove the newsroom door open and run toward the building's exit.

My hands are shaking so badly I can barely fit my key into the car ignition. I tear out of the journalism building parking lot and race the short distance toward the dorms. I'm praying Megz will be there.

20

CONFRONTATION

Keegan

I can see from the end of the hall that Megz' door is wide open. I want to barrel in with fists clenched and a snarling face—Killer Keegan, raining justice down on Megz' lying, thieving, friendship-destroying head. But I can barely pick my feet up; it feels like I've already been running for miles and miles.

By the time I step into the room, Killer Keegan has crumpled into Lame-Ass Crying Keegan. I sit on the bed that used to be mine and glare through my tears at Megz. She's slouched against a pile of pillows on her bed, holding a red Solo cup and staring stupidly at a half-empty bottle of Jack on the desk. Mascara streaks run halfway down her cheeks.

"I was expecting you," she slurs, raising her cup in my direction before taking another swig and then setting the cup back on the desk. She still hasn't looked at me.

"I'll just bet you were." The last word comes out all weak and quivering. *Dammit.* I try again. "Megz, how could you do this to me? How *could* you? *Why* would you? Why?"

She finally raises her eyes and looks at me. I think I see, for just a second, regret pooling there. Her mouth, for just a second, is trembling. But then her face hardens and when she speaks, the words cut into me. "Says the rich little brat who had everything handed to her

her whole fucking life. You have no concept of how the rest of us have to live, do you?"

I'm on my feet, lunging at her as I scream. "You know that's not true, Megz! You're just making excuses! You really think you can blame this on *me*!"

She pushes herself off the bed and comes at me, shoving me. Before I know it, I've slapped her so hard my arm vibrates all the way up into my shoulder. I've never hit anybody before. That's not the kind of person I am. But when my hand smashes into Megz' face, some part of me feels a deep sense of satisfaction. I want to wipe away her sneer, make her feel some of my pain.

I expect Megz to hit me back. I think maybe I *want* her to hit me back. Her eyes flare; she curls her lip and raises her hand, her fingers forming a fist. But then the hand opens, and she rests the palm on her red cheek and stands up straight, giving me this cold, defiant stare. "You've never been hit, have you, KeeKee?" She says it softly, bitterly. "Never once in your whole life, I bet." She lets the hand fall to her side. We are still standing just inches from each other, both of us breathing heavily. "You want to know how many times *I've* been hit?"

I don't answer.

"Well I couldn't tell you. So many times that I couldn't even begin to tell you." She blinks back tears and picks the cup up, downing the rest of it. "So you just slap me all you want, KeeKee. I can take it. But it won't change anything." She throws the cup on the floor and slumps back on her bed.

I am not going to let myself feel sorry for her. I shake my head, determined to hold on to my anger. "Why didn't you ask me if you needed to borrow some money, Megz? Why'd you think it was okay to steal and then, and *then,* help them screw me out of everything I worked so hard for? You think things have been easy for me? Huh, Megz? My mother died, my dad fell apart, my brother went to prison! You think that was *easy*?"

Megz just stares up at me for a minute. "I've been a charity case my whole fucking life, KeeKee," she scoffs. "I've had to take whatever hand-me-downs, whatever scraps of time and money people like you decided to give me to make you feel good about yourselves. I didn't *want* a loan from you." She sits up and points at me. Now she's the one shouting. "You have no *clue* what my life has been like! You have no clue about *anything*, you stupid, privileged bitch!"

I take a few steps backwards, my hands up in a gesture of dismissal. But Megz isn't finished. "I'm sorry your mom died," she says more calmly. "I really am. But at least you had a mother who gave a shit about you. And you still have a dad who'd do anything for you. I don't even know who my fucking dad was, who he *is*. And my mother only cares about drugs and whichever loser's her boyfriend at the moment. Do you know what my mother let her boyfriends do? To me? You want to tell *me* how hard things have been for you, KeeKee?"

I gasp, understanding what she means. "Megz..."

"I don't want your fucking pity, don't you *get* that? I take care of *myself*. I took a pair of scissors and stabbed one of the boyfriends. I stood up for myself." Her voice shakes. She can't keep the child's pain out of her words. "And when I did, my mom threw me out like I was a piece of trash."

I close my eyes. "Megz, why didn't you tell me?"

"I just said I didn't want your pity!" She's practically spitting the words at me. "People like you and your rich grandma and Pastor Seth. I hate all of you! And even if I'd wanted to tell you, KeeKee, you were always gone. You were always at that fucking newspaper. That's all you care about!"

"That's not true."

She rolls her eyes. "Yeah, whatever."

There's a long moment where we glare at each other. A movement out in the hall catches my eye, and I turn to see a couple of girls lingering nearby. We hadn't thought to close the door. I look back at Megz. She's seen the eavesdroppers too. "Heard enough, bitches?" she yells, and the girls scamper away. Megz crosses the room and kicks the door closed, then falls back on the bed and puts her arm over her face. "Beautiful. Just fucking beautiful."

I stand there, staring at the Pulp Fiction poster on the wall: Uma Thurman stares right back at me, cigarette smoke curling above her head. The smoke and her black pageboy haircut, as well as something in Uma's up-yours expression, reminds me of Kendra. Someone else who's had a tough life. But Kendra didn't let it turn her into a criminal.

"I still don't understand." I clear my hoarse throat. "I don't understand how, *why*, you went along with Lugner and Jason, Megz. Okay, so you got busted for shoplifting. You couldn't have just faced the consequences and then moved on? I could have helped you, somehow. Maybe Virginia could have done something. Why did you have to..." I hate that I'm crying. "Why did you have to *ruin* my life, ruin my plans for the future?"

Megz still has her arm covering her eyes. "You still don't get it, do you Kee? I didn't *want* your help or Virginia's help! And even if I did tell you, it wouldn't have done any good. I had no choice."

"You're so full of shit!" Every bit of empathy I've been feeling for Megz has vanished.

"Yeah, well, I'm not the only one."

Neither one of us says anything for a moment. I hear my phone ding. Megz sits up and stares at her pink socks. "Do you have any idea how hard it was for me to graduate from high school with a good GPA, KeeKee? When I was being moved from one foster home to another? From one school to another? No, of *course* you don't." She pulls another cup from a package under her bed and pours out more Jack, then takes a long drink. "Well, it was almost fucking impossible. But I did it. And I got a full scholarship to Ikana. I thought I'd made it. I thought I could finally control my own life. But then I get *here...*" the wounded, childish tone makes her voice wobbly again, "...and everybody's got great clothes and nice cars and lots of money to do stuff. And I've got *shit.* My school expenses were paid, but nothing else. You know how all the rich-Daddy bitches on campus looked at me when I was walking around in hand-me-downs?"

"So you started stealing."

Megz belches, then laughs. "Yeah, I started stealing. And I liked doing it. I liked getting away with it. Until I got caught. A criminal record would mean no scholarship, no college degree, *nothing* for me. And there you were, Miss Blog, Miss It's Up to Me to Save the World, Miss Rich Bitch with your Lilly Pulitzer sheets, writing in your fucking diary with a$300 pen."

"I told you my dad worked his ass off to buy me that as a special gift, right after my mom died. You're jealous of my pen? You're unbelievable!"

She laughs again, takes another swig and speaks to the ceiling as if she doesn't hear me. "A fucking $300 pen. And she says she feels *my* pain." Her gaze falls on me again. "And then for over a year, I've had to sit and watch you vomit all your shit into your *journal.* 'Oh, my rich granny is mean to me. Oh, I hope I get to be editor, that would just be so peachy.' Please. Such a nauseating little brat."

"You've been reading my journal? All along, Megz? How could you?"

Megz crumbles the cup in her hand and fixes a cold stare on me. "Of *course* I've been reading it. What did you expect? And it worked out really well for me that I knew you wrote *everything* down in your ridiculous journal. *And* that you'd made enemies, KeeKee. Lucky for me, those enemies of yours could make sure I didn't lose my scholarship. All I had to do was tell them where you were, whether what they were doing was working, whether you were getting scared enough to quit."

She smirks and licks her lips. "Did you like the whole Tyler angle? That was my idea." The softer Megz I'd spotted, the one who regretted what she'd done, the person I thought I knew, is nowhere in sight now.

"Why would you try to get Tyler in trouble like that? He never did anything to you."

"Well, his daddy sure did."

"*What?*"

"Just another story you weren't around to listen to, Kee. I knew they'd figure out pretty quick it wasn't Tyler, and then you'd be even more scared, thinking there was some lunatic trying to kill you. But at least for a little while, it would give Pastor Seth heartburn."

I shake my head and put my hands up again. I am done with Megz. I've just grabbed the doorknob when her voice, tinged with the slightest hint of remorse, stops me. "I told Lugner I wasn't going to do it anymore. Before I read your journal at the house. I tried to stop. But he threatened me. He said he'd make sure I was convicted, that I lost my scholarship, that I lost *everything*. He said I had to give them *something* that would make you resign. I didn't have a choice, KeeKee." She put her face in her hands.

"Bullshit!" I say. "You had plenty of choices. You're just wallowing in self-pity, aren't you, Megz? And I handed you everything you needed on a silver platter with what I wrote about Blue, didn't I? You've put Blue in danger. You know that I love him. But you didn't even think twice about it, did you? *Sisters before misters.* What fucking bullshit!" I notice the diamond bracelet sparkling on her wrist. I've never seen it before. I point at her arm. "You get that bracelet from Lugner? Is that some kind of reward?" Then I hiss, "or did you steal it?"

Megz flinches like I hit her again, and for a second, I regret my words. But then she raises her head, and I see the malice flooding her face. "Actually," she says evenly, "*Hunter* gave me this bracelet."

"Does Hunter know all about this? Does he know what you are? Of course he does. He's just like you. I guess that explains the attraction."

She clenches her fists and stares me down. "No, he doesn't know about it, KeeKee. Or about Blue." She laughs. "I really can't believe you're going to look down your nose at Hunter when *your* boyfriend is a killer. And a liar. *Your* boyfriend belongs in jail."

"Shut the fuck up!"

"Truth hurts, doesn't it KeeKee? Well, you keep your mouth shut and get out of town, and you can keep your criminal coward of a boyfriend. At least 'til he dumps you."

I almost slug her for that. But she raises up her face like she wants me to. Like she welcomes it. I pull the door open and see a group of girls scrambling away. They've obviously been standing right by the door, listening. The tears are streaming down my cheeks now. I don't even bother trying to hide them or control my shaking voice.

"I will *never* forgive you for this, Megz. And it may take time, but I will find a way to pay you back. I promise you that. And you know something? Your mother was right. You *are* a piece of trash. You're nothing but fucking trash!"

I slam the door and then hear the bottle of Jack shatter against it.

Blue

I'd just jotted down the last note in the last song of the set I'm writing for Keegan when I hear a car door slam and then steps pounding across the front porch and into the living room. Keegan bursts into my room, and I barely have time to set aside my guitar and flip over the notebook that has BAR GIRL scrawled across the top in a Sharpie pen. I'm planning to record the whole set as a Christmas gift for her, and I don't want to give away the surprise.

She throws herself into my arms; she's shaking, and her face is swollen and red. "Hey, what's wrong? Did something happen? Keegan?" I kiss her eyelids and run my thumbs over her cheeks. "Why didn't you wait for me? It's not 10 yet, is it? Keegan, what's wrong?"

She's gasping and sobbing. I don't say anything else for a few minutes. I just hold her until she calms down a little. And then the whole ugly story pours out. I stand there, kissing her, trying to soothe her. I loosen her ponytail and run my fingers through her hair. I let her talk. But all the time she is speaking, her words are tearing me apart.

I should have known. I did know or at least I sensed that Jason and Lugner were dirty. I should have made the connection with Megz. I should have pursued it, figured it out, exposed all of the lying motherfuckers. And I should have kept my big, stupid mouth shut about what happened in Afghanistan.

Keegan waits until she's told me all the other details before, finally, telling what she's done, what they made her do. Because of me. I try to stay calm, stoic; I try to remain the rock she needs to cling to. But I can't stop the fear that knots my stomach and spreads in waves throughout my body. It's stronger even than the rage. I can't stop myself from trembling like some candy-ass little boy. I end up clinging to Keegan as much as she's hanging on to me. I am scared of what might happen to me. But I am determined *not* to let her sacrifice herself for me.

I grab her shoulders. "Why did you do that, Keegan? Why did you resign? I can't let you drop out, throw it all away. I can't let you give it all up for me!"

"Blue."

"You need to call them, email them, all of the people you sent the resignation to. The president of the college, the police, everybody. You need to tell them the truth."

She's shaking her head. "Blue."

"I can't let you give up your dream for me. I *won't* let you do it. If you don't tell, then I will!" I am crying. I'm fucking crying.

Keegan puts her hands on my face. She's crying too. "Blue," she says fiercely. "*You* are my dream. I don't want the rest of it without you. They can *have* the editor job. We have no idea what might happen to you if the army found out. I *can't* let them put you in danger, not if I have a way to stop it. None of it means anything to me, not if I can't have you!"

We stand there, forehead to forehead. I don't know what else to say. *Not true.* I know what I should say. But I don't say anything. I don't want to.

Instead, I pull her into my arms again. I feel her breath, warm and sweet, on my neck as she speaks. "Blue, we can run away. We can just leave, go somewhere else." She pulls back and puts her hands on my face again. I close my eyes. "You can play your music," Keegan implores me. "You're so good, you can make a living playing your music. And I can make a living doing freelance writing. I'm a good writer. I know I can get freelance jobs. And even if I can't, I don't care. I'll scrub toilets if I have to. Just as long as we can be together."

The hopeful, childlike lilt in her voice breaks me down completely. I stand there letting my tears roll down into Keegan's fingers. *I should never have let this happen. I should never have gotten involved with Keegan in the first place.* My gut's been screaming at me for weeks to end it, to do the right thing. I've tried. But I don't seem to have it in me. Not if it means giving up Keegan.

"Blue! It's okay. We'll have so much fun. We could go around the country. We could even go to Europe. Bum around, backpack across Europe. It'll be great."

It takes forever just to force my eyes to open and my mouth to curve into a smile. "That does sound awesome." I don't sound very convincing.

She squeezes my face with her hands. "Blue, promise me. Promise you will come with me. Tomorrow. Promise you'll run away with me." Her voice breaks. "You promise me right now, Blue!"

There's a roaring in my ears; for a moment, my vision narrows so that all I can see is her mouth, moving in slow motion.

"Blue!"

I kiss her, and the roaring subsides, at least a bit. "I promise, bar girl. I promise."

It's after midnight when we curl up together on the roof. Keegan wanted to go out there "one more time." She'd run her fingers over my guitar strings and asked me to sing to her. So we went up to her room and crawled out the window, and now I'm playing, again, the theme from *Somewhere in Time.* I've never seen the movie—and I'm pretty sure you need a vagina to really appreciate it—but I kind of dig the song. And I know Keegan loves it.

I pull off my jacket. It's a clear night and mild, for December, with a full moon. I play slowly, glancing at her face, trying to make each note a caress. I can see her lips moving slightly. It's all I can do to keep playing. Even now—with all we're facing, with what Keegan has been forced to do for me—I am distracted by my dirty thoughts. My head fills with a picture of what else Keegan's lips could be doing. I guess the dick wants what the dick wants.

When I finish the song, I stretch through the window and place the guitar on the floor. Then Keegan nestles into the curve of my shoulder, and we lay there looking up into the stars.

After a few moments, I feel something wet on my arm. "Are you crying?"

She snuggles against me and nods, and I hug her to me. "I called Megz a piece of trash, Blue. After she'd just told me her mom threw her out like trash. And what her mom let other people do to her." She shivers and squeezes my arm. "I know I should hate her for what she did to me. I *do* hate her. I can't believe the things she said to me, the things she's been doing to me all this time while she was pretending to be my best friend. I wanted to hurt her the way she'd hurt me. I told her I'd pay her back. And I mean it. I will pay her back. I'm going to figure out a way to make all three of them pay."

She lets out a sob. "Megz told me she was a foster kid, but I never really thought about what that meant. What she might have been through."

I let her breathing slow before I speak. "How do you even know Megz is telling you the truth about what happened to her?"

She raises up to look at me, and her hair tickles my neck. "I guess I don't. But it felt real. You should have seen the way she looked at me, the *jealousy* she had toward me. I had no idea she felt that way." She runs a finger down my cheek and across my lips. "She could have been making it all up. It felt real, though, the jealousy and the pain. I think it really happened to her. And if it did, no wonder she's the way she is. It's not an excuse for what she's done to us. No way in hell. But I guess it makes me understand her a little better. She's been screwed her whole life by the people who were supposed to take care of her."

She settles back down on my chest. "I just wish I hadn't called her *trash,* that's all. I have every right to hate her after what she's done. But I still wish I didn't call her that. I'm just confused, I guess."

I kiss the top of her head. "You're such a good person, Keegan. I don't think you even realize what a decent person you are." My voice catches. I'm trying not to sound as desperate as I feel. I have my own plans for revenge, but I don't yet know how to carry them out without putting Keegan at risk. "I don't think you have any *idea* what you've done to me, bar girl. How you've changed me, even in the short time we've been together. How much I love you."

She sits up, her fists in my shirt, and gives me a long, deep kiss. Then she takes my hand and pulls me through the window and on to the bed. We remove each other's clothes without saying a word. And we make love. No other way to describe it. It's not just *sex*. It's sure not *fucking*. It's love: created, brought into existence sigh by sigh, heartbeat by heartbeat.

Keegan falls asleep soon after, but I just lay there staring at the ceiling, comforted by her slow, steady breathing, memorizing the feel of her skin under my fingertips. I couldn't have slept if I wanted to. My mind is spinning, veering back and forth between choices, thinking, one minute, that running away is *out* of the question. I cannot let Keegan throw everything away for me. It would be unbelievably selfish.

But then, because I want to so much, I bounce back the other way. We love each other. We're meant for each other. Keegan needs me. I can't take the chance that we'll be separated, maybe forever. Besides, I promised I'd run away with her. And it would actually be a lot easier than she realizes. I won't have to sing for my supper. She won't have to get freelance gigs. We can storm Europe in style. Because I have a trust fund with $5 million, just sitting there waiting to be spent. Yeah, I'd called it blood money. Yeah, I'd told Bill I would never touch a penny of it. But things have changed. Everything's different now.

The first streaks of dawn are lighting up the room just enough for me to see when I edge away from Keegan, sliding one knee and then the other over the bed. I stay like that a few minutes, on my knees, watching her sleep. Then I creep out the door.

21

FRAGILE FEELINGS

Keegan

I wake up alone. My fingers know it before I do. They've been clutching Blue's body all night, and even before I open my eyes, my fingers grasp at the empty air and sound the alarm. They drag me out of the hot, Blue-blazing dream I am having. I just lay there a minute, staring at the Blue-barren sheets, until my brain finally starts working.

I sit up and look around. No Blue in the bedroom. I yank the sheet off the bed, wrap it around my body and stumble across the hall. No Blue in the bathroom. I go back to my room and look out the window. Blue's car is gone. A little jolt of panic makes me shudder.

Don't be ridiculous. He's just gone for coffee. And donuts. He's definitely gone for donuts. I sit back on the bed and stare at my charging phone on the dresser. *Don't be one of those girls who can't go 10 minutes without texting her boyfriend.*

I walk around the room, still dragging my sheet. I sit back down on the bed and will the phone to ding or ring, do something.

I throw off the sheet and tug on my jeans and wriggle into a sweatshirt. True to its crazy reputation, the Oklahoma weather has once again changed overnight. It's overcast and chilly. The oak tree, long shed of the colorful leaves adorning it when I moved into the Embassy, looks naked and dead. I'm shivering.

It's been no more than 10 minutes since I woke up, but I can't stand it any longer. I grab the phone. It is turned off. *Duh.* I forgot that I turned off the phone the night before so I wouldn't be tempted to answer questions from all the people who received my resignation. I turn on the phone and listen to my heartbeat pounding in my chest as I wait for my home screen to appear. Thirty-two missed calls. I don't even try to count the texts and emails. After sending out that WTF email, I'm about to slink out of town under cover of darkness. It will destroy my reputation. But I have no choice.

I text Blue. *Hey, where are you?* Then I add a smiley face, just to soften any impression of stalker-girlfriend tendencies. No response for15 minutes. Fifteen agonizing minutes.

And then, finally. *Just needed to take care of some things before we leave. I have to talk to Bryson too. I owe him an explanation. I can't go without talking to him.* I stare at the phone, trying to dissect my uneasiness. Then he texts me again. *Go ahead and get your stuff packed up. I'll be back soon. Love you.*

Now I feel better. Now I have a plan of action.

Max scratches at my door, and I let him in, kneeling down to run my fingers along his back the way he likes. "Oh Max, what are we going to do about you?" We hadn't thought about Max. He nuzzles me, staring back with his wise, brown eyes. "We'll take you to the ranch." I cuddle his face and kiss the top of his head. "You'll love it there."

I spend the day packing up my stuff, putting it back in the boxes I pulled it out of not so long ago. I cry, a little, over having to leave behind the furniture Blue bought for me. I clean out my portion of the fridge. Just for something to do, I scrub the bathtub and sweep the floors.

I pass Kendra a couple of times, and we make indifferent small talk. She seems distracted. I debate whether to tell her we're leaving. We have to tell her *something.* Maybe it would be better, though, to just leave a note, along with an extra month's rent for both of us, so she has time to find new roommates. I decide to wait for Blue, see what he thinks we should do.

I don't see Hunter; he's probably with Megz. I don't intend to ever say anything to Hunter again.

Blue is taking a long time to do whatever he's doing. It's all I can do to restrain myself from picking up the phone. *Just leave him alone. Don't panic.*

But by late afternoon, I'm in full panic mode. I call Blue's phone twice; I text him five times. No answer. I pace the house like a caged animal. I go into Blue's room twice, the first time just to inhale his scent, just to calm down. Then I go back in there, thinking I'll pack up his possessions, make it easier for him. I get some more boxes out of the garage and place them on Blue's bed, looking around, trying to figure out what to put in them. I don't see his guitar. He must have it with him. I pull some clothes out of drawers and place them in the boxes. My hands tremble.

I sit on the bed, pile my hair on top of my head and take several deep breaths, willing myself to relax. It doesn't help. Walking to the desk, I scan the papers on it, wondering if I should just dump them all into a box. I pick up some pictures stacked in a corner: old photos of Blue in his Scout uniform, with a much younger Maria; Blue on a horse, grinning wide and showing a mouth full of braces; a surly-looking teenage Blue slumped on a bed, with long black hair falling into his face; and one of him in fatigues, his hair shorn, standing next to a hard-looking man in front of the house in Tulsa. That must have been his father, Bill. Both of them stare stonily at the camera, both unsmiling.

I clutch the pictures against my chest and sit back down on the bed, shaking all over. I should be happy. I *am* happy. But it's the uncomfortable, fragile-feeling happiness that always turns out to have been hovering on the edge of something different. Something *unhappy*. I'd give anything *not* to be feeling what I'm feeling.

I put the photos back on the desk and race out of Blue's room, taking the stairs two at a time, grabbing my phone off my dresser. I'm not waiting any longer to call him. But the phone goes right to voice mail. "Hey, just trying to see how much longer you're going to be." I try to make the message sound casual, but it's obvious from my voice that I'm scared. "Call me, Blue. Where are you? What's going on? Okay, call me."

The sun's way over in the western sky, looking cold and remote, when I shuffle out to the front porch in my slippers, a blanket over my shoulders. I've paced the entire house and can't stand being inside any longer. Kendra is on the porch swing, moving slowly back and forth.

"Hey."

"Hey."

Awkward silence, broken only by the creak of the swing's chains. Kendra stares at her feet. She's barefoot, wearing sweatpants and a T-shirt. *She's got to be cold.* She sighs and, as if she read my mind, crosses her arms and shivers. "So, we haven't really talked at all about this thing with your brother," she says tentatively

And right now, I so don't want to.

"I know it's ridiculously fast," she goes on. "I know it must seem like I'm robbing the cradle, and that it's just about sex." *Dear God, stop talking.* "And I'd be lying if I said it wasn't mostly about the sex at this point. I mean, Buick is unbelievably hot and..."

I put my hand out as if I can grab the words coming out of her mouth and stuff them back in. "Kendra, you have *no idea* how much I don't want to talk about this now. Or at all. Buick's my little brother. And besides that..."

And then Blue's car rounds the curve and drives slowly toward us. The rush of relief that surges through me leaves me barely able to stand; I have to grab one of the wooden posts on the porch for support. Blue is back. I feel like I can breathe again.

The setting sun hits the windshield and makes it impossible to see Blue's face inside the car. I can't help grinning. I'm sure he's grinning too. He's been playing games with me, making me wait so long, not answering his phone. "I'm going to kill him," I mutter. But I don't mean it.

Blue's car turns into the Embassy's driveway, and the sun's glare slips off the windshield, leaving the interior suddenly, brutally, visible. And the air around me seems to wobble and spin. I sink down to the porch step.

"Keegan, you okay?"

But I don't answer Kendra. I only stare at the man getting out of Blue's car. The man who is *not* Blue.

Frasier Bryson stands in front of the car, looking from me to Kendra, his face troubled. He holds two envelopes in one hand and the Coupe keys looped around a finger on the other.

"Why are you driving Blue's car? Where is he?" I don't care that I sound rude. Bryson stares at his cowboy boots for a moment, the lines on his forehead deepening. My breathing gets shallow; I can't seem to get enough air. I must have made some kind of sound because Bryson looks up quickly.

"Are you all right?" He takes a step toward me.

"Just tell me where Blue is!"

Bryson places one of the envelopes in my hand, then walks up the porch steps and over to Kendra, giving her the other envelope and the car keys. I sit there unable to move, unable to think; my mouth's open, but I can't seem to make it speak.

"What… Why are you giving me Blue's keys?" Kendra asks.

"Just read the note." Bryson's eyes are fixed on me. I hear Kendra tearing open her envelope; the sound hurts my ears. I watch her reading and see her mouth make an O in surprise. Her eyes fly up to meet mine.

"He's giving me his car. Says he's not going to need it. What the hell? Where is Blue? What's going on?"

Bryson doesn't answer.

I rip open my envelope and pull out the piece of paper and the flash drive inside. I thumb through the money that's in there too: several hundred dollar bills.

"He spent all day recording in my studio." Bryson's voice is drenched in sorrow. I just stare numbly at the device in my hand. "The songs, they're … *incredible.*"

The flash drive dissolves before my eyes. I blink away the tears and try to focus on what Blue has written.

Keegan:

By the time you read this, I'll be on the bus that goes to Fort Sill. I can hardly make myself write these words. I never wanted to hurt you and now I can see your face as you're reading this and I know that I am hurting you. I'm hurting you very much and I hate myself for it. I am so so sorry. I meant it when I promised to run away with you. I was going to do it. I swear.

But then I went to Bryson's office and when I walked in, he was sitting there playing one of his songs, one that I used to listen to all the time when I was a kid. It's a song about what true courage is, about what true love is. I used to wish Bryson could be my father instead of Bill. But when I was standing there listening to the song today I realized nothing Bill ever did was as bad, as cowardly, as what I've been doing all this time. I realized I can't go on like this, lying, running away. I can't let you pay the price for what I did. That's what Bill did to people. And I've been acting just like him.

I have to tell them what really happened in Afghanistan, Keegan. I have to do it. I have to face this. I'm sorry not to tell you in person. But I wasn't sure I could walk away from you if I did. I didn't trust myself even to tell you over the phone. I don't think I could stand to hear your voice.

I promise you that I will be back. I will come back to you!! But until I do, I need you to fight back.DO NOT give up the paper, DO NOT drop out!! Use the talent you have, use your writing ability and fight back. Make Lugner and Jason pay. Tell everyone what they did.

Use this cash to pay my part of next month's rent. The landlord's name and address are on the fridge. You guys will have to find somebody to move into my room.

I love you. I love you. God, I love you Keegan! Please forgive me. Please.

Blue

P.S. I wrote all these songs for you. I meant to record the set and give it to you for Christmas. I hope you like them. Bryson said they are really good. I think he meant it. I told him everything.

I love you.

"If there's anything I can do." I raise my head slowly and watch Bryson twisting his hands as he speaks. "There's got to be something I can do." His voice falters. "Blue has become like a son to me."

I say nothing. My mind's full of cotton, and my tongue feels too big for my mouth. But then, as if I'd grabbed an electric fence, a shock jolts me to my feet. I run into the house and up the stairs to my room, kicking off my slippers and yanking on my boots, then grabbing a coat and my purse. I'm pulling my keys out of the purse when I get back to the front porch.

"Where's the bus station?" I yell at Bryson, running toward my car.

"Corner of Birch and Sequoyah," Bryson calls back, sounding alarmed. "But it's too..."

I slam the car door and turn the key, shoving it into reverse.

"Keegan!" I hear Kendra shout. But I just shift into drive and press hard on the gas.

Only a couple of people—one man, one woman, several empty seats between them—are in the bus station when I yank open the door.

They don't even look up, just keep staring at the dingy gray floor tiles. I've never been in a bus station before. For some reason, in the seconds I stand there blinking under the harsh fluorescent lights, trying to figure out what to do next, I think of Megz. How many times has she been in places like this, all of her meager possessions in a cheap suitcase next to her? She'd told me once she's never been on an airplane. She looked ashamed over that.

I step up to the ticket counter and wait for the plump, middle-age woman sitting behind safety glass to look up from the magazine she's reading. When she finally does, I find myself speechless. Whatever I planned to say has just skittered out of my brain like a cockroach suddenly exposed to the light.

"Yes?" Her tone's so indifferent it makes me even more nervous.

"Um … I…" The man and woman in the worn-looking vinyl chairs are now staring at me.

"I need a ticket. I think." I closed my eyes for a second. "Look…"

The lady behind the counter raises one bored eyebrow. I take a breath. "My boyfriend is on a bus to Fort Sill. At least I think he is." I'm speaking in a rush now. "And I have to find him before he gets there. I have to talk to him." I'm starting to cry. "He left without telling me, and he's going to do something that I know he'll regret. And…"

The attendant looks slightly less bored.

"I think he already left on a bus from here going to Fort Sill, and I need to catch up with him and get on the bus and talk to him *before* he gets to the base. So I guess I need a ticket? Or I need to know what to do. I mean, can you tell me if he's on the bus? His name is Blue Danube."

The woman purses her lips and sighs. "I have a daughter your age. You girls, you just don't get it, chasing after these useless guys." Her face softens a bit, and her voice follows suit. "Honey, they're not worth it. Believe me."

"This one *is* worth it." I pull out a credit card and slide it under the glass. "Can I catch up to the bus somewhere?"

She shakes her head, but picks up the card. "I can't tell you who is on that bus, honey. All I *can* tell you is that there's a bus that's already left here," she looks at her watch, "about half an hour ago, and it's going to make three more stops before it gets to the town nearest to the base. So if you were to drive straight to the town of Percy, you'd probably beat the bus there."

She pauses, waiting for me to say something. "So do you want a ticket from Percy to Fort Sill?"

I swallow. "Yes, yes I do."

A few minutes later, ticket in hand, I floor it as I steer my Nissan back on to the highway, driving—as my Grandpa would have said—like a bat out of hell toward the town of Percy.

22

FIVE MINUTES

Keegan

The Percy bus station is smaller and shabbier looking than the one in Hickory Flats. I park under one of the few working lights and glance at the clock on the dashboard before getting out. 9:10 PM. My ticket says the bus is due to leave Percy at 9:30.

I walk into the station, remembering just as the door swooshes shut behind me to hit the Lock button on my key fob. I haven't really considered what to do with my car if I'm taking a bus to Fort Sill. I haven't really considered a lot of things.

No one's waiting inside the ticket office. Another woman, a bit younger than the first one, sits behind security glass, earbuds in, moving her head to the music. I finger the ticket in my coat pocket and feel my heart fluttering in my throat.

Water. I need a bottle of water. I have to feed a crumpled dollar three times into the vending machine before a bottle drops into the bottom. I pull it out and unscrew the lid, gulping half of the water down. When I start to put the lid back on, it slips out of my fingers, hits the dusty floor and rolls under the machine. No way I am fishing it out.

I go outside, looking up the road, hoping to see the bus arriving. A guy in torn jeans and a hoodie is leaning against the wall, dragging on a cigarette. His eyes crawl all over me. My heart starts beating faster and louder. I go back inside. I've just taken another gulp of water when I see, through the dirty station window, the bus lumbering into view.

I pull out my ticket and go back outside, standing on the curb, bouncing up and down on my toes, not sure if I'm excited or terrified. Or both. Creepy guy takes another drag and throws his butt on the ground, then smiles at me. The smile does not reach his eyes.

You sure as hell better be on that bus, Blue. I choke on the exhaust that spews out of the bus as it comes to a stop in front of me. When the doors open, I hop on and then fumble in my purse when the driver asks for ID. Creepy guy's standing so close behind me that I can smell his beery breath.

I steal a glance into the darkened bus as the driver processes my ticket. I don't see Blue.

Clutching my purse against my side, I walk slowly down the aisle, looking for Blue. Not many people on the bus and most of them seem to be sleeping.

"Want to sit together?" Asshole is right behind me, his lips brushing my hair. He reeks of smoke and body odor.

I pull away from him, curling my lips in disgust. "My boyfriend is on this bus. Back off."

"Sure he is."

I am beginning to panic. I can feel it seeping in as each step brings me closer to the back of the bus.

And then I see Blue. He's only a couple of rows from the rear. He's asleep, his head leaning against the window, the orange-tinted light from outside slanting across his face. I stop next to his seat and turn to glare at the guy behind me, who makes a point of brushing against me as he slouches into the seat across from Blue.

I stand there staring at Blue. His face is drawn, and he looks exhausted, even in sleep. I study his profile, the faint stubble that runs all the way from his sideburns down to the soft part of his throat. I want to cradle his face, kiss away the strain. But so many emotions have seared my spirit in the last few days. I am reeling from all of it.

Anger ranks pretty high up there as one of those emotions. Some part of me is definitely pissed off.

I'm still holding the water bottle with about a quarter of the liquid in it. I don't choose what I do next. Not consciously anyway. But my hand surges forward of its own accord, and I toss the water in Blue's face.

Blue

It might as well have been propane, followed immediately by a lit match, that hits me full in the face. I come roaring up out of my seat before my eyes are even fully open, my skin burning, in full flashback mode. I accidentally knock the bottle out of Keegan's hand. My hands automatically go for her throat and have already begun to tighten before I realize who it is, where I am.

"Blue." She doesn't even raise her voice or try to wrench my hands away. She's crying. "Blue, it's me."

And I go from blazing hot to ice cold, just like that. "Keegan." I can do nothing more than whisper. "Keegan." I grab hold of the seat back in front of me to steady myself. "What are you doing here? What the *fuck* are you doing here?"

"I'm going with you, Blue. If you're determined to do this, I'm going with you."

"No, you're not."

"Yes, I am."

"Keegan." I place my hands on her shoulders, still trying to catch my breath. "You can't."

"Everything all right back there?" the driver calls, and some dude next to us laughs.

"I guess her boyfriend really *is* on the bus," he says sardonically.

I have to wipe a finger across my eyes to clear the water that's blurring them. "Why did you throw water on me?"

Keegan goes, in an instant, from speaking quietly to yelling. "Because I'm so mad at you!" She pounds her fists against my chest. "How could you take off like that, Blue? How could you just sneak out of town and leave me with some stupid piece of paper? How could you?"

She keeps pummeling me, and I let her. I want her to. But then she collapses against me and buries her face in my neck. "I can't do this without you, Blue!" she sobs. "I can't do my *life* without you. You've changed me too much. I don't want to. You have to take me with you. I can help you."

I wrap my hand around her arm and begin to pull her toward the front of the bus. "No!" She yanks her arm out of my grasp. "I'm staying on."

"Keegan!" I clench her arm again, my fingers digging into her skin. I don't want to hurt her. But I have to get her off the bus. She pulls back again, but this time I hold on.

"Hey!" the driver yells. "What the hell is going on back there?"

I drag Keegan down the aisle with me. "Dammit, Blue! Let go of me." She starts kicking me. I manage to get her to the front and stand panting in front of the driver. I'm still holding Keegan in an iron grip.

"If you two can't settle your little domestic dispute in the next minute, you're both off this bus," the driver says, eyeing us with disdain.

I fish around in my pocket, trying to open my wallet and pull out a bill with one hand. I lift the bill up so I can see it. A fifty. I shove it toward the driver. "Please," I say in a low voice. "Five minutes. I just need five minutes with her, outside, and then I'll get back on." I thrust the fifty at him again. "Please. Five minutes."

Keegan's stopped struggling; tears run down her cheeks. It breaks my heart. I release her arm. "Keegan, come talk to me outside for five minutes. If you still want to come with me after that, I won't try to stop you."

She nods, and I inch the fifty-dollar bill toward the driver with my fingers. He glances swiftly back at the other passengers, then crumples the bill in his hand. "Five minutes, and this bus leaves," he says.

I take Keegan's hand, leading her off the bus and over to the side of the station. As soon as we get out of sight, I pull her into my arms, my fingers on her face, and kiss her. It's a desperate, greedy kiss; I push my lips against hers so hard she stumbles back against the wall of the building. Then I shove my tongue into her mouth, exploring, memorizing. She moans and matches her tongue to mine, her lips to mine. She grabs my face and kisses me back so hard, so completely, that for a moment, I weaken. Maybe there's a way. *No. There is no other way.*

We rest our heads together for a few moments, then kiss again, this time softly. I can taste tears, but I don't know if they are mine or hers.

"I know what you're doing, Blue." She clutches my hand. "You're saying goodbye. You … *bastard* … you're saying goodbye."

I close my other hand around the back of her neck and whisper into her ear. "Listen to me. There's no way for you to go with me. Not now. They won't let you on the base. You'd be stuck there, and I couldn't help you. There's nothing you can do for me right now."

She's sobbing and shaking all over. "We can still run away, Blue. My car is right there. Come with me. Dammit, come with me!"

"I can't. I just can't. I *have* to do this, Keegan. There's nothing you can do for me right now, but there's something you can do for yourself. Like I told you in the note, you have to fight back. Use your gift. You're a journalist. Use that gift. Don't you dare give it up."

I've just taken her face in both hands when I hear the driver's voice yelling. "This bus is leaving!"

Jabbing my eyes to clear them, I focus on each feature of Keegan's face, locking them into my memory. "I have to go now, Keegan, okay? You have to go back to campus. *Okay*?"

Very slowly, she nods.

"I love you, bar girl. I will come back to you."

It's the hardest thing I've ever done, pulling away from her. Her sobs burn my eardrums as I walk toward the bus. I hate myself. I fucking loath myself at that moment. She deserves better.

I've got one foot on the first bus step when I think of something that makes me turn to see if Keegan has followed me. She's standing a few feet away, watching me with an expression of such agony that my legs go weak. I grab the railing and start to just get on. But then I turn back to her.

"I need you to go to Tulsa." I can barely speak. "Tell my mother. Tell her everything. And … will you take care of Max?"

Tears are spilling down her face. "Yes."

I mouth the last words because no sound will come out of my mouth: *I love you.* And, just as the bus doors close, I hear her shout, "I love you, Blue!"

Keegan

My heart is already broken. It cracked in two the day my mother died. I can still remember the pain in my chest, a chisel cutting through my brittle teenage ribs and slicing the blood-pumping muscle in half as I watched her fingers slip out of my hand and turn white. It had healed, as most broken hearts eventually do—or so they tell us.

This is different. Watching the lights of the bus taking Blue away from me until they disappear causes my heart to implode. It doesn't just break; it falls in fragments, dropping piece by piece from its place nestling between my lungs to somewhere around my feet. It hurts like hell. I want to die. I want to just give up and die.

But Blue wants me to fight back. He wants me to be strong. *Fine. I'll fight back. I'll fucking fight back.*

An idea's already forming in my mind, a plan. I swallow the lump in my throat and wipe my eyes, then pull a tissue out of my purse. I blow my nose with one hand as I search the Contacts list on my phone with the other. I need the ranch's main number. I haven't called it in so long that I no longer have it memorized.

It rings about a dozen times before the housekeeper answers. I ask to speak to Virginia and walk quickly back to my car while I wait. I've just gotten in and clicked the car door to lock it when I hear my grandmother's voice, husky from sleeping and worried.

"Keegan, what's wrong?"

"Virgi … *Grandmother,* I need your help."

AUTHOR'S NOTE

Thank you for reading *Tangled Up in Blue*! I hope you liked it. It is Book One in my **Ikana College** series. Book Two, *Shelter from the Storm,* will be available soon. It continues (and concludes) the story of Keegan and Blue, and takes us into the passions and problems of other colorful characters who live at the Canadian Embassy. Want to be notified when Book Two is available? Sign up at JDBrick.com.

Please spread the word to your friends, family, even random strangers who look like they're romance readers, about *Tangled Up in Blue.*

Visit **JDBrick.com** for more information. Thanks again!

J.D. Brick

ABOUT THE AUTHOR

Yes, J.D. Brick is a pen name. I am a wife, mother, corporate refugee, ever hopeful if seldom successful gardener, and slave to great books and good coffee. I've been a journalist, technical writer and intrepid humorist, which is the only kind of humorist worth being.

Want to get in touch? Please visit JDBrick.com.

Made in the USA
Charleston, SC
03 August 2015